Promise

Regina E. Williams

Main Street Publishing
SUMMERVILLE, SOUTH CAROLINA

Promise by Regina E. Williams

Published by
Main Street Publishing
Summerville, SC

ISBN: 978-1-0880-0308-4

Printed in the United States of America

Cover Art: Adapted from the screen print, "*Protection During the
Middle Passage*" by artist Winston Kennedy.

In Memoriam

Dawn C. Gill Thomas
Robert Ishmael

CONTENTS

INTRODUCTION

My early years were spent in the Bedford-Stuyvesant section of Brooklyn when it was an immigrant community. The population included Caribbean people from Barbados, Jamaica, Trinidad & Tobago and Haiti. Also represented were Hasidic Jews from Eastern Europe, Poles, Russians, and Estonians. And there were African Americans from the South. One memorable "benefit" of having been segregated was that all our professionals –doctors, nurses, dentists, teachers, lawyers, plumbers, and electricians– lived and socialized right in the neighborhood. I was more than fortunate to grow up feeling cared for and protected, not only by my family, but by my community as well.

There were memorable people like the Reverend Mister 'Puddin' an' Tane.' He was a very fair complexioned older gentleman with watery grey eyes and a shock of white hair. He always wore a black suit, tie, and vest no matter the season. He always wore a broad smile too as we children gathered around to listen to his delightful tall tales.

Another neighborhood character was the rotund gentleman with the wild eyebrows, matching bushy mustache, and beard. He wore overalls and smoked a pipe. The bowl of his pipe had a cut-out where a tiny hula dancer was encased. When he drew on the pipe, the dancer would shimmy up and down, much to our delight.

Always present were the windowsill women. They leaned on cushions in their windows gossiping from one brownstone to another. They often wrapped coins in a handkerchief along with a note of what they wanted us to buy from the local store. The tiny bundles would be dropped from their windows. We were rewarded with a small tip or candy for running their errand.

My grandmother's door was always open, and the stove was always filled with large pots. She cooked to "feed the walker," those people who had no permanent residence or who were down on their luck. Gram did not believe that anyone should go hungry and that whatever we had should be shared. That brought many colorful visitors to the table and into our lives.

It is from this place that I came to understand and enjoy the power of the story. It is a place where I could imagine 'what if,' or come to terms with a hard truth. Or not. In essence, each story became a (re)searching.

I believe we come into this life knowing what brings us pleasure and pain; what we want and need. We are then taught to distrust what we know. It is only in the university of life that we slowly regain our knowing, where we begin again to trust our instincts and those things our bodies tell us to be true; where we experience pain, joy, grief, pleasure and hopefully, love.

The stories in this collection take place from the mid-50s to the present. The work represents an array of situations and locales, but the reality is that place matters only in our consciousness, in our memories. These stores are brief reflections of some of life's markers on the journey from self to self.

1955

Daddy didn't say nothing about lynching when he put me on the train going south. I was going to visit my brother Sean and his family, who lived in a small town in North Carolina. Sean had mustered out of Air Force there. Even though I was fourteen years old and had lived and traveled around in Spain and Germany, it was the first time since we'd returned to the States one year ago that I'd be traveling such a long distance alone.

At the train station Dad had a conversation with a very nice Pullman porter. "This is the first time my daughter will be visiting the south. Would you be good enough to keep an eye out for her?"

"Certainly. She'll be just fine as long as she follows the rules." He said he'd make sure I moved to the rear of the train when we reached Washington, DC and that I got off the train at the right station. They shook hands.

Mr. Porter had kind eyes and a sweet smile. He took my suitcase and led me to a seat by the window where I could wave to Daddy. I held tightly to the bag with my lunch and other snacks. I was so excited and feeling like such a proud and competent traveler that I forgot to ask why I had to change seats when we got to Washington.

The train took its time leaving Penn Station and then we were in a dark tunnel for a long time. But eventually we were rolling through what looked like industrial areas and then farmland. It reminded me of Spain and the bullfighting bulls grazing in the fields.

I must have fallen asleep. Mr. Pullman Porter was waking me up to move to the rear of the train. He was nice, but he didn't have time to explain how "it came to be" that Negroes had to ride in the rear of not just trains, but buses too. "If I have time I'll come back to tell you about this particular history," he promised.

While I was settling into my seat, I remembered that Mom had told me to listen to the sound of the train on the tracks. She said I would hear the rhythm of the blues. She'd played blues music for me sometimes, but I'd never heard it live myself. To me the train's rhythm sounded more like the thump, thump twang of the traditional Ethiopian music.

I was still humming some tunes I knew to the sound of the train when Mr. Pullman Porter came to get me. I'd arrived in North Carolina. My brother was there to meet me.

Sean, who was twelve years older than me, had married Mae-Lee. She was country and afraid of everything – the dark, lightning and thunder, snakes and especially white people, "Cara," she said, "I don't know nothing 'bout that fancy northern cooking y'all do, so I hope you like chittlings and hog maws and the like."

She cooked with fatback and lard, two things I'd never heard of. With a hardworking husband who always seemed to be hungry and three-year-old twins, who ate everything in sight, it was a good while before anyone noticed that I wasn't eating very much.

One afternoon Mae-Lee took me with her uptown to buy fabric at the Five and Dime. "We'll go to the movies afterwards," she said. She also told me to stay close to her in the store. But I was curious, so when Mae-Lee was absorbed in buying fabric and thread and stuff, I wandered off in spite of her nervous watchfulness. I wanted to buy something pretty for my mother. Some jewelry caught my eye. I took my time browsing before I found some pearl earrings and a necklace that Mom would like.

The sales lady watched me like a hawk. When I was ready to pay she rolled her eyes at me, folded her arms across her chest and turned away. I called her several times but she ignored me.

Two white women came to the counter. The sales lady was all smiles. It finally sunk in that she had no intention of waiting on me. This really made me mad. In all of the places we had lived, this had never happened to me. I threw the jewelry down and shouted, "I didn't need this crappy stuff anyway. Your loss."

I ran out onto the street, stomping down the sidewalk. Hot tears ran down my cheeks and I stumbled down the sidewalk. A very large white man with a red face, bib overalls and a baseball cap yelled at me, "Get your nigger ass off the sidewalk. You belong in the gutter. This sidewalk is for white folk."

"Don't you yell at me, you dirty ole drunk," I screamed back.

He steadied himself before he vowed, "The Klan will ride tonight!"

"I don't care if your clan rides! You ain't the only one with a clan. I belong to the McDonnell clan and we don't take no mess!"

All the shouting brought Mae-Lee running. She was beside herself. "Cara, what's wrong with you?"

She pulled me down the street. I was hopping mad now. "What about the movie you promised?" I tried to pull my arm away but Mae-Lee had a tight grip.

"Movie? Girl, you done lost your mind." Her eyes were wild and she made me real nervous. She finally turned me loose and ran past me to a telephone booth outside the gas station. She called Sean at his job. I couldn't hear what she said, but her arms were gesturing wildly.

As frightened and frantic as she was, we didn't go right home. First we stopped at Mae-Lee's sister Ruby's house where the event was recounted. Then we stopped at several other neighbors' houses. By the time we reached home, Sean was pulling up in the driveway. It seemed everyone was suddenly in motion: Mae-Lee loaded the children into the car to take them to her mother's a few miles away; Ruby began gathering and packing my belongings; Sean was checking guns, ammunition, and lanterns. He pulled down the window shades even though it was still light outside. I still didn't understand. This time of day Sean was usually at work; Ruby would have been home in her own house with her teenage boys and me and Mae-Lee would be on the front porch playing with the twins. All of this activity upset me and nobody would tell me what was going on. Or why.

"Sean, what's happening?" I pressed. Never one to talk much, he shifted himself so that he faced me. "Not now Sis, there's no time. Everyone is in danger but I promise to tell you about it when everything has quieted down. Okay?" I nodded, although I wanted to say otherwise.

The hustle and bustle didn't stop until it was dark and Mae-Lee had returned. I was packed into the car, along with my luggage. The sisters drove way out into the country. After a while there were no houses or street lights. The car finally stopped. We were in the middle of nowhere. Just pitch-black darkness and silence. I was so scared, the sweat running down my back was making me itch. Ruby took a lantern from the trunk. Mae-Lee pulled my suitcase from the back seat. We waited.

"Why we out here in the dark? Where we going?" I wanted to know. "'We' ain't going nowhere." Ruby replied. "You're going back home." I started to protest but was told to stop all the prattle. I didn't much like Ruby at all right then but I knew better than to suck my teeth or let her know what I thought.

We waited in silence until a speck of light could be seen a good distance down the tracks. As the train got closer, Ruby began waving the lantern. A man in a uniform leaned out. There was a brief conversation and he pulled me up onto the train.

Both Mom and Daddy were waiting for me at Penn Station. Daddy was not happy. His normal wide smile and playfulness were absent. Mom's lips were pressed tightly together. Daddy picked up my suitcase and started walking. We followed. I was eager to talk about my trip but it seemed like the silence of North Carolina had followed me to New York City.

Even after a week Daddy seemed distant. "Mom, what did I do? Why is Daddy so upset with me?" At first Mom gave me a stern look, then –realizing that I had no idea of what was going on– took my hand and led me into the living room.

"Your father is not angry with you. He was terrified of what could have happened to you." Tears welled up in her eyes. "And the rest of the people in Sean's community as well."

I looked at her, puzzled. Mom handed me a copy of Jet Magazine. There was a picture of someone named Emmett Till, in an open coffin. His body was bloated, discolored and disfigured. His head seemed really big. It sent a chill through me. I tossed the magazine aside, looking at my mother for an explanation.

Mom sighed, twisting her hands around. "Some white people in that small town in Mississippi claimed that Emmett, a 14-year old Negro boy, got fresh with a white woman. He was kidnapped, beaten, shot and lynched with barbed wire then thrown in the Tallahatchie River. His mother wanted the world to see what they had done to her son. That could have been you, Cara."

"But Daddy's white! He wouldn't do that to anyone Mom. I know he wouldn't." Now I was crying.

"No baby. He wouldn't, but until the murder of Emmett Till, your father didn't understand the depth of the racism here in this country." I was still puzzled, but she continued. "Your father was born and raised in Ireland so even though there were cultural problems, it was different. I was born in the States, although not in the South, so I have a different sense of American racism. As nurses, working for world health organizations, we've seen a great deal of violence but he just couldn't believe something like this could happen here, in the United States, especially not directed at a child. He really thought such intense racial hatred had ended. Maybe he had simply hoped it had…." Mom's voice trailed off.

"Mom, what about Sean, Mae-Lee and everybody? Are they okay?"

"We don't know. If we haven't heard by tomorrow, your dad and Uncle Sonny will drive down to check." Mom looked worried.

"Can I go?"

"No, not this time," she replied softly, but her eyes shifted and by the way her hand gripped my shoulder, I knew I'd never again go South. And I also knew that that image of Emmett Till's body would always be with me. Always.

THE HOLY SPIRIT

My daddy was an important man at the Mount Sinai Baptist Church. He collected the money and counted it with the rest of the deacons. And he sang in the choir, too. A lot of people in church really liked him. He got invited to lots of dinners, recitals and baby christenings. Daddy liked to take me with him.

One Sunday daddy was going to sing a solo. I put on my very favorite Sunday dress: pink with a white ribbon sash and a pink bow for my hair. We headed to church early. Since he was going to be with the choir, I was to sit with Miss Etta Mae. She was nice and always smelled of talcum powder. On this day, Miss Etta Mae had on a dress the color of key lime pie and wore a yellow hat.

Me and Miss Etta Mae ended up almost at the back of the church; I couldn't even see daddy 'cause all the ladies had on big hats. Miss Etta Mae gave me a really nice fan though, to keep me cool. It had a picture of Jesus holding a baby lamb. Jesus had big blue eyes. Carlos, a boy in my class, said that the right way to say Jesus was "Haysoos." He said Haysoos ain't white. We got into a big fight.

After the preacher preached the choir began to sing. The choir swayed back and forth in time to the music and people started clapping and tapping their feet. Somebody was playing a tambourine. And then daddy started to sing. Everybody kept clapping, shuffling their feet and fanning themselves. A pretty hefty lady took to dancing in the aisle. More people started jumping up and down until the floor began to shake. Soon ushers and nurse ladies came down the aisle and made a circle around the dancing lady. But that made it worse. She was bouncing closer and closer to me and Miss Etta Mae. She was shout-singing words I didn't understand. I was getting scared but Miss Etta Mae seemed to be paying me no mind. She was clapping hard, her eyes shut and her head thrown back.

I couldn't get around Miss Etta Mae so I crawled under the pews and made it to the back of the church. I wanted to get outside but a tall usher-man with white gloves stopped me.

"What's the matter, Little One?"

I pointed at the lady jumping around. All the ladies in white were trying to hold her down.

"Don't be frightened. She just got the Holy Spirit."

Twist and turn as I might, he wouldn't let me go. Daddy finally finished his solo and came to get me. His forehead was wrinkled and he looked very upset.

"Explain yourself, young lady! All I could see from the podium was your bottom crawling at breakneck speed up the center aisle. What has gotten into you?"

As soon as he spoke, I started to cry. I didn't like to upset my daddy.

"Well, maybe it was the Holy Spirit!" volunteered Mr. Usher-man.

I rolled my eyes around to see what daddy thought of that. He took me by the hand and led me to a room next to where the deacons counted the money.

"We have to have a come-to-Jesus meeting Miss Missy! You are too old for this kind of behavior."

Daddy talked and talked about how the Holy Spirit does this and does that. He went on and on. I was quiet. I was waiting for him to take a breath so I could ask some questions: Was Jesus's real name

Haysoos and was he white? What I really wanted to know was if Jesus did the Holy Spirit dance like the ladies in church.

I know my daddy knew the answers. I'd just have to wait 'til he got to that part.

THE DATE

His father owned a tailor shop and did alterations. His mother, a housewife, spent most of her waking hours hanging out of the third-floor window of their brownstone gossiping with other windowsill women. Benjamin, their son, was of fair complexion, with wavy hair (aka 'good' hair), and long teeth like his mother. He attended classes at Pace University and worked in his father's shop. Perhaps that's why my mother thought Benny a good prospect for marriage.

Marriage? I hadn't even entered college yet!

As a senior in high school I was more focused on graduating and going to college than in dating anyone, least of all Benny. I had no interest in him – at all. He had no personality, and he had an awful nasal voice. He was just plain boring. He didn't play sports, had no interest in theater, art or music and didn't skate or dance. What would we even talk about? He wasn't even easy on the eye. His complexion was pox marked and sallow; his eyes were owl-round and his glasses, also round, magnified his vapid stare.

My mother had decided, as some mothers do, that Benny was a decent and responsible person and one I should have an interest in. He was, as she constantly reminded me, "a good catch." But who would want to catch him? I wondered.

I was puzzled when our mothers arranged a date.

"If Benny is such a great catch, why isn't he arranging his own dates?" I asked. Mom's eyebrows arched, letting me know that I was stepping into dangerous territory.

Benny arrived promptly at 7:00 pm in a sports jacket, white shirt and tie. He handed me a small packet of flowers which I handed to my mother. Mom and I were informed that we were going to have dinner at a restaurant in Manhattan – in the Village. I was expecting to take the subway, but Benny escorted me to a long black car parked at the curb. This made me nervous. I hesitated. I know my mother didn't know about this! Benny opened the car door and nudged me gently into it: "I know you'll enjoy the ride. It's new."

We drove across the Brooklyn Bridge and onto the FDR Drive, exiting at Houston Street. Conversation was predictable, although in fits and starts. He asked about my school and what I was planning to do after high school; what college I'd attend, what I planned to major in. He said little or nothing about his course work. Cruising through the East Village he stopped talking, paying closer attention to the heavy traffic. I welcomed the silence and the sights. The neighborhood pulsed with the sounds of street musicians, tourists and locals going about their Friday night business.

The restaurant was on the second floor above a retail store. The gentle wafting of music welcomed us. We were seated at an elegantly appointed table with starched white tablecloth, more forks than I thought necessary for one meal and a simple but beautiful floral arrangement. Benny ordered white wine and escargot. I requested a shrimp cocktail appetizer. The rest of the menu was a bit of a riddle to me but Benny translated several items and made suggestions, brief as they were. So, maybe he did have some redeeming qualities, I mused.

"How do you like Pace?" I inquired, more of a way to initiate conversation than real interest.

"Fine."

"Had you thought of going to college outside of the City?"

"No."

"I'd been thinking about attending Amherst."

"Umm."

The man across the table from me lacked even the most basic social graces and it was beginning to annoy me. Why did he even bother to invite me out? He wasn't interested in getting to know me. What in heavens name did he want?

After dinner we took a very silent walk through Washington Square Park before returning to his hearse-like limo. Benny suggested a ride across the Verrazano Narrows Bridge; there was something special he wanted to show me. *On Staten Island?*

"Listen Benny, I know I'm not experienced, but I do know that there is nothing on Staten Island to see. I'd greatly appreciate if you took me home."

"Soon. There really is something I'd like to show you." He smiled, exposing his long, sinister looking teeth.

I repeated my request. Benny was ignoring me and it was beginning to seriously unnerve me. He turned on the radio to a classical music station and continued to drive. Even unnerved, between Benny's lack of conversation, my boredom, and the music, I was lulled into a twilight state – somewhere between wakefulness and sleep.

I was startled into full awareness. The car was speeding over a bumpy dirt road. On either side of the car stood tall grass, and more of the same ahead, obscuring any other view of where he might be taking me. Benny slowed the car suddenly, making a sharp left into a patch of land that looked as if it had been carved out specifically for the size of the car. There was nothing to see, except more tall grass!

"What is this place, Benny? Why have you brought me here?"

Benny didn't answer. He rolled down the window, turned sideways and with very strong, focused hands began fondling me. I attempted to stop his hands from their exploration, but quickly realized that he was stronger than he looked. It was as if the entire evening had been a prelude to this moment. He was not going to be convinced and no amount of shouting would bring me help – we were alone in the middle of nowhere. His intent was clear. I was scared but I knew I needed a more useful strategy than continuing to struggle.

I relaxed and smiled. "Since there is no place for me to go, why don't we get more comfortable? The back seat?"

He liked that. He quickly released me, removed his jacket, tie and shirt. I pretended to unzip the back of my dress. Benny removed his glasses and placed them on the dashboard before he hopped out, launching himself into the backseat where he hurriedly began unzipping his trousers. Just as quickly I scooted into the driver's seat, hit reverse, shifted gears and sped down the solitary road we'd been on.

I drove as fast as I could, not knowing where I was or where I was going, or caring that I was stripping the gears, but only that I was moving. Benny shouted for me to stop, to give him his glasses. He flailed about in the backseat while trying to put on his clothes. The jostling of the car did not make it an easy task. "Give me my glasses!" he shouted. He continued shouting but I wasn't listening.

Ahead, I could see speeding traffic. It looked like a highway. *Hallelujah.* I slammed on the brakes, stopping under a very bright streetlight next to a gas station. I removed the car keys.

"You take me home right now, with no other shenanigans or I get out and call my dad and brother to come get me. I will also call your parents, and tell them exactly what you just tried to pull."

If his eyes had been intense before, they were moreso now. He was slow to speak until I opened the driver side door and began walking toward the gas station.

"Okay, okay." He got into the driver seat. He began searching for his glasses, which he found on the floor on the passenger side of the car. "Where's the key?"

"Okay what?" I demanded.

"I'll take you directly home."

I remained fully alert and eager to get back, scrutinizing every turn he took. Although I was fuming inside, I kept my eyes open and my mouth shut on the way home. He had assumed that because he treated me to an expensive dinner, that I was bought and paid for – that he could do whatever he wanted to do to me. The more I thought about it the angrier I became but I was focused on getting home safely.

It wasn't until we were crossing the Brooklyn Bridge that I began to worry about what I would tell my mother. Telling the truth could ruin the relationship between my mother and Benny's mom. And if confronted he could say that I'd led him on and then didn't want to follow through. It wouldn't matter whether that was rational or true.

Mom was waiting for me. "You're way past your curfew."

"Benny got caught in traffic and then got lost." I turned away so Mom couldn't see my face.

"On the subway? You know that system like the back of your hand." Mom was scrutinizing me closely.

"No Mom, he drove his new car."

"Car?" She continued studying me. I could tell that she had questions she wanted to ask but had decided to hold off for the moment.

"Did the rest of the evening go well?"

"Dinner was nice and walking through Washington Square Park was fun, but he wasn't really interested in me. He was more interested in…" I stopped, almost forgetting myself. "It was all about him. He was more interested in impressing me with the expensive restaurant and showing off his new car."

I scurried past my mother to the safety of my room. I comforted myself with the knowledge that Benny would never ask me out again. And that makes me incredibly happy.

BLIND SIGHTED

The girdle pinched but Urielle was determined to fit into her favorite red dress. She'd not been able to fit into it for over a year but she'd been dieting and today she had something special to report. She walked carefully to minimize the sound of her chafing thighs. Perspiration trickled down her back. Sweat pooled beneath her breasts, but she ignored it – she was late. She arrived just as the meeting of the Savior Church of the Redeemer Women's Guild was being called to order.

Smiling demurely, extending a well manicured left hand, Urielle smugly announced, "I AM ENGAGED! At age 29. Finally."

Joyce was loud. "Let me see that ring! How'd you meet Mr. Charming? What's his name, what does he do?"

The meeting agenda had been commandeered but no one minded. Urielle raised her hands to quiet the happy chaos. "I met Sam at the movie theater, my favorite place, after church." It was the one place where she could completely relax, forget about wearing 'proper foundation' garments; where she could eat chocolate, candy, popcorn and drink soda to her heart's content; where she could laugh or cry unashamedly. It was where she could revel in the darkness.

"I dropped my gloves at the concession stand," she continued. "The gentleman behind me picked them up and asked if they belonged to me. Lord have mercy, he had gorgeous light brown bedroom eyes, a well-manicured mustache and wonderfully full, kissable lips. I was speechless."

She thought back to that moment and recounted the meeting to her guild mates:

"Miss, are you alright?" he asked.

"Oh, sorry, yes I'm fine," I stammered.

"Indeed you are!" he smiled as I blushed.

"I didn't mean to be so forward, or to embarrass you. May I sit with you in the movie, or have coffee afterwards?"

I nodded, "Yes."

"Which one?"

"Both," I managed to say.

"That's how it began," she concluded and sat back in her chair, remembering.

Even though it was October they had gone to Coney Island – something she hadn't done since she was a child. They ate hotdogs at Nathan's, walked the boardwalk and returned for clams on the half shell. He took her to Radio City Music Hall for the Christmas Show; the African Burial Grounds, the Merchants House in the Village, the Brooklyn Museum, the Museum of Modern Art.

In the evenings they frequented Sam's favorite jazz haunts: The Blue Coronet to hear Miles; Pharoah Sanders at The East, and a jazz violinist at Slugg's, on the Lower East Side. The Red Rooster, Town Hill in Brooklyn, Town Hall in Manhattan and Obi's in Harlem for breakfast after a night of music and fun. Sam introduced her to a city she'd been oblivious to before he entered her life.

She adored the pipe tobacco, Bay Rhum scent of him, the intensity of his eyes, the baritone of his voice. There was nothing about him she didn't love.

The wedding, 18 months later, was held at the Morris-Jumal Mansion in Harlem, followed by a honeymoon in Barbados. Upon their return, Urielle and her Guild sisters had fun decorating the bright, airy fourth floor apartment on President Street in Brooklyn. Sam fit right in with the Guild husbands.

Sam left the apartment while it was still dark to go fishing. She planned to have lunch with Mavis. Since she hadn't been able to go back to sleep after Sam left, she used the quiet hours to make a dress for herself. In spite of constant dieting, her body continued to expand. By the time Mavis arrived, Urielle was wearing her new dress.

"Girl, when were you going to tell me about Sam? I am so sorry. What can I do?" Mavis swept past Urielle and arranged herself on the edge of the sofa, awaiting a response.

"Tell you what?" Urielle replied, feeling her forehead crinkling, hand still holding the open door.

"When did Sam go blind?" Mavis demanded.

"Blind? He's not. What are you talking about?" Urielle's voice was shrill.

"Then what was he doing in front of Macy's wearing dark glasses, holding a cup and a white cane?"

"Mavis, you're mistaken. Sam's fine."

"Well, it's none of my business, but I know what I saw. If you say Sam is fine, then fine he is!"

The subject was not broached again that afternoon.

The following morning Urielle took the subway to 34th Street. She exited the subway directly in front of Macy's. She emerged into the bright sunlight, about six feet away from her husband. Sam's face was turned upward, enjoying the warmth of the sun. Urielle gasped involuntarily. Sam turned towards the sound, its familiarity. Urielle was already descending the subway stairs.

Disbelief, denial, shame, hurt and betrayal volleyed for Urielle's attention. Everything had been a lie! By the time she reached their apartment she was seething. She frantically pulled his clothes from closets and drawers, tossing everything into a pile on the bedroom floor. *If he thinks he's going to make a fool of me, he'd better think again.* Urielle paced and ranted until she collapsed from sheer exhaustion. *You don't deserve my tears*, she screamed as she wiped at her face. The streetlights were now the only illumination in the room.

The ringing telephone forced Urielle to turn on the light. There was an envelope addressed to her propped against the lamp.

"Mrs. Thompson, Mrs. Samuel Thompson?" the voice asked.

"Yes."

"Mrs. Thompson, your husband has been injured in a bus accident."

Without thinking Urielle hung up, shoved the letter into her purse and rushed from the apartment.

When she arrived at the hospital, she peppered the doctor with questions: "Doctor, what happened? How long has my husband been here? What is the prognosis? Will he recover?"

Although the doctor had advised her that her husband's condition was serious, she was unprepared for the comatose man plugged into so many flashing and beeping machines and monitors. She repeated the Lord's Prayer like a mantra – touching his face, holding his hand.

It was hours before she remembered the letter.

My sweet Love,

I never thought I'd meet someone like you and even more surprised that you would love and marry me. You saved me from myself. You've done nothing but make me happy. But I've lied to you – a lie of omission, but a lie nonetheless. I tell you now because we are soon going to be parents. I know you haven't realized it yet, but you, we, are pregnant! And I'm elated. (You haven't noticed my morning sickness during the past months have you?) But first I must share my "truth."

Seven years ago I lost my sight. It began like an allergy – like sand in my eyes, and gradually grew worse. My hands become my eyes. All the things I took for granted like traveling, cooking, doing laundry, had to be relearned. After two years I lost my job with the insurance company. Disability wasn't very much. I picked up some work playing piano at some of the clubs and even made some money tuning pianos. "Selling pencils" came after everything else failed. It was what kept me on course and has been my source of income all this time – not the insurance company job I allowed you to believe I'd returned to.

Two years ago my sight was restored. The doctors were and are mystified. I was and am grateful. I was just getting used to being sighted, somewhat afraid of losing my sight again when I met you. I was still pinching myself when you said you'd marry me! I kept finding excuses for not telling you....

Sweetheart can you ever forgive me? More than anything I'd like to be a husband and father worthy of your love.

Yours always,

Sam

With tears flowing, Urielle climbed into the bed next to her husband, cradling him until his body was no longer warm.

SOYBEAN, FAT AND SALT

I

Everyone in the Gilliam family could shoot. Except me. Daddy had no intention of me ever needing to shoot a gun so he never taught me. That is until we went to visit Aunt Betty, who lived in the country in a small town in Virginia.

Even though I knew Aunt Betty and her husband Elgin were professional hunters, visiting them was always traumatic. The house was filled with guns; long guns, short guns, practice pistols, miniature guns. Guns hung on the walls, leaned behind doors, sat atop dressers and nightstands, and sheltered in closets. Guns were everywhere. And I was afraid of guns. Uncle Elgin knew this so he always removed the guns from the room I'd sleep in. This time though he was visiting his sister in Atlanta.

My aunt believed that since I was my father's daughter, I too should know how to use a gun. She did not appreciate my fear. "Rosa Lee, you got something against guns?" she asked one day. I scanned the room looking at what I perceived as an excess of equipment. "Yes ma'am. They kill people."

It's not the gun, Rosa Lee, it's the people handling the gun that can be the problem. Guns can be a protection."

Aunt Betty was looking at me intently. "You're 12 years old. When I was your age me and my brothers were bringing home rabbits, squirrels and possums for dinner. You're too old for this nonsense. Come with me."

In the kitchen she placed several items on the table. "Soybean, fat and salt," she announced. These she stuffed into an empty shell casing and then loaded it into the chamber of a shotgun. She loaded the remaining chamber with live ammo.

"What is soybean and that other stuff going to do Aunt Betty?"

"Cut and sting but it won't kill."

"Sting?"

My aunt gave me a long look "Well, 'sting' may be a bit of an understatement. It would be like pouring salt in an open wound."

It was getting dark by the time Aunt Betty told me that she and my father had to go into town to take care of some business. "We won't be long. If anyone comes up the driveway, you'll hear their car on the gravel. You yell out, 'Who's there?' If you don't get an answer, shoot in the direction of the sound, ya hear?"

"Yes ma'am." I was terrified. Aunt Betty was well over six feet tall and powerfully built. I didn't know which was more frightening, the gun or my aunt. My entire body was quaking.

"If they keep moving in your direction, you shoot the live ammo."

With that she handed me the gun and went to find my father.

What business could they be taking care of in the dark of night, I wondered, but dared not ask.

Everything was quiet. The evening remained hot. I kept peering into the darkness, hoping they would return quickly. I paced the short hallway, entered the front room, the dining room and back through the kitchen, into the front room, and checking the window. Then I'd start the march all over again. It remained as quiet as only nighttime in the country can be. The stillness wrapped around me like a blanket of fear and trepidation. I was sweating. And then I heard it. At first I wasn't sure what the sound was. It moved slowly, as if trying to muffle the noise of tires on the gravel. I picked up the gun from the table. It was heavy. I turned off the light, moved to the window and sang out, "Who's there?"

I sounded like a wounded bird. Positioning the gun against my shoulder I repeated the question louder, trying to sound more assured. The car kept coming. Closing my eyes and pointing at the sound I pulled the trigger. My arm flew up into the air, the pain shot up through my shoulder and I fell backwards, landing on the floor. The next thing I knew Aunt Betty and my father were standing over me. Dad was lifting me. His face was contorted with anger. "Betty, what did you think you were doing?"

"That child is too old not to know how to use a gun. She's a Gilliam. As her father you should have taught her."

"You couldn't have achieved that with target practice? You know how I feel about this. We've talked about it more than I care to remember."

Aunt Betty glared at him. "You have your way and I have mine."

II

Getting married while still in college, and having a baby, were probably not the best-timed choices that I could have made but I'd made them. Sometimes I think I should have waited until I'd finished school first, but Jamal was a kind, caring person and we loved each other. Of course, being very pregnant in the sweltering heat of August was awful and I tried hard to remember that he was the love of my life. And I tried not to blame him for my misery. (But we all know, it's his fault, right?)

Where was Jamal when my water broke? Somewhere with his phone turned off – on call no doubt. He did reach the hospital before Amy Li was born though. And he really was a most devoted father. And why wouldn't he be; our daughter was the most beautiful child in the entire world. We were both elated.

***

"Rosa Lee, your mom called to remind you she and your father are coming to spend the weekend with us," Jamal called out from downstairs. "They should be here this evening. I'll probably have to pull a double since we're so short-staffed. I'll let you know. Love you." He was out the door.

The birth of our baby, just like our engagement and wedding had been announced in the local newspaper. Once again we were besieged by paper advertisements, emails and door-to-door salespeople. This go-round they were selling everything from baby furniture, toys, baby books, clothes and even savings plans for our child's college. So I was not surprised to find yet another saleswoman ringing our bell.

Something about the woman who was trying to sell a specially coated set of stainless-steel pots did not seem quite right. Maybe it was the way she kept trying to look around me into the house. Or maybe it was the dark green convertible sports car parked at the curb. An import. Her simple skirt and jacket fit the bill but not the 18-carat gold earrings and necklace or the large emerald and diamond ring she wore on her exquisitely manicured finger. *I can't remember the last time I've had time for a manicure. Selling door-to-door must be quite lucrative,* I thought. Amy Li's loud wail rescued me. I made my excuses and sent the woman on her way.

That green convertible was near the pediatrician's office later that morning. It was at the rear of the parking lot. The driver was a white haired older man. Maybe it wasn't the same car. *But you don't see those kinds of cars often.*

I decided to skip my other errands. Parking in the driveway would have been my routine, but I decided to park in the garage instead since it was attached to the house and provided a sense of safety, false though it might be.

Mother called a short time later to say that traffic on the highway was at a standstill; there was road construction delaying them, but they were on their way.

After feeding Amy Li and drinking two cups of tea I felt better, but was still a bit jumpy. Ignoring my nervousness I chose to at least try to complete my special project for the day; planting the daffodil bulbs. First though, I went to the attic and retrieved the gun and gun case Aunt Betty had gifted me on my 13th birthday. I loaded the gun and propped it inside the garage next to the phone. Just in case.

After settling Amy Li in her bassinet the two of us went out to the back garden. The weather was delicious. We were luxuriating in the crisp air and bright sunshine when a white panel truck began moving slowly down the alley behind the garden. It was not unusual for gardeners, painters and other service people to use the alley so I was not particularly alarmed. The van parked two doors away. I checked on the baby and went back to planting. The phone inside the house rang. Just as I picked up the extension in the garage, I heard the front gate squeak open. The hair on the back of my neck stood up. I dropped the phone and reached for the double barrel shotgun.

As I stepped around the side of the house the saleswoman was running toward the front gate carrying the bassinet. Glancing behind me the white van suddenly backed up, blocking the back gate. A white-haired man was at the wheel.

Running toward the front I stopped, stood completely still, aimed and shot the front tire of the green convertible. The woman dropped the bassinet and ran. Amy Li's scream was shrill, piercing. My second shot caught the woman in the hip. She staggered and slowed but continued to run, dragging her leg. The white haired man who had entered the garden changed his mind, jumped back into the truck and sped up the alley.

I was still shaking when the police and my parents arrived. The woman wasn't hard to find; they simply followed the trail of blood.

The police notified Jamal about what had happened. When he entered the bedroom looking every bit of the 16 plus hours he'd worked, I was sitting up hugging Amy Li and rocking. My eyes must have been red and puffy. Jamal took Amy Li, placed her in her crib and then gently guided me back to bed. He held me. "Do you want to tell me about it?"

"Give me 'til the morning. It's been one hell of a day. Why don't tell me about yours instead?"

So Jamal began telling me about his night in the ER. Often this was soothing or perhaps distracting when I couldn't sleep.

"Tonight the ER was like trauma city," he spoke softly, continuing to hold me. "The police brought in a handcuffed woman. She had a really nasty gunshot wound to her hip. And she was very vocal about the searing pain. I wondered what she'd been shot with. By the time I got her stabilized they bought in an older gentleman who'd been in a one car crash. He'd driven into a tree. Anyway, it was quite the night," he concluded.

"Soybean, fat and salt," I mumbled.

"What?"

"I shot that bitch with soybean fat and salt."

"Rosa Lee, what are you talking about?"

"I'll tell you about it in the morning."

I kissed him and was asleep before he could ask another question.

MANNY'S KOSHER DELI

Manny's Kosher Deli is directly across from my junior high school, in front of a bus stop, and around the corner from home. For Manny's business that means great foot traffic; for me it means getting a root beer, Mary Jane, Baby Ruth or other goodies on the way to or from school. My dad, Emanuel McBride, would often pick up a hot pastrami sandwich and a few beers after work and before Mom got home, or just spend some time sitting outside in front of the store chatting with Manny.

Although Manny is Jewish and Dad's Baptist, they're cut from the same cloth. They're about the same size -- large. Both favor chunky work boots, plaid flannel shirts, leather caps and corny jokes.

Every once in a while Manny's wife, Miss Rebekkah, helps out in the store. The opposite of Manny, she is tiny and cautious. She spends most of her time spinning around in the middle of the floor trying to figure out where to shelve an item. Often she looks completely befuddled. Manny will walk up, hug her and point to where something should be placed. He doesn't seem to mind. He's just elated that she's there with him. You can see him steal a glance at her and smile. She blushes. This after 25 years of marriage. Maybe it's because they only have each other; they both lost most of their families during the Holocaust.

My father is a bus driver, but on Friday evenings he closes the store at sunset and opens and operates it on Saturdays. He manages Manny's Deli during these times because the Jewish Sabbath observance begins at sundown on Friday and concludes on Saturday at sunset – a time when observant Jews refrain from work activities.

My mother, Grace, and Miss Rebekkah are close too; they share a lot of recipes. While I love potato pancakes, cheese or berry blintzes and matzah brei, my favorite snack is plain matzah and butter with tea. Sometimes on Sundays Manny, Miss Rebekkah and my parents get together for brunch: lox and bagels or salmon croquettes and grits, are their all-time favorites.

Today, after the school kids have gone home and before people return home from work, a young man wearing a stocking mask attempts to rob the deli. Manny is willing to give him the money but the man is nervous and mistakenly thinks Manny is reaching for a gun. He shoots Manny as he's turning to open the cash register. Miss Rebekkah hears the shot and sees her husband fall sideways behind the counter. She pulls Manny's gun from a drawer below the counter and shoots the robber twice before she falls to the floor, cradling her husband in her arms.

Manny dies on the way to the hospital. So does the would-be robber.

Miss Rebekkah is distraught. She calls Dad. Dad calls the rabbi who makes arrangements for Manny's burial which by tradition has to take place within twenty-four hours of this death.

Dad hires a caterer for the seven days when the family and other mourners will sit shiva. He asks Mr. Sweeney, the neighborhood plumber and a friend of Manny, to put a notice on the door of the shuttered deli.

Since Miss Rebekkah can only sit and rock, Mom rummages through Miss Rebekkah's closet and finds appropriate clothing for her to wear for Manny's funeral and then during the ritual mourning period. Afterwards Mom cooks and makes sure Miss Rebekkah eats.

Several weeks later Mom broaches the subject of Manny's clothing still hanging in the closet. Miss Rebekkah simply waves her hands around vaguely. Mom arranges for a local charity to pick up the clothing. But Mom is worried. Miss Rebekkah has lost interest in everything – she doesn't make her bed or care what she wears. Her eyes always hold a distant, vacant stare. She neither reopens the deli nor inquires about it.

"Bekkah, I know it's hard, but it's been a two months since Manny passed, what are you going to do with the deli; with the rest of your life?" Dad asks.

"I never thought about life without Manny," she says. "He took care of everything."

At that, Dad pushes his cap to the back of his head and frowns. Mom looks bewildered and I can almost see her thoughts: she's worked hard every day and taken care of me and Dad. She's never had such a luxury.

When the store reopens Dad is behind the counter. He's taken a leave of absence from work until Miss Rebekkah can decide what she wants to do. Mom, a postal worker, heads back to work.

Dad shows Miss Rebekkah how to keep inventory, how to order groceries, stock the shelves, tally up at the end of the day; how to make out a bank deposit slip, how to write a check. I come after school to help out. So does Mr. Sweeney when business is slow. Miss Loretha and other neighborhood folk also pitch in. But it's clear that without Manny, Miss Rebekkah has little focus.

Since I spend so much time in the store Dad sets up a table in the corner so I can do my homework. Some of my friends start dropping in to do their homework as well. Miss Rebekkah helps us, especially with math. Sometimes in the evenings, a few neighborhood women drop in to keep Miss Rebekkah company. They gather around the table to play mahjong. Or Chinese checkers. Or bid whist. Or to talk about whatever crosses their minds. Miss Rebekkah begins to smile, to relax.

It isn't long after that when Miss Rebekkah discovers she is pregnant. She fluctuates between quiet joy and sudden bouts of weeping; from morning sickness to a period of blissful wellbeing.

Mom talks to Miss Rebekkah about possibly selling the store and moving to Florida where she has some distant cousins. Miss Rebekkah says she hates the humidity in Florida and she is not close to her cousins. Miss Rebekkah's pale blue eyes move from my mother to my dad.

"You two are stuck with me. You're my family now." She flashes a nervous smile.

Miss Rebekkah delivers a healthy five-pound girl but dies in the process.

While Miss Rebekkah may not have known how to run the deli, she was very thorough in making sure that all the legal "t's" were crossed and "i's" dotted in her last will and testament. And that is how my parents, African Americans, become the owners of Manny's Kosher Deli in Bed-Stuy, Brooklyn and I become the big sister to Sarah Rebekkah Mankowsky-McBride.

And in honor of Manny and Rebekkah and in recognition of the Jewish Sabbath, the deli still closes at sundown on Friday until sunset on Saturday.

PICTURE PERFECT FUTURE

Kaleef had trouble waking up. Even the shrill blare of the wind-up clock seemed remote. Eventually, the sound faded and Kaleef returned to the business at hand – sleeping.

Immediately, or so it seemed, the distant sound of the phone disturbed his sleep. It was a muffled sound. As he awakened the volume increased; he opened his eyes, listening. His feet swung to the floor and his body staggered toward the noise. Before he could reach it, it stopped. Standing in the middle of the hallway, still dazed, Kaleef realized that today there was something special he wanted to do…but first breakfast.

In the kitchen, Kaleef poured cornflakes, mounds of sugar and milk into a plastic container. Putting the lid in place, he shook the concoction thoroughly. Climbing up to the table, Kaleef ate while studying the picture of President John F. Kennedy on the wall calendar hanging across from the table. When he was finished eating, he carefully placed the container and spoon in the sink.

Quickly he went to the bathroom to wash himself; returned to his room and found the clothes his mother had laid out for him: blue overalls and a white tee shirt. No, he didn't want to wear that. Today was too special for the clothes he usually wore; he had finally saved up enough to buy his mother a present. Kaleef pushed a chair into the closet, climbed atop it and found a pair of long blue pants. From the drawer he took out a yellow shirt, a clip-on blue and red bowtie and rainbow suspenders.

He dressed quickly. Before putting on his shoes though, he retrieved his hidden treasure – 90 cents in dimes, nickels and pennies. He placed the coins inside his sock and then put on his shoes. It would be uncomfortable but he had learned the hard way that in this neighborhood, money was not safe in his pocket.

Looking at himself in the bathroom mirror, he was satisfied with his appearance: kinky, close-cropped hair and neat, clean clothing. Although he was only six years old, his appearance was that of a little adult.

Kaleef checked the apartment to make sure that all of the windows were locked and that the jets on the stove were turned off before leaving. Since he didn't have a key, he had to be sure everything was in order and that he had everything he needed before closing the door.

He really wanted his own key. He'd asked several times, but each time his mother had said that it wasn't safe for him to have one. He might lose it, or worse yet, one of the rough kids might take the key from him and rob their apartment. "Maybe when we move," his mother had promised. He often imagined where that might be as they rode the bus downtown. Maybe near the Dime Savings Bank clock tower, or close to Junior's Restaurant where he'd always be able to get cheesecake.

Since it was a school holiday, he was supposed to go directly to Miss Clarissa's, the sitter, and call his mother at work to let her know that he had arrived safely. But he'd do that later.

As Kaleef left his building, he peered up and down the street. No rough kids were around. He threaded his way past a puffy-faced woman who was sitting on the curb washing her face from the open hydrant. Her male companion sat on the hydrant watching between nods. He sprinted past a group of old men sitting at a rickety card table playing Dominoes and another group of younger men shooting craps nearby. Kaleef slowed his pace as he approached the snowcone vendor, who was preparing his cart for the day's work, loading block ice and filling the syrup containers. At the corner he waited for the light to turn green and then made sure that no cars were moving. He crossed the street at a trot. On the next block he maneuvered around an old man sweeping the sidewalk and dodged some residue falling from overhead. Rubbing his eyes, he looked up to discover a dust mop being shaken from a second floor window. The mop wagged to the rhythm of loud electric rock music. He scurried on, blinking from the falling dust. A woman pulling a shopping cart loudly advised him to watch where he was going.

A few paces further, a wild-eyed dog was scavenging in the trash. Having eaten all there was to eat, or perhaps having found nothing, the dog riveted its attention on Kaleef. The mangy hound slumped low to the ground, bared his teeth and growled. Kaleef froze. The dog advanced. Kaleef's eyes were wide with fright. The dog moved closer. Kaleef was about to run when a large soup can sailed past him and struck the dog squarely between the eyes. The dog yelped and ran down the alley. Kaleef ran too, in the opposite direction – all the way to Broadway.

Broadway. There it was! The store he'd passed many times with his mother. His face brightened. He stepped inside and was amazed at the assortment of toys and other colorful items on the shelves.

When Kaleef emerged from the shop, he carried a large yellow envelope and had a bounce in his step. He hurried, via another route, to Miss Clarissa's.

All day he played quietly, away from the other children, checking the window frequently and constantly asking the time. All day he waited for his mother. Finally, when he saw her turn the corner, he bolted for the door, stopped, felt for the envelope, swung open the door and bounded down the stairs. Miss Clarissa called after him to no avail.

Ruth Ann, his mother, was tired. As usual. Tired of her "no pay-ing" job at the lampshade factory; tired of the winos and junkies and the garbage lining her street. Tired of the roach-infested apartment to which she always returned. Tired of the abandoned buildings now used as gambling dens, drinking holes and shooting galleries, and God only knew what all else. Her eyes swept across the familiar, loathsome sight.

"Momma, Momma, you're here!" Kaleef beamed up at her. Ruth Ann smiled and bent to hug him. She wondered why he was on the street. Automatically, she looked up to the sitter's window, frowning. The sitter shrugged wearily.

"Boy, why you got on your good clothes? How many times do I have to tell you…" But Kaleef interrupted her. "I have a present for you Momma. Come on." Kaleef took her hand and skipped alongside his mother, happily leading her home.

At the kitchen table Ruth Ann lowered herself into the chair with a sigh. Kaleef climbed into the chair next to her and handed her the envelope. Propping his elbows on the table, he rested his chin on his hands and closely watched his mother's face.

Ruth Ann opened the envelope slowly, watching the anticipation build on her son's face. On the greeting card was a picture of a lone, white stone house in the country surrounded by a stand of tall trees. In the foreground was a freshly plowed field. It was so very tranquil. Her eyes skipped over the words. Her mind drifted to her own childhood on a farm. Her tired expression softened into a smile.

"Oh Kaleef, it's so beautiful. Thank you, Baby."

Kaleef bounced up and down in his chair.

"Read it to me, Momma, read it."

Ruth Ann's voice was soft, pleading, "Baby, you know words don't come easy to me."

"Read me the picture Momma!"

Ruth Ann's eyes began to smart. She always bought Kaleef picture books and made up stories to go with the pictures. She thought when he learned to read he could teach her. Ruth Ann drew him into her lap and began to read the picture to him.

"One day, you and me are going to move from here. We'll move to the country and live in a lovely white house where there are lots of trees, where we can grow our own food. We'll have lots of chickens in the yard, and plenty of fresh eggs…"

Kaleef was pleased that his mother loved her gift. He couldn't see the faraway look on his mother's face, or the tears cascading down her cheeks. He felt good – it was nice to make his mother happy.

TRANSITIONS

Makaida possessed special 'spiritual' gifts. As her grandmother said, she'd been born "with a caul over her face." In spite of her gifts, she had no sense of time. She seldom knew what hour of the day it was, or for that matter, the day of the week. Events were remembered as "the summer the daylilies didn't bloom," or "the fall the robins ate all the berries from the fire thorn."

When asked her age she had to stop and calculate: If it was the year that Tomas proposed, she would have been sixteen – the year he gave her a silver, heart-shaped necklace. The mother of pearl heart was surrounded by marcasite and overlaid with a marcasite cross. And if it was the year they got married, she would have been eighteen, 1958. That she remembered.

Sometime after that she noticed the fullness of her breasts, her newly formed roundness of hip as well as her abundance of energy. These symptoms she attributed to having "reached womanhood." It was at Tomas' insistence that she finally went to the doctor and learned she was pregnant.

With her girlfriends moving out of state to attend college or working she was grateful for the visits of her spirit companions. Sometimes she'd be reading or meditating in the garden when one of them might interrupt, "Psst, Makaida, you don't have to close your eyes to see us." or "Don't you think it's time to cut the rose bushes back?" When she asked their names they shrugged, adding that they'd had hundreds, perhaps thousands of names over time. She'd taken to calling these two Earl and Lady Grey since they often made their appearance while she was having tea in her garden.

Her thoughts drifted to other times – of Tomas playing basketball – making it look like ballet. His muscled, dark body seemed to freeze in mid-air, poised for time eternal in her mind's eye. Tomas, the only man she'd ever known; black as a rosary, smooth as the hymn his body chanted. Tomas, who knew the rituals of manhood by heart. He'd glide through the bushes in the park, collecting the sun-kissed weeds, presenting them to her as a bouquet, promising gardenias when he got a permanent job. He had a way of always massaging her when they sat alone watching television or in the movies -- whenever he held her. His fingers always seemed to find her stomach – to knead her into willingness. She loved his hands.

Her mother Jasmin had other thoughts.

"Boys only want you for one reason. They don't mind soiling you, but they ain't about to keep no dirty laundry around as a reminder. Besides, Tomas is too black, and his eyes are too slanted to mean anyone any good."

But Makaida loved Tomas and had married him.

The sound of a car horn brought Makaida back to the present.

"I'd better pull these clothes in off the line before I have to wash them again," she muttered to herself. She studied the clothes, but made no move to collect them. Tomas, her rosary, her rock. Tomas, who had promised to take care of her, always....

The doorbell rang. It was the mailman. All bills. Opening one as she walked back to the kitchen, she read: total balance due...turning over your account to the collection department. The next one said that their telephone service would be disconnected. There was a note advising of additional charges for reinstatement of service. Makaida's hazel eyes flashed sienna; her light brown complexion rouged deep red, the color of her hair. She tossed the envelopes onto the kitchen table and poured herself a cup of tea. "Why doesn't Tomas pay these bills? He got paid last week."

She wondered if he were gambling again. He'd promised to stop. As much she wanted to believe him she was becoming weary of his excuses. She wondered if she should remind him, or simply tell him of her own plans.

***

Tomas didn't like pushing the heavy racks of clothing through the rain, snow or blistering heat. Although he had the broad shoulders, massive arms and muscular thighs required for the work, he didn't like the crowds, the trucks belching black smoke or the noise of people shouting over the din. He liked least of all the pay. In order to make ends meet, he'd been stealing and selling the designer clothes "freelance." He didn't mind stealing as much as he hated having to sell the items. Each client was a potential stool-pigeon. Tomas didn't like his job, but he had promised to take care of Makaida.

***

Chi was a quiet man. He had appeared in the neighborhood two years before, from Chicago, he said. No one had ever questioned him about his past. And he did not speak of it. As a matter of fact, no one knew his real name. He'd simply been dubbed "Chi," short for Chitown.

Chi's intense eyes and unsmiling face did not invite inquiry. He seldom spoke. The truth was he chose to blend into the scenery. And he did, with the exception of his eyes which boldly took in his environment, especially people.

Makaida had first encountered Chi at her friend Doreen's card party. Makaida didn't play cards, but often made money by cooking for house parties. Chi had bought a fish dinner and had complimented her cooking. He had asked what her favorite records were and before returning to the game, had stacked the record player with her choices. He had not said anything else to her, but for the rest of the evening his hooded gaze followed her.

Makaida ran into Chi often; in the park, on the bus to the beach, at the library. She welcomed the company. In the beginning he listened to stories she made up that took place in faraway places like ancient Dahomey, Timbuktu and Brazil. He soon began telling her about places that he had been like St. Louis, New Orleans, and Savannah.

Makaida enjoyed her sojourns with Chi but she found him elusive, like wind or sand, never leaving a clear impression. Although he never uttered a harsh word or treated her roughly, Makaida sensed something cold and menacing about him; something she could not articulate. It was just there, like his slow, rare smile. Maybe it was his smile. His lips would stretch back to expose small, slightly crooked teeth. But his eyes never smiled, they were always guarded, alert. They took in everything, while giving away nothing.

***

On the way home from the doctor, Makaida watched the setting sun. It had already given up its warmth. Now, using its last bit of energy and color, it slid out of sight. The moon had already made its appearance, pale, like the beginning of a new idea. Makaida walked slowly, while pondering the gentle wave-like rhythm in her belly. She felt good, smug. With each step, she envisioned the child she would have in four months. She always imagined the baby as a miniature version of Tomas. The thought made her happy.

It was after midnight when Makaida put the dinner away. She had already telephoned Tomas's mother twice and was embarrassed to call again. She'd called several of his friends, without finding him. She undressed, propped herself against two pillows and tried to concentrate on the book open before her. She turned on the television. Too late for news. She walked to the window. Parting the venetian blinds, she peered out into the night. It was raining. Just as she was about to drop the slat, she saw a flash of light from a car across the street. In one movement she snapped out the lamp and lifted the slat again. Two people were seated in the car, deep in conversation. The driver's back was to her. It was impossible to tell if it was a man or woman, yet Makaida instinctively felt she knew the person. The other person she saw only in silhouette. It wasn't until the passenger lifted his cigarette and lit it that she recognized Tomas. She tensed.

Tomas finally opened the car door, but seemed reluctant to lift himself from the seat. He looked back at the driver. His appearance, even in the dim light, frightened her. When he did move, his shoulders, normally proud and broad, seemed to have fallen; his hands were pushed into his pockets, his steps were reluctant. Halfway across the street, he glanced toward their bedroom window. Makaida dropped the slat and stumbled into bed. She prayed Tomas would not come directly into the bedroom.

Tomas entered the house like a cat. He neither turned on the lights, nor removed his jacket. He found the sofa by instinct; sank into it as if the cushions would absorb his state of mind. He didn't hear Makaida approach.

"Tomas?" She turned on the light.

"Tomas!" His head followed the general direction of her voice. With no change of expression, he rolled slightly to one side, reached into his pocket and brought out a fist full of money.

Makaida gasped. "Tomas, where did you get all that money, and who was that in the car?"

The mention of the car brought his eyes into focus. Like a cornered feline, he sprang forward as Makaida fell back. Without as much as a sideward glance, he shot past her and into the bathroom, locking the door. Makaida followed, pounding on the door, demanding an answer, but received only silence.

Makaida cried herself to sleep on the sofa. Now her back and legs ached. Remembering Tomas, she rushed towards the bathroom, stopping abruptly at the sight of money scattered about the floor. Tomas was gone.

***

She remembered fingering her door key, remembered the red glow of the setting sun on the door of her home, falling slow-motion to the pavement and the flow of blood pumping from her. She couldn't remember any pain, only panic, and an inability to call for help.

Nothing in her nineteen years prepared Makaida for the stark, shimmering glare of the white room in which she found herself. Overhead was a light that reminded her of a visit to the dentist. When she tried to move, she couldn't. There were four or five people swathed in pale, dull green, faces covered with white masks. Trying to sense her stomach, thighs, the only sensation she could muster was numbness. And her thoughts floated in and over any subject or object on which she tried to concentrate.

It was a slow movement, as slow as her vision trying to focus; the massive glaring equipment, the soundless green-clad people and the awareness that she was in their control. It was slow – the fear that took root in the pit of her stomach, seeping through her half-opened eyes and culminating in a low, escalating scream that echoed through her being but made no audible sound. There was no escape. With her last moments of consciousness, Makaida summoned her grandmother and all of the saints to watch over her and her baby.

Opening her eyes slowly, she saw that the glare was gone. The room was dusk. In the corner sat her grandmother, Lilyanne, erect in a straight-backed chair, hands folded, mouth moving in inaudible prayer.

"Grandma, what happened? My baby, how is my baby?"

"Birthin' ain't never been easy, Makaida."

"Grandma, you had five children."

"Yes, and lost two."

"Grandma, my baby?"

"They tried Makaida, you were in surgery a long time. It's only by the grace of God that you're still with me."

Makaida could not be consoled. In spite of what she was told, she felt her child, ever present, in and around her. She knew what the doctors did not: that her baby's spirit was searching for her.

***

While Grandma Lilyanne helped Makaida dress, Tomas made a great display of paying the bill, in cash. He had dressed for the occasion: gray slacks, gray silk shirt, a large platinum chain with medallion, large platinum bracelet and watch, gray patent leather shoes. He was proud -- not needing charity.

As they reached their home, a delivery truck was unloading. The deliveryman approached their door just behind them with a large box. Grandma Lilyanne went to the kitchen, hat still perched on her head, to make tea. Tomas opened the box as Makaida read the note:

Dear Makaida,

Sorry I have to leave without seeing you. My partner arrived from upstate ahead of schedule so it was time to split. I know the cradle is a little old-fashioned, but thought you'd get a kick out of it.

I won't have a forwarding address, but I'll be in touch with you and Tomas as best as I can.

Chi

Tomas's face contorted, his body stiffened. "What the hell... that lowlife SOB..." Tomas was beside himself with anger. There was no doubt in his mind that the cradle would be returned if he didn't smash it to bits first.

Makaida seemed oblivious to anything he said. She fitted the cradle with the blanket and pillow she had made and moved it into the bedroom along with the rocking chair that had been in the nursery. She spent long hours rocking the cradle, humming tuneless melodies. She spoke when spoken to.

"Makaida, I'm sorry we lost the baby, but when you're stronger we can try again. Besides, it will allow us time to move to a larger place, or buy a car."

A car? It made no sense; she was unanchored, adrift and uncertain of where she or her marriage was heading. When Tomas came home from work he had no joy, no interest in what her day had been... But he found time for gambling and his friends at the local bar. She wanted the Tomas she'd married, her rosary, her rock...

All through the fall she tended the loss of her baby and the relationship with Tomas. She watched and listened to the building and falling of the winds; the withering of the flowers, the ebb and flow of the ocean. She watched, listened and prayed. It was the end of familiar sounds, the beginning of new ones that she heard.

Sometime during the winter months Tomas returned home to find Makaida dismantling the crib and humming to herself.

"Makaida, are you alright? Has something happened?"

She looked up, smiling. "Yes. He's happy, he kissed my cheek; said he'd been my mother last time."

"Who?"

It took a moment for Tomas to realize that the "he" she referred to was their deceased child.

"Baby, you're confused."

"No Tomas, I'm comforted."

It was difficult for him to understand how Makaida had come to that conclusion and he was even more bewildered that she would be comforted by it. Tomas shook his head. But at least, he reasoned, Makaida was beginning to resemble the woman he'd married.

"I understand." He patted her shoulder.

Makaida smiled shyly but knew that Tomas did not truly understand although he was trying to be a good husband and father. In his mind that meant being able to financially take care of them. For Makaida it meant so much more...but she could no more explain it than could he. She'd never known her father so she had no one to compare Tomas to and her mother had given up trying to fill the void left by the loss of her husband.

Makaida began sending for college catalogues, vocational training courses and reading want ads for jobs. At first Tomas simply threw them away. When they continued to appear he confronted her. "You know as well as I do I want my wife to be just that – my wife. Isn't that enough for you?"

To say that it was not enough would mean an argument. She knew that behind all of his bravado was Tomas' fear of losing her, a fear they shared. She was afraid of losing herself too.

"Tomas, I want to visit my mother for a while."

"Really?" Tomas was clearly amused. "And what will you do for money to get to Silver Spring?"

Her eyes involuntarily focused on the closet where the box of money had been stored. Following her gaze, Tomas' body stiffened.

"You don't know where the money came from do you, Makaida?" He did not wait for response. "Remember Chi?" At the mention of Chi's name Makaida had averted her face, but it was too late. Tomas grabbed her arm. "What's the matter? Is Chi something special to you?" He released her; he had her full attention.

"Chi is cold-blooded. Said he'd heard I could use some extra cash. Said the word 'round the way was that I was having a rough time – kid on the way and all."

Tomas snorted and continued. "He had an arsenal of guns -- taught me how to use those guns, how to break them down, how to clean, store and hide them."

He paused. When he spoke again his voice was low and he spoke as if speaking to himself. "I was scared as hell on that first job, but we got through it okay. But the fear began to settle in. You ever see someone shot at close range, Makaida? A young security guard. Chi just shot him. Didn't faze him at all. Never mentioned it afterwards either. He split for a while after that, visiting his 'business partner' who was in prison upstate. Then he disappeared again, but not before sending that damned cradle. The only good news was that the security guard didn't die."

Makaida was not surprised by Chi's actions; she'd sensed his hard undercurrent. Tomas's involvement left her disappointed, but not shocked. Not really. He'd always liked flashy, expensive things. And he did want to create a home for their family. More than anything, though, Makaida was sad, weary. It felt as if everything she held sacred was falling away.

It was several weeks before Tomas realized a change was taking place in Makaida. The house was always clean and supper was always on the table when he got home from work, but when he attempted to touch her she pulled away.

"Baby, what's making you so unhappy? What can I do?"

There was an aloofness that had never been there before. No matter how often he asked she refused to answer his questions. He was becoming distraught.

Finally Makaida realized he deserved some answers. "I don't like who we're becoming. It's as if we don't know what we want. Tomas, are you comfortable with our marriage?"

Although Makaida had stopped speaking, Tomas knew there was more. "Is that what all these past weeks have been about?"

"I'm leaving, Tomas. I have to take control of myself, figure out what I want…"

"We agreed that you would stay home and…"

"There are no children to raise Tomas. Maybe this is the time we should be raising ourselves."

Tomas managed to look angry and hurt at the same time but Makaida was not frightened nor was she sympathetic to the boyish look of hurt that took over the features of his face.

***

Although Makaida thought she knew the neighborhood, just two miles from the home she shared with Tomas, the realtor called the neighborhood "transitional." Makaida wondered what it was transitioning from and more importantly, what was it trying to be. There was a gourmet grocery store but no supermarket, a wine store with fancy displays and barrels of new inventory but no fish or meat market, a Laundromat that doubled as a newsstand and a candy store, and a funeral parlor but no church. The bottom line was that the apartment above the florist shop was what she could afford with what she'd saved from her grocery money. Her original plan was to surprise Tomas with a trip to Cancun or some other romantic place, but that was before she'd left him. She shook her head to focus on her immediate situation – finding work. It had already been three weeks with no job in sight, and no backup plan.

Facing up to read the florist shop sign and her thoughts elsewhere she collided with someone. "I'm so sorry…" she began and quickly stooped to pick up the sign that had fallen to the ground. The older gentleman was dazed but grateful to still be on his feet.

Makaida read the sign: "Help Wanted. Inquire Within."

"Really?" she said, pointing to the sign.

"Why yes, do you know anyone who might be interested?"

"Yes, me."

The old man's eyes twinkled. Although she didn't recognize him, there was something about his energy that was familiar; perhaps it was the mischievous twinkle in his eyes.

"I'm Mr. Taliaferro. Come tomorrow."

Before she could ask any questions, he was gone.

That night Makaida had difficulty falling asleep. She had never worked and wasn't sure of what to expect. She was giddy with anticipation. While she didn't know very much about operating a business she certainly knew flowers. She had gardened from the time she was a child trailing behind her grandmother in the backyard. And she'd always had a gift for growing and arranging flowers. She especially liked to put flowers in unusual containers. She fell asleep arranging an exquisite floral arrangement in her head.

The next day Mr. Taliaferro asked her to make three arrangements: one for a sweet sixteen party; one as a thank you gift, and one for a bridal reception. She was pleased with her work but looked at Mr. Taliaferro for approval. He simply nodded and asked how much she would charge for each arrangement. She had no idea.

"I will teach you."

"I have the job?"

"When can you start?"

"Is now too soon?"

Mr. Taliaferro and Makaida worked together easily. He made sure she understood the business -- when he placed orders for supplies or invoiced customers, he made sure Makaida understood the "what" and "why" of each transaction and advised her which accounts to use. When she created her floral arrangements he watched quietly, offering suggestions, tricks of the trade. She suggested smaller, less expensive arrangements that would be accessible to a larger clientele. On her days off she went to secondhand stores and yard sales, buying unusual containers which she used for her arrangements.

Excited to show off her accomplishments, Makaida invited her grandmother, Lilyanne, to the florist shop. Before long Lilyanne was a frequent visitor, especially around holidays when the shop was busy. "Where is this elusive Mr. Taliaferro?" she asked whenever she visited. He was always away on business or traveling.

"You mean he leaves you to run the shop alone?" Lilyanne frowned, but held her tongue. She was uneasy about her granddaughter being left alone in the shop, so decided to make her visits more frequent. She'd been watchful from Makaida's birth. Because Lilyanne recognized the special gift her granddaughter had been born with, she had taken her to the Yoruba priestesses to be blessed and protected. She was not about to stop her attentiveness now.

Before long the shop took on a different ambiance. Makaida bought a bistro table set and placed it in a corner where she and Mr. Taliaferro could have afternoon tea. She asked Mr. "T," as she'd taken to calling him, if she could order a few tea sets. These sold well. Makaida put containers of cut pussy willows and forsythia outside the front door, which attracted new customers. Mr. Taliaferro seemed appreciative of Makaida's natural business acumen.

In quiet moments, Makaida thought of Tomas. She wanted to call him but to do so would be to acquiesce to the very things that she didn't want in her life. She noted that he had not called her either.

One day Mr. Taliaferro made a pot of tea and asked Makaida to join him.

"Have you talked with Tomas lately?" he inquired.

"No."

"Nothing is carved in stone, Makaida. Both of you are young. Youth is a time for learning. If he was so awful, would you have married him?"

Makaida made grunting sounds that could be construed as anything the listener wanted to hear. Mr. Taliaferro shifted gears.

"What do you think the possibilities are for the vacant lot next door?" he began. "Any ideas?"

"That lot is a mess; it's been used like a junkyard for years it seems, but I can envision any number of things…"

"Like what?"

"Once cleared, it would be a great place for a community garden with a greenhouse at the back for winter gardening. It would give folks an opportunity to have fresh vegetables. And if we got the neighborhood kids involved they might enjoy it too – a chance to learn where their food comes from. Maybe we could experiment with a small hydroponic garden." Her mind was already racing with so many ideas. She stopped abruptly.

"Is the lot for sale?" she asked.

"I don't know, but I'm sure I can find out. In the meantime will you sign these papers? I'm putting your name on some company papers so when I take a little trip to Florida, you can run the business without a problem. You are, after all, one of my most trusted employees!"

"Mr. T, I'm your only employee!"

As Mr. T made travel plans, Makaida thought of Tomas. How and what was he doing – had he started dating? Did he still have the same job? She wanted to tell him about all of the new and wonderful things going on in her life, the new skills she hadn't known she had and the confidence it brought. But she didn't want to be a postscript in his life. It may have been alright before… but not now. And yet she missed her best friend and yearned for some portion of what had been.

Makaida finally called Tomas. He answered on the third ring.

"Is that you Makaida?"

"Yes, how have you been? Are you still working in the same job?"

"No, I quit. Now I buy the clothes from the manufacturers and sell to the clients I've built up over the years."

"Is it going well for you?"

"It would be better if you were with me. I miss you babe."

Makaida was gladdened by his words but she was just getting used to her independence and didn't want to be just a housewife.

The first week of managing the shop alone was a bit taxing but exhilarating. Every day she set aside time to make a pot of tea and sit quietly, to daydream plans for the vacant lot. If something perplexed her, she'd ask herself, what would Mr. T. do and wait for an answer. By the end of the second week she'd even drawn up several possibilities for the vacant lot. By the third week, she wondered if Mr. T would ever return. She called Grandmother Lilyanne.

"Grandma, I haven't heard from Mr. T. I'm worried. Have you heard from him?"

"You're the only one who 'hears' from Mr. T., Makaida. Obviously he's a man of great mystery. What's going on? Are you okay?"

"No."

By the time Lilyanne arrived at the flower shop, a neighbor was consoling a very pale Makaida.

"Makaida, are you alright? You look awful."

Instead of responding, Makaida handed her grandmother a stack of papers. There was a last will and testament and deeds to properties including the flower shop and the adjacent vacant lot. Makaida was the sole beneficiary.

"Where did these come from?"

"They were here on the counter when I came in. I didn't notice them initially. Grandma, look at the dates."

The documents were dated eleven years before.

The kettle whistled. Since neither of the women had put the pot on, Makaida almost expected Mr. T to step out, holding the teapot.

Lilyanne broke the silence, "Makaida, what did Mr. T say the last time you talked to him?"

"I don't remember exactly. He said he had accomplished what he'd come to do and would now move on. But the way he said it frightened me. I wondered if he was ill, so I asked about his health. He just laughed and said, 'I'm quite well, now.'"

As Makaida tried to fully understand what was happening, she distinctly heard Mr. T say, "Be well, daughter."

She smiled. She didn't doubt she would be.

'SPLANATION

Emma and Sissy, both middle-aged thick, separated themselves from the other mourners leaving the church. Arm-in-arm they walked to the waiting automobile in the churchyard.

"I ain't never heard a such a thing! A funeral where the deceased ain't in attendance. It ain't like he died at sea. He died right at home, in his own bed, with all his kin lookin' on!" lamented Sissy.

"Heard tell he already been buried," volunteered Emma, the older of the sisters. Sissy's beady eyes bulged.

"You know that cain't be true, Emma. Why you choose a time like this to exercise your humor is beyond me. You bein' very un-Christian."

"Well, you see a hearse? 'Sides, the reverend kept callin' the service a 'membrance' or some such thing. That mean the buryin' already been done."

Having seated and arranged herself in the automobile, Sissy folded her arms in front of her ample bosom and addressed her sister in a tense voice, "Well, if you hadn't a been so long gettin' dressed, we just mighta got here in time to sit up front and hear 'cisely what was goin' on 'stead of bein' out here supposin.'"

"Never-you-mind," Emma tried to sooth her sister. "Things will 'splain theyself when we get to the Weems's house."

"You bes' believe Hattie Weems gon hafta do a good bit of 'splainin ta satisfy me" Sissy grumbled.

In a small hamlet, outside of Henderson, North Carolina, nestled among tall ancient trees, was the Weems house. Hattie Weems rocked slowly in the swing on the back porch, listening more to the rhythm of the conversations going on inside than to their content.

"Yes, Billy Weems was a righteous man. Gon' really miss him. I 'member when he got me my job ovah ta the mill. Way back then you either farmed or worked the mill. Either way, we was always jus' one step ahead a hunger."

"Well, Reveren," bantered Sissy, "the way I heard that story, Billy was forced ta getting' you that job. He coulda' either listened to your constant preachin' or get you somethin' new to talk about." Before the Reverend could reply, Spider Jesse sauntered in, holding a plate of Hoppin' John and neck bones in one hand and a cup of white lightning in the other. Slowing his pace, he loudly proclaimed, "Well, Billy musta' growed inta sainthood whilst I was in D.C."

Continuing across the room, Spider eased his tall, pot-bellied body into a comfortable chair. "The Billy I know'd had a good corner on some genuine hell-raisin'. I 'member clear as day how we usta buy our corn ovah to Sadie's and then head straight to Jackson's juke joint. Shoot, many a night we hadda fight our way outta there – 'specially if that big-legged Keeley gal was around."

"Man, what you talkin' was 'fore he and Mae got married," cut in the Reverend, "and you could show some respec' for the occasion that brings us here."

But Spider was just getting warmed up. "Oouwe! I 'member one evenin' I was sittin' out on Billy's porch waitin' for him ta get home. He come down the road bobbin', weavin' and singin' at the toppa his lungs. When he reached the gate, he winked at me and commenced to shout, 'Woman, I'se home. My food ready?'

"Not bein' a pure fool, I figures I'd bes be getting on home. Lawd, I wudn't home five minutes 'fore little Hattie comma runnin', yellin' for me ta 'come quick.' When I gets there, Billy Jr. was doing all he could ta separate them two. Why Mae had Billy by the collar with one hand and was poundin' the livin' daylights outta him with t'other. An' she wasn't sayin' a word, min you. It was Billy keeping up the ruckus! It took three of us menfolk ta get her offin him. If memory serves me right, that was the las' time Billy let his liquor do any talkin' for him round that house."

Sissy moved out to the back porch. "Sho woulda liked to have looked on Brother Weems one mo time 'fore he crossed ovah." Her body stood rigid with her arms folded across her chest, taking up the entire doorway. Hattie smiled up at Miss Sissy.

"Poppa was ailin for quite a spell. The Reveren made the announcement in church. Elder Pugh and Loretha Jones came ta see 'bout him that very day. Why didn't you come then? You was mo' than welcome."

"That ain't exactly what I'm talkin' about. Some of yo daddy's friends feels cheated. We come to the funeral 'spectin ta say our las' good-byes and finds out that he already been buried. It jus ain't our way. It ain't right.

"When yo momma died, y'all had a right decent funeral. I 'member it good 'cause Mr. Burton had just got a new fleet a limousines – powder blue they were – such a pretty sight. Was leas' thirty cars in that procession. Folks still talk 'bout that funeral and how grand it was. Yo momma was put away in style. Seem like to me yo poppa deserve at leas' as much respect."

Hattie rolled these words around between her thick plaits and her thin fingers. In the dimming evening light, her deep-set eyes took on a bright light.

"Uh huh, you right Miss Sissy. It sho' was sumthin. And that was what Momma wanted. Me and Poppa talked a lot 'bout that since. Matta fac, Poppa talked a lot 'bout a time when folks took care of they own birthin' and buryin' an everything in between. Seem like folks wasn't scared ta touch they own life an those 'round 'em. Poppa tried for the longest to figure out why we embalm our kinfolk and then stare at the body tryin' to measure how close a likeness they come ta they real self." Hattie chuckled to herself.

"An?"

"Poppa wanted folk to 'member him the way they knew him."

"You tryin ta tell me yo Poppa wanted this, this..."

"Yes, ma'am."

"That don't sound nothing like the Billy Weems I grow'd up wid. He know'd how we do things, the way we always did things. The way things 'spose to be done."

"That's the point, Miss Sissy."

"What point?"

"The way things are done can change Miss Sissy."

Spider came out to the porch to find the two women staring: Hattie staring off into the night, and Sissy staring at Hattie.

"Hattie, I jus wants to 'spress my condolences."

"Thank you, Mr. Jesse."

"Chile done grow'd into a 'spectable young lady, ain't she Sissy? Spittin' image of her daddy, even talk like him."

"Hump," followed by the slamming of the screen door is all Spider and Hattie heard as Sissy returned to the living room.

"I say sumthin' wrong?" asked Spider Jesse.

"Nah, don't think so."

"Then, what's wrong with Sissy?"

Hattie was quiet for a few moments. "Guess times a changing an' Miss Sissy ain't takin' kindly to it."

"Ain't many ole dogs takes kindly to new tricks."

"Poppa didn't have no problem wid new ideas."

Spider smiled. "Yeah, but yo daddy was, uh, unusual, a bit ahead of his time."

"Mayhaps, but I always thought of him as always being right on time."

Spider Jesse grinned, "I reckon."

Author's Note: *A version of 'Splanation was published in Faith Journey Series, Level III, Youth and Young Adults. Jointly published by the Board of Educational Ministries of the American Baptist Churches in the U.S.A; the Division of Publication, the United Church Board for Homeland Ministries, The United Church of Christ; the General Assembly Mission Board, Presbyterian Church (U.S.A.); and the Program Agency, Presbyterian Church (U.S.A.)*

COUNT IT ALL JOY

For Marguerite Lewis

Fundi was a beauty by any cultural standard. She was the color of burnt almonds with a touch of cinnamon showing through. Her round face held heavy eyelids and slanted eyes, high cheekbones, full sculptured lips and a smile that made her face sing. Everything about Fundi was round and she favored fish-tailed dresses that accentuated it all.

Wherever she chose to live in "my town" as she called Brooklyn, she took her plants, cooking pots, wooden bowls and spoons, wood carving tools, fabric and all manner of mementos collected over the years. Her new apartment was large – four bedrooms all having floor-to ceiling windows. There were two working fireplaces, one in the master bedroom and the other in the living room. All of the rooms reflected Fundi, from the paisley velvet sofa and chair that she'd re-upholstered, the cane-bottom rocking chair which she'd found on the curb with the trash and refurbished, to the old picture frames that she called "found treasures."

These frames were now fitted with sepia-tone photographs of family members and friends. In her workroom were stacks of fabric, wicker baskets, blocks of wood, broken tables, discarded doors (which sometimes served as workbenches), and anything else she thought could be restored or repurposed or just made beautiful anew. And her prized possession, her mother's antique sewing machine, stood in the center of it all.

Fundi walked slowly into the living room, trying to ignore the pain in her shoulder and neck. She stacked the record player with treasured records from "'ome," red and blue translucent disks that held the music of Calypsonians Lord Flea and the Mighty Sparrow. To these she added Billie Holiday and the Duke. Popping her fingers to the music she continued her chores, lighting incense and arranging flowers for the party. The apartment began to take on a festive air.

In the large, airy yellow and white kitchen, Fundi moved amid earthenware jars of dried herbs and seeds, wooden canisters of grains and flours, along with baskets and bowls of vegetables and assorted fruits. No cookbooks or recipe cards were in evidence. Fundi cooked by her own measure – the way she lived her life.

As she mixed, stirred, chopped and kneaded the ingredients before her, she flirted with the shadows and designs the sun cast on her busy hands. She listened to the music and the counterpoint rhythms created by the bird-like children in the courtyard below her window as they chanted to their rope jumping, "2-4-6-10-2, 22...." I was the Double Dutch queen not so long ago. The recollection heightened her spirits.

The front door opened and slammed shut, interrupting her thoughts. The familiar footsteps of her niece, Mariamma, clicked their way down the hallway. She made her way into the kitchen cradling a towel-wrapped tray in one arm and a shopping bag draped over the other.

"Hey Aunt Fundi, do I smell codfish? You making coo-coo and codfish? I.... What happened to your eye?" Mariamma gasped at her aunt's swollen, almost closed, purple/maroon eye.

"Your grandmother, my mother, the one and only, Laurel. It was an accident though."

"Aunt Fundi, would you please tell me what happened?" With this she moved carefully around her aunt trying to get a closer look.

Later. Let's talk about that a little later."

"But what about the party tonight? How will you explain that eye?"

"Explain? With the new dress I've designed, I doubt anyone will notice." She paused for the briefest of moments. "On second thought, maybe I'll design and decorate an eye patch I've got tons of sequins...."

"Aunt Fundi!"

"I thought you said you'd be here early."

"It is early, isn't it?" Mariamma checked her watch.

Fundi sidestepped her niece and began rummaging through the shopping bag. "Never mind, you're here and bearing goodies."

Mariamma moved to the stove, lifting pot lids, peering into the oven and finally retrieving a pitcher of sorrel from the refrigerator and sweetbread from the counter.

Fundi's hands moved from Mairamma's bags back to chopping vegetables. She never stopped moving, while her eyes studied her niece. Mariamma looks a lot like me, except she's slender and her movements are quick, abrupt – like America. Only the second generation and already we move differently, Fundi mused to herself.

Mariamma unloaded the remaining contents of the shopping bag. At the bottom, she retrieved a dozen decks of cards. "Why do you need so many playing cards?" she asked her aunt.

"Medical expenses, darlin'. The shop is holding its own, but it's not enough for the rent on this grand apartment and my mounting medical bills. Which reminds me, Reggie will deal one table, but I still can't reach Dalton. If I have to deal that second table, I may well miss my own party – and I don't intend to miss this one."

Mariamma's eyes rolled back in her head as she mumbled through her full mouth, "If Gramma heard you talking about gambling and playing 'tuk,' real devil music..."

"Never-you-mind Gramma. 'Dis here is important work getting ready to 'appen. Besides, it's part of your education. Pay attention darlin', the weekends you spend with me are important educational resources." Fundi winked at her niece.

"Just weekends?" quipped Mariamma. "What about the time we spend in the shop, doesn't that count?"

"Chups," said Fundi, sucking her teeth. "Dat livelihood, dis livin'."

"So when did you start making such distinctions?"

"Since we Americans now. Ain't dat how we do, nuh?"

The two women laughed at their playful Bajan-English parlance.

"I know the craft shop is your first love, Aunt Fundi."

"Eh, eh, I did t'ink t'was Cyril!" Fundi said.

"I'll bet you've invited all of your menfolk to the party."

"Well, almost all" replied Fundi, reaching for the covered tray.

"Those are Miss Odessa's fishcakes," said Mariamma, pointing. "She said she'd bring the rest later. But there's no telling when; Mr. Pittman had a grip on her!"

"What? Where'd you see Mr. Pittman?"

"On Miss 'Dessa's stoop debating the political ramifications of current events in the colored community." This Mariamma said with her head held high, one hand on her hip, the other held aloft in the air, her speech clearly mocking the Caribbean orators she'd seen and heard around the neighborhood.

Fundi laughed at her niece's dramatization. She began grating coconut. While she worked, she prayed that she'd have enough time to do all she needed to do; that Mariamma would be as strong as she'd need to be to take care of Momma, to carry on the business, to make something of herself, to pass on the trade…

"Oh, Aunt Fundi, come look at my latest project," Mariamma said as she pushed Fundi playfully toward the workroom.

"It's not finished yet. What do you think so far?"

Smiling, Fundi turned the carving around in both her hands – the mahogany was heavy. "Love the movement of it and the attention to detail. What's with the head?"

"That, Aunt Fundi, is something unique that I'm trying to work out."

"I think you are about to surpass me with your carving skills, my dear niece." Fundi put the sculpture back on the pedestal and headed toward the kitchen. "We have a party to prepare for, remember?" The truth was she could feel her strength waning but hoped Mariamma wouldn't notice.

"So what happened to your eye, Aunt Fundi?"

"Well, it was an accident."

"You've already said that!" Mariamma exclaimed, anxious to get to the crux of the matter.

"Momma and I were talking about my Going Home Party. Up until then I hadn't told her what my real plan for the party was. She just thought it was another of my "very un-Christian fetes." Fundi glanced up in time to see Mariamma's eyebrows arch in alarm.

"'This is my farewell party Momma,' I told her. 'It's going to be the grandest of them all. I intend for this gathering to be instead of a funeral or memorial. And I've made arrangements to be cremated. If the family needs something concrete to look at I can order or design an urn to hold the ashes.'"

"Oh my…what did Gramma say?"

Fundi could see Mariamma was clearly shaken. She lived with her grandmother and knew that the party was insult enough but to be cremated was well beyond what her grandmother's religious sensibility would abide.

"At first she didn't say anything – it was as if it didn't register immediately so I continued mixing the batter for the cake I was making. I bent down to get the Bundt pan from the cabinet. At that moment the realization must have set in. Momma stood up abruptly, slamming her hands down on the counter. She was livid. Her hand came down on that large, heavy-duty spoon – a spoon from hell. It flew into the air just as I was attempting to stand up. It caught me right in the eye, sending me sprawling onto the floor." She winced. Even recalling the incident caused her pain.

Fundi continued. "'I did not raise a heathen,' Momma screamed, before she realized I was unable to rise from the floor. She got me into bed and got an icepack for my eye."

What Fundi did not say was that she had had a very difficult conversation with her mother after that but she didn't want to upset her niece further. As she reflected on that conversation she wondered if she had been too hard on her mother.

"Momma, this is my life" she remembered saying. "Maybe you would like to have a traditional funeral but that would be a sham. That's not how I've lived my life. You probably think I'm a heathen, but, truth be told, everything you taught me has kept me from falling apart."

Laurel had raised an eyebrow, waiting. Fundi, clearly in pain, opened the nightstand drawer to retrieve a Bible. She flipped deftly through the pages and read:

Count it all joy, my brethren, when you meet various trials, for you know that the testing of your faith produces steadfastness.And let steadfastness have its full effect, that you may be perfect and complete, lacking in nothing. (James 1:2-4)

Laurel had been surprised her daughter even owned a Bible. This one was dog-eared, marked with highlighter and with notes scribbled in the margins. Laurel offered a small smile, but her eyes registered confusion.

"Where does this party fit into that, Fundi?"

"It fits with how I've lived my life, Momma. I've never liked all of that sanctimonious talk that ends as soon as Sunday service is over. I prefer to celebrate life every day." She offered her mother a hopeful smile. "And I don't want any pity. No well-intended but often insincere words of sympathy or empathy. Or tears. I've cried enough for all of us. The bottom line is, I want to be remembered as I am now — however people interpret that.

Smiling through her tears, Laurel had embraced her daughter, holding her tightly. "A mother isn't supposed to bury her children!

I've already lost one daughter, Ena, and her husband to a drunk driver. Now this. I've spent my life on my knees praying for my family, for your protection, for enough to keep you all fed, clothed, healthy. I've tried to teach you the right way to live." Laurel's voice lowered, barely audible but Fundi could hear her speaking to herself. "How have I failed? Dear Lord, how have I failed? Take me, I've lived long.... leave my daughter and grand baby to live a full life…"

Reggie and Dalton were the first to arrive. Their movements seemed synchronized – arranging the card tables and chairs in one of the side rooms, stacking boxes of new playing cards and setting up a mini-bar in one corner. They were making sure the gamblers need not be distracted by the party going on down the hall. Odessa arrived next with two additional pans of codfish cakes and a bowl of potato salad.

Laurel arrived next with a pinched look on her face. Fundi gave her a hug, trying to smooth over their previous disagreement. Her mother merely grunted.

Cyril wasn't far behind, carrying a huge floral arrangement, which he placed in the center of the refreshment table. Heading into the kitchen he greeted Laurel and Mariamma, "Greetings lovely ladies. You both look enchanting."

Mariamma blushed. Laurel smiled a thin, impatient smile.

Moving down the hallway Cyril tapped lightly on Fundi's bedroom door. "Do you need any help Sugar?"

Cyril pushed open the door. Fundi turned her back to him, indicating she needed him to zip up her dress. "My word woman, you look ravishing!" A second later: "What the hell happened to your eye Fundi?" His body tensed, prepared to fight the unknown villain.

"It's okay Cyril. It was an accident."

"Who caused this…accident?"

"Momma."

"What?"

"That's a story for another time." She seated herself. "Can you help me with my eyepatch?"

Mariamma had stacked the record player with records and sorted through the music collection to select the next cycle of dance tunes. It wasn't long before everyone was on their feet dancing, including Fundi. She could feel Cyril watching her closely. If he sensed her energy was waning or if she was in pain, he'd cut in, holding her securely or sit her down and bring her sorrel or ginger beer. He made sure she didn't have anything alcoholic since she was on morphine. At some point in the evening he carried her to her bedroom, undressed her, tucked her in, and kissed her forehead. "I'm not going anywhere Fundi, so rest. I'll be here when you wake up." She did not protest.

The next morning Laurel rose early and headed to the kitchen to make coffee. Considering the number of people who were here, she mused, the place is not nearly as discombobulated as I'd anticipated. She poured coffee into her cup, just as she realized that Cyril was filling the doorway with his tall, muscled body, arms folded across his chest. How long has he been standing there staring at me? He's a fool. What does Fundi see in him?

"Is there enough for me?" asked Cyril.

Reluctantly Laurel filled another cup and slid it across the table. Where did he sleep? she wondered. Laurel's hands were a tight fist, challenging her coffee cup's breaking point.

"I know you don't like me and I'm sorry you don't," Cyril said. "But I'm not here to convince you of anything. I do want you to know that I love Fundi and intend to take care of her however long or short that time may be. We've been together for six years and, if God willing, there will be many more years to come."

"Really? 'More years to come?' My daughter's time is short. She doesn't need you. She's got us – me and Mariamma."

"I'm not challenging your love or position in Fundi's life, but I'm not going anywhere." Cyril took his cup of coffee and left the kitchen. A few minutes later he returned. "Why don't you like me?" he asked as he placed the cup in the sink. There was no heat in his question.

Laurel straightened her back and glared at him. "You're a ruffian, you're seldom 'dressed' and you never say much. I can't get a feel for who you are."

Cyril's laughter erupted loudly and unashamedly. "I'm a stevedore. We don't load and unload ships in business suits! No, there has got to be something you're not saying. You're being disingenuous." He seated himself in front of her.

Laurel glared at him for a long moment before refilling her cup. "You remind me of my former husband. He didn't say much either. He worked the docks too. He made good money and made a good home for us, but money wasn't all he brought home. He brought home VD – more than once. And I'm sure he has children outside of our marriage." She began to weep. Cyril handed her his handkerchief but did not attempt to comfort her.

When Laurel drew herself up her face was closed. "I wanted more for my daughters."

"I assure you I am not like your ex-husband." Cyril rose to leave. "Thanks for your candor." His voice was measured but his eyes were hard, cold. It was an hour before Laurel saw him ease into Fundi's room.

"Okay beautiful lady, are you planning on getting up any time soon?" Cyril asked. It was late afternoon.

Fundi rolled over, opening one eye to test the amount of light in the room. "Ummm" she crooned softly. She moved gently to the edge of the bed. Cyril wrapped her robe around her and led her to the sofa. He poured coffee for her.

"How long have we been together, Fundi?"

Fundi didn't respond immediately; she wasn't sure of the purpose of the question.

"Well?"

"Six years. You know that Cyril."

"It must be time then," he said. He reached into his pocket and produced a ring with an emerald center stone surrounded by diamonds. "Fundi, will you marry me?"

Instead of a response, she burst into tears and covered her face. "Babe, I've got stage four cancer; I'm dying. You know that. Why are you tormenting me? Just stay with me until the end. Please."

"Who told you that you were dying? Yes, you have cancer, but that isn't what defines you or our relationship. And, the length of your life is not something you control, is it? Or mine. Or anyone else's. The question is, do you love me, Fundi?"

"Yes Cyril, you know I do!"

Cyril did not wait for additional conversation. He took her left hand and slid the ring onto it. It was a perfect fit. Fundi's tears turned to tears of joy.

They wasted no time in letting their families know of their wedding plans – which would be in two weeks.

Laurel bent forward slightly as she studied the gold-edged Bible in her lap. She read and reread Judges 5:24-31 -- The Song of Deborah. Her lips moved silently, mouthing the words, as if in a trance. Jael's killing of Sisera lifted Laurel's spirit. Her body rocked gently to the rhythm of her inaudibly mouthed words. She did not hear Mariamma enter the house.

Mariamma paused. Something in the feel of the house wasn't right. Walking through the living room, kitchen and dining room didn't make her feel any better. She did not ponder long: she went to her room to retrieve a sage bundle, which she lit. Carrying the smudge stick in her right hand she used her left hand to fan the smoke – to smudge all entry points in each of the rooms, to remove the negative energy. Her grandmother's room was last. Out of habit and respect she knocked, but pushed open the door before there was a response. The sight that greeted her made her step back. The strange energy she'd felt emanated from this room, from her grandmother.

"Grandma, what are you doing?" she asked in alarm.

"Just my daily devotions."

Mariamma gave her grandmother a weak smile in return but held her ground for another second before entering the room to continue her task. Laurel did not object.

It was too much for Mariamma. She quickly completed her task and fled – all the way to her aunt's home. Cyril was in the kitchen preparing supper while Fundi sat at the counter watching. She smiled when she saw her niece but it quickly faded.

"What is it Mariamma?" Fundi asked as she rose to embrace her niece.

"It's Gran. She's doing something weird and the whole house has a strange energy. No, a negative, hateful energy. I smudged the place, but I'm frightened."

Cyril spoke calmly. "Mariamma, you give it power when you accept that it has power and act or react accordingly. Your grandmother is afraid – afraid that her only daughter is being taken away from her. Even though I've told her otherwise, she's having a hard time with that new reality."

"But she's doing something weird!" Mariamma insisted. Fundi comforted her niece while Cyril set another place at the table.

After the meal they sat together to try to figure out what to do. Cyril was for confronting Laurel immediately. Mariamma was afraid of what that might unleash. Fundi was quiet. She remembered the last time her mother had behaved this way. It was when her mother decided she'd had enough of her husband's philandering. Laurel had taken to burning strange powders and oils. Each night she placed a glass of water under his bed with a sheet of paper with something written on it. In short order he'd left. It was clear to Fundi her mother was now trying to frighten Cyril.

Fundi reached for the phone. "Momma, I know what you're trying to do and if you continue, you won't have to be concerned about Cyril pulling me away from you. I will remove you from my life -- not Cyril. The wedding is in one week. You're welcome to attend if you stop this foolishness. Otherwise you will not be welcomed. No one is doing anything to you. You're creating a web of destruction all by yourself." Fundi hung up without hearing her mother's response.

Fundi's next call was to the Yoruba priestess, Ayo, who promised to visit later that evening to perform the necessary protective prayers and rituals. Fundi began the clearing process. She retrieved her salt box from a kitchen shelf and carried it to the apartment door. She sprinkled salt on both the outside and inside floor mats.

The following evening Fundi was visibly happy while Cyril was apprehensive. He paced the length of the living room and watched the clock impatiently.

"Come and sit down, Cyril. This is not the Inquisition."

Cyril nodded but continued his restless walking.

Finally, the doorbell chimed and Fundi went to answer it. Cyril seated himself and lit a cigarette. The dark-skinned wiry gentleman who entered kissed Fundi on the cheek and walked directly to Cyril. He extended his hand and offered a toothy smile.

"Good evening, I'm Lazarus, Fundi's father."

Cyril greeted him warmly. They spent the rest of the evening getting acquainted, beginning with their shared work as longshoremen. Cyril told Lazarus about how he'd met Fundi at a Sunday soccer match; how he'd pursued her each Sunday for three weeks before she agreed to date him. The two men talked as if they'd known each other for years. Fundi sat back and enjoyed being with two of her favorite men.

The wedding chapel was small but quietly elegant -- just what Fundi hoped for in her future with Cyril. The bridal party was small: Mariamma, maid of honor; Reggie, the best man; Fundi's father; and the Presbyterian minister, Rev. Sheldon Jamison. They'd not heard from Laurel so Fundi had no idea if she would show up. Cyril's parents, who were aboard a cruise ship, would visit with them in a few weeks on their return.

Laurel was late. The Rev. Jamison had almost completed the nuptials when she arrived. She was all smiles until she saw Lazarus. Dropping her eyes, Laurel nodded an apologetic greeting to all. Fundi knew from her mother's stiffened back and the forward thrust of her chin, that she was not pleased and was probably plotting some retaliatory action. But Laurel remained quiet during the remainder of the church service and the wedding supper.

Cyril made sure that Fundi was settled and that Mariamma needed no further help in preparing coffee for the gathering before he flopped down next to Lazarus. A sense of well-being enveloped him; he felt he'd come full circle; that everything had gone well and he and his wife could relax into their new life together.

Laurel watched them with a slow growing rage. How dare he return as if in control of something; his ease with Cyril, his smugness. How dare he, after all these years to walk back into my child's life as if he'd never left. How dare he befriend that, scoundrel, Cyril. She rose from her chair, traversed the wide living room as if in a trance. When she was within reach of Lazarus she bent down so that her face was inches from his. "You know this boy here?" Her finger pointed at Cyril although her eyes never left Lazarus' face. "You remember him?"

Lazarus was nonplussed. "No, I'm afraid not. I met him yesterday, although I've heard about him for several years now from Fundi and Mariamma. And I do recall we spoke a few times on the phone."

"Liar!"

"Laurel, what is wrong with you? Why are you acting as if someone has done you harm? What do you want from everyone? You always make it seem as if you and only you are the center of the known universe. What do you want?"

Rearing back on her heels Laurel's voice escalated. "You don't recognize your own son? He is your son, isn't he?" And she smiled wickedly, gratified that she'd finally said what had been in her heart and what she had intended to declare when the minister asked if anyone objected to the marriage.

"What in the hell are you talking about, Laurel?" Lazarus stood and propelled Laurel into a corner where he roughly sat her down. "You need to clean this crap up Laurel. Now!" His voice had taken on a dangerous edge. Laurel saw Cyril rush to Fundi, who was on the edge of her seat attempting to get up. He gently eased her back into the chair.

Laurel continued her tirade. "Remember when you used to tip out on me? Well, I followed you. Every Wednesday and every Saturday you visited that woman on Hancock Street. Nyla, wasn't that her name? Isn't that Cyril's mother's name? Didn't they live on Hancock Street?"

Laurel stared at Lazarus with a sense of complete vindication. Lazarus laughed. "Woman, you are a fool, a mean-spirited, controlling fool. You see what you want to see. You create stories that suit your purposes. All these years….Yeah, there was a Nyla. The daughter of the man who taught me to play chess, who helped me get into the longshoremen's union. Truth be told, I went there twice a week to avoid being in the house with your negativity; with you trying to turn my children against me."

Lazarus walked back across the room. "I apologize to all of you for Laurel. Her need to be in control has made her difficult, to say the least. But I leave for Charlotte in the morning. You two will have to figure out how you want to handle her antics, if at all. I am so sorry you have had to experience Laurel at her worst – at a time when we all should be celebrating your marriage."

Laurel looked on silently. Cyril shook his head in disbelief. Fundi spoke softly – a controlled softness that belied her obvious anger. "Momma, go home, just get out!" Her body was shaking. "I'm not sure I'll ever want to see you again!"

***

Cyril had wanted to take Fundi to the Caribbean for their honeymoon but believed the flight would be too much for her so he'd rented a beach house on Fire Island. In the mornings they enjoyed the surf along the ocean. In the evenings they enjoyed the calm of the bay.

Three days later, as they were having lunch on the deck, Mariamma called.

"Uncle Cyril, is Aunt Fundi okay?"

"'Uncle' is it?" he smiled.

"Yes!"

"Well, niece, all is well here. Fundi seems to have gained strength and vitality being around all of this water!"

"That's good to hear. But Uncle, someone's life is ebbing away. I can't 'see' whose it is, but it's someone close. I feel it. Since it's not Aunt Fundi, I guess I'll wait on it. Either it will reveal itself or when I get home I'll meditate on it further."

Later that evening Mariamma called again. She'd found her grandmother dead in front of her altar. Apparently she'd been performing some rituals – various herbs and root jars were open around her. And there was a fire still smoldering in a ceramic bowl.

Fundi did not believe in funerals. Death is such a private matter – between the person transitioning and what or whom they expect to return to. An agreement between two entities A funeral was anything but. It's a spectacle, an unwarranted intrusion at best and an assault against the memories of the mourning family. But Fundi knew a funeral, a grand affair, was her mother's wish; Laurel at the center of the drama – one last time.

Fundi's immediate concern was for Mariamma; as it was for Lazarus, who was on a flight an hour after his granddaughter had called. Cyril, too was concerned for his new niece. At the same time, Fundi knew that Cyril understood instinctively not to crowd her – to give her space -- to be there when or if she needed him.

The funeral was a blur. The repast following the burial was a crowded, catered event. Only the soft recorded music kept the volume of so many people from being overwhelming. Fundi just wanted it to be over.

Mariamma thrived. She met a spirited young man who had many ideas for expanding the shop that she and her aunt owned. He was a sculptor. He made her sing out loud...

Fundi and Cyril returned to the tranquility of their home. Each day Fundi grew in vigor – even as the leaves began to vacate the trees and the winds chilled. Each day she enjoyed the ever-changing flora of the nearby botanical garden. Sometimes she sat in meditation in the Japanese rock pavilion where the white stones gave the illusion of water running over river rock.

And each evening she and Cyril discovered each other anew, knowing it had never been about time, but rather the joy and beauty they brought to that time.

NO GOOD DEED GOES UNPUNISHED

James-Edward was not just light but bright-skinned with curly hair and long eyelashes. He thought very highly of himself and was not shy about sharing his illustrious thoughts. But he was short. Short in height and short on personality. At least that was my view. Loreen, my best friend since college, loved everything about the man. I figured her infatuation would eventually evaporate. That is until the day I came home to find Loreen on my steps, her tiny frame shaking and eyes swollen from crying. "Eventually" had arrived.

He was two-timing her, she whimpered. Since the man had always presented himself as someone who could, would and did have the willingness and capacity to take on more than one woman, Loreen's lament was surprising to me. The rumor, which I too had heard, was that he was seeing a woman from Trinidad who was very vocal about James-Edward being "she man." From all accounts her declaration sounded more like a threat to any other woman interested in him than a simple statement of fact.

Loreen was hurt and I was angry with him for hurting my friend. My anger was perhaps colored by the fact that I suspected my boyfriend of being unfaithful, too. (The lowlife!) Whenever I asked Renaldo if he was seeing other women, his response was always the same, "Did you see me with someone? Did you touch me?"

While Loreen wept and tried to compose herself over a glass of wine, I was plotting James-Edwards comeuppance. The plan required that Loreen get from hurt to angry. It didn't take long.

James-Edward spent most Friday evenings at the local bar. After calling the bar to ensure that he and Trinidad were there, Loreen and I went to the home of the deceitful lowlife pimp where I very efficiently used a metal nail file and bobby pin to unlock both the outside door and the one to his studio apartment. Once inside I took off my clothes down to my underwear. Loreen scouted out a hiding place near the door. We then planted ourselves at the window to watch for their arrival.

Although my heart was beating very loudly in my chest, I couldn't let Loreen know how nervous I was; she was already a wreck, pacing up and down, questioning the wisdom of my plan.

A taxi pulled up. A smartly dressed man got out and entered the house directly across the street with a key. It was Renaldo! My heart leapt into high gear. I knew just where he was going. It was the home of our friend, affectionately named Slick. He was older than our group, a longshoreman who always had lots of cash, lots of women and lots of parties. But Slick was out of town. So what was Renaldo up to I wondered. I was having a hard time remaining calm. And before I could reflect on Renaldo's arrival, another taxi pulled up. Loreen's sister, Angela, emerged. Renaldo was at the door in a flash. He wrapped his arm around her and guided her into the building. I was now rocking from foot to foot trying to contain my fury. Loreen kept instructing me to "breathe!"

James-Edward and Trinidad arrived almost at the same time. I peeled off my underwear and climbed into the bed. Loreen got into position near the door.

They entered laughing and talking. It seemed an eternity before he turned on the light. They were still laughing when I eased out of the bed, "Sweetheart what took you so long?"

"What the hell? Who are you?" His eyes bucked, his jaw dropped. He stuttered, closed his mouth and began the process of trying to speak again. Meanwhile, Trinidad spun around, poking him in the chest and demanding to know what kind of game he was playing. As they argued, I quickly retrieved my clothing and sprinted out of the door that Loreen had already exited. By this time Trinidad was no longer talking; she was boxing him like she was a heavyweight and he a featherweight. He kept trying to duck, to hold out his arms to protect himself. "Trying" was the operative word – his arms, like everything about him, were short. Trinidad, being tall and big-boned was introducing "she man" to a new version of hell.

I dressed quickly while enjoying the drama going on inside. But time was of the essence; we had to get out of the building before Trinidad tired of the exchange and looked for a new sparring partner.

Once outside, I suggested Loreen get a taxi and wait for me around the corner.

Nail file and bobby pin in hand I crossed the street to repeat my entry skills. At the door to Slick's apartment, I listen for a few seconds. They were still talking; soft pre-intimate cooing. I rapped firmly on the door, hoping it sounded like one of the male tenants. Renaldo opened the door in his shorts. He was too stunned to speak. Before he could recover I took a page out of Trinidad's book and punched him squarely in the eye, hard. He staggered backwards. I reached in, grabbed the doorknob and slammed the door shut. I ran down the stairs and raced to the waiting cab.

At the first telephone booth, I stopped the cab to call Slick's telephone number. Renaldo answered. "You've been seen and touched. I'd suggest you get out of harm's way before Angela's old man finds you. Enjoy if you can."

Loreen and I were giddy with elation in spite of my now painful, swollen hand. We returned to my place to celebrate our double victory, albeit bittersweet, with a bottle of champagne.

A BLUES RIFF

I arrived in St. George, Staten Island on a sunny May afternoon in 1971 to begin my new job as a librarian. André was the first neighbor I met. He lived five houses down the hill from me and appeared to be around the neighborhood at all hours. At fifteen years old, he had the carriage of an old man, and the presentation of a child -- peering deeply at things that intrigued him. He totally lacked inhibition: "Where you live before here? Why you come here? Got any kids? You like music?" The questions rolled out without pause for response.

With his scrawny frame and dull complexion he could easily have been a poster child for Feed the Children. The whites of his eyes were brown. And he smelled of cigarettes. Still, there was a vibrancy and charm about him.

Within six months he'd become a fixture in my living room, when not roaming the streets, where he discovered my record collection. He studied each album cover carefully, asking questions about the instruments and the musicians. Although he'd never heard any of them before, he clearly had a special passion for Coltrane, Dexter Gordon, Lady Day and the World Saxophone Quartet. He was like a locust eating through the collection, ever hungry for more. I'd never seen a child listen to music with such intensity. He had absolutely no interest in the myriad books spilling off shelves and stacked in every available space around him. I was disappointed by this, but I was sure I'd figure out a way to interest him in improving his reading skills.

One Saturday afternoon André brought along his friend. Fourteen-year-old Leah was plump-pretty and shy. She looked at me; studied him. Her eyes held no judgment. She accepted whoever it was we chose to be.

"Leah, listen to this, you gotta hear this!" he said as he selected a tune from Miles Davis's "Filles de Kilimanjaro." The title tune began to play. He sat back on the sofa putting his arm around her. He disappeared into the music.

"What's the name of that song?" she asked after a few minutes had passed. Something in the way André handed her the album cover made me realize he couldn't read. All of his questions to me had been shrewdly designed to elicit information about the musicians and what was being played without revealing his handicap.

On his next visit he admitted he couldn't read and that he no longer attended school.

"Why not? Is your mother aware that you don't attend school?"

"It was boring. Yeah, Mom knows."

"And your mother is okay with it? What about the school? Don't they send truant officers to find out where you are?"

André shrugged.

So, what do you do all day?"

"You know…. hang out with Moms in the morning; sometimes my crew comes by…. We listen to music, play cards, watch TV; sometimes we go to the arcade -- just hang out."

Since I was working full time and was still trying to unpack, it took a few weeks before I broached the subject of teaching him to read. He was not enthusiastic. He would rather have had a guitar.

Although the idea of buying a guitar for him seemed out of line, I also thought it would be a chance to coach him in math and reading. I found a guitar in a pawn shop and some illustrated books on the finger positions and cords. What he couldn't figure out from the pictures, he stumbled upon on his own, to his great delight. And, happily, he did not hesitate to ask me questions when all else failed.

Often Leah would sit quietly while he played guitar and sang to her. She listened to whatever music he introduced to her. She scanned the bookshelves. Whenever she found something of interest, she read. She cried through Their Eyes Were Watching God, and grew sad reading Ann Petry's The Street. When she read she always sat where she could see André and determine his shifting moods.

Leah's musical preferences were more in the R&B and pop range: The Temptations, LaBelle, and Nina Simone. When she visited me on her own, which grew more frequent, her romantic side showed itself; she'd play Lady Day and Johnny Hartman.

Sometimes my music perplexed her: The Julius Hemphill Live from the New Music Café elicited a "What kind of music is that?" Steve Toure's Sanctified Shells garnered a "What kind of instruments are they playing?" It was during these times that I got to appreciate her quiet ways, keen observations and uncanny intuition. One day, I was lamenting André's illiteracy. As I finished in obvious frustration, Leah observed, "He's fine, in his own rhythm, that's all."

"But how will he support himself as an adult without the fundamentals of education?" I asked pointedly.

"He's resourceful, Miss Val. He'll figure it out."

Something in the way she spoke – her calm assurance and centeredness – struck me as someone who, as the elders would say, was an old soul.

An only child, Leah had asthma from infancy, spending a large part of her young life in hospitals. She grew up watching, listening and reading. Since there was no one to talk to most of the time, she read, drew and painted what she felt. Leah read the way André listened to music.

On a beautiful, crisp, February afternoon with fresh snow clinging to the tree branches, André appeared at my door. His face was contorted in pain as he gingerly held his arm. His shirt was dirty and his trousers torn.

"Take me to the hospital Miss Val, please!"

"What happened?"

"I fell. The brakes on my bike failed." He winced.

I had already grabbed my coat, purse and car keys when it occurred to me that the emergency room would not care for him unless I had proper documentation.

"André, is your mother at home? You're a minor. I'm not your legal guardian. I can take you, but your mother has to come and bring proper ID and insurance papers."

Mrs. Jordan opened the door. A blue cloud of marijuana smoke engulfed us. I was too stunned to speak. André pushed past his mother, grimacing in pain. He came back with a plastic bag containing his medical papers.

"Let's go," he said to me. There seemed an unspoken agreement between them that she would not accompany us.

At the door of the emergency room André got out. "Thanks Miss Val, I'll call you later."

"Wait a minute. Don't you want me to come with you?"

"I got this. I'll call you."

With that he disappeared into the hospital.

A week later André appeared at my door wearing a cast and a wide grin. "What are you so happy about?" I wanted to know as the strong scent of marijuana filled my nostrils. "And why do you smell like reefer?"

"I'm gonna be a father!" he gushed, ignoring my question.

My mind went into high gear with one question after another crowding the one before it for attention.

"You're only 15," I began lamely. "How can you take care of a child, you're still a child. What have Leah's parents had to say?"

"Leah?" He looked puzzled.

"Well who's the mother-to-be?"

"Peewee."

"Who's Peewee?"

You know, the girl I was talking to in front of the arcade. You remember, you said it was late and we should go home."

Indeed I remembered. It had been a group of about six or seven boys and girls. André had had his arm wrapped around a little unkempt girl who looked to be about 12 years old. Lord, Lord have mercy. Before I could frame my next question, André had sprinted out the door, waving happily. "Tell you all about it later."

I had help from the wind getting down the hilly avenue, but then, when I turned into my even hillier street, the wind had shifted and all I could do was hold onto a fence. André came up behind me and began to push me with his one good arm. We laughed as we finally stumbled breathlessly into the house. I headed to the kitchen to make cocoa.

"Guess what? Leah is having my baby, too."

"What?" It took a moment for me to connect with his words. I was unable to disguise my incredulousness. "How can you be so completely irresponsible and pleased with yourself at the same time?"

My rant did nothing to deter his joy. Trying to collect myself, I asked how far along in the pregnancy the two mothers-to-be were and if they were receiving prenatal care.

"What's that?"

"What's what?"

"Prenatal care. Ain't you happy for me, Miss Val?"

Ignoring his "happiness" I explained prenatal care and its importance. Neither girl had yet told their parents, seen a doctor or been to a clinic. He wasn't sure but thought both girls to be about four or five months pregnant. And according to him, both girls were excitedly looking forward to being mothers.

"How is that possible?" I wondered aloud.

Peewee's parents were duly upset. According to André their confrontation with his mother had not gone well. They forbade Peewee from seeing André and were, however futile, trying to keep her locked in the house.

Leah's mother had made no attempt to speak to Mrs. Jordan.

I felt utter helplessness but thought a conversation with Mrs. Jordan might, if nothing else, make me feel better.

It took a moment for her to recall who I was. Ushering me in, she apologized for the condition of the house, which appeared quite tidy to me. Perhaps she was referring to the dozen or more potted marijuana plants in front of the window. Mrs. Jordan eased her overweight body into a straight-backed chair and rested her cane on the edge of the side table. Noting my attention to her plants she volunteered:

"I got sugar, fibromyalgia and I need a hip replacement. The social worker has set up appointments with the doctors, and they take tests and prescribe pills, but," nodding in the direction of the plants, she added, "That's the only relief I get."

"I am so sorry…" I began, but was cut off.

"You come here to talk about my health?"

I paused – I hadn't expected hostility. "There are two young girls who are pregnant by André and it occurs to me that he doesn't realize the seriousness of the situation. In fact he's elated about being a father."

"What you think I can do about it?"

Her response, while not unexpected at this point in the visit, annoyed me.

"You could talk to him about the role of fatherhood and the fact that he's too young and unprepared. Talk about what he, you, both of you might do to be helpful. If nothing else you might want to talk to him about using condoms."

"Sounds like closing the barn door after the cow done run out."

The conversation was going nowhere and my anger was growing. "You know, he could be charged with rape."

Mrs. Jordan sat up straight and her eyes refocused at the mention of rape. Before she could respond, I rose, wished her well and made my exit. I felt no better.

I seriously doubted the girls' families would seek legal counsel or charge him with rape. Still, I couldn't fathom everyone's lackadaisical acceptance. Was I missing something?

A month later I returned from work to find André sitting on my porch, crying. The façade of an old man had left him; he was crying unashamedly, like a baby.

"Botha ma babies dead; ma babies dead, Miss Val! What'd I do wrong?" He repeated the refrain over and over. I had no answers.

Peewee's mother thanked me for my concern, but, "no," I could not see Peewee; she was resting. Her tone and her scathing look told me she thought I was somehow involved in her daughter's fall from grace.

Leah was still hospitalized, in critical condition. She was attached to several monitoring machines and an intravenous drip. Her mother greeted me with a furrowed brow and a worried smile. She mumbled something about Leah's diabetes and asthma.

Leah was conscious but weak and pale. When I took her hand, she opened her eyes.

"I lost the baby." Her voice was just above a whisper.

"I know."

"There won't be no more," she stated even more softly.

I tried to think of something to say, to ask what she meant.

"I've always known my life would be short. I was hoping though that my baby…."

Tears welled up in my eyes. Leah squeezed my hand.

"I'm a little tired Miss Val. Come tomorrow."

But there was no tomorrow, Leah died that night with her mother and André beside her.

**

Have you ever put something away carefully so as not to lose it and then not be able to find it? That's how I felt in the months that followed. I transferred to a job at the Grand Army Plaza Library in Brooklyn and moved into a nearby apartment. André and I kept in touch for about a year after which his mother's telephone was disconnected and my notes to him were returned with a postal stamp that said, "No forwarding address."

Whenever I thought of André, Leah, Peewee and my Staten Island experience I felt as if I were being held hostage by a memory, with no power to influence the past, the present, or the future.

Five years later, during the holidays, I received what I thought was a Christmas card from a Lisa Pettway. I didn't recognize the name. Inside was a copy of a GED in the name of André Jordan. There was also a copy of a birth certificate for Monet Jordan -- mother, Lisa Pettway. And there was a ticket to a blues concert in which Andre would be featured. The accompanying note said that she had decided against marriage even though André had wanted to. Three-year-old Monet was doing well. Lisa had not seen André for several months but he always showed up, eventually. She would be entering nursing school the next cycle. The note was signed "Peewee."

There was no return address but I had a feeling I'd be seeing Andre soon.

BENEDICTION

The attendants were very gentle in carrying Thea from the ambulance to her bedroom, but her eyes were stretched wide in terror. She clung tightly to the gurney.

"Oh Sweet Jesus," moaned Sylvie as she tried unsuccessfully to pry Thea's fingers from the railing.

The attendant very patiently addressed the older woman. "Mrs. Simpson, we're going to put you in your own bed now, okay?" Thea's glazed eyes moved in the direction of the voice. She loosened her grip.

"Ready?" On the count of three the attendants slid her from gurney to bed, smoothing the blankets and raising the bed's side rails securely before departing.

Sylvie watched in silence as her mother's eyes panned from one side of her room to the other. Extending a long, bony finger and raising her head slightly, Thea exclaimed, "See them there, jumping rope?" Sylvie looked where Thea pointed but saw nothing.

"Lord, Lord, Lord," muttered Sylvie, while mentally acknowledging Thea's worsening dementia. She tried to visualize Thea in a nursing home, but the idea of her mother anywhere except in her own home was too unsettling. She already felt guilty for having brought the subject up several months before…

"A nursing home? I have a home, and it's paid for, too. I'm quite comfortable here with my things, my memories."

Thea's voice had dropped low, digressing into a rambling conversation with herself. Sylvie remembered too that she'd shouted at Thea, had physically taken her by the shoulders and tried to shake her back into the present. That was before anyone realized Thea had had another stroke, her fourth.

Sylvie's fingers slid absently over her rosary beads, her lips silently shaping the words of a mantra, as she watched her mother's vacant eyes seeming to scan the photos of family members and friends, the piano, antique dolls, and souvenirs from her travels abroad.

Thea would not open her mouth or her eyes when Sylvie tried to feed her. She was flushed, hanging on tightly to the bed rail.

"When did you start calling me by my Christian name?" Thea asked quite suddenly.

"When you stopped answering to 'Ma.'"

Thea focused watery eyes on her daughter. In a weak, flat voice she announced, "I'm dying."

"Lord Jesus..." Sylvie began, then stopped and took a deep breath. "We're all dying," Sylvie finally managed to say in a controlled voice. "Have you checked this out with God?" she added as an afterthought.

Sylvie could see she had her mother's full attention. She continued with more confidence. "You taught me that God is in control, so it seems to me that you ought to be in touch with God. Pray Thea, pray on it."

As Thea rested her head on the pillow to reflect, Sylvie began her incantation anew, "Oh my dear Lord, help me in my hour of need... Lord, Lord, Lord..."

"Sylvie?" Thea interrupted in a whisper.

"Yes, Ma."

"That's the wrong prayer. 'My will be done' is the right one."

Sylvie waited for her mother to explain, but Thea offered nothing more, except a deep exhalation of breath. She was smiling. It was her final benediction.

MRS. TOUSSAINT'S HOUSE

Initially it looked like the rest of the brownstones on the block until I was standing directly in front of the small yard. A sign suspended from an ornate wrought iron post in the center of a rather disorganized assortment of tiger lilies, irises, lavender, some kind of wild looking grass, broken pottery, a brass treble clef and other collectibles read: "Piano Instruction."

Interesting, I thought as I checked the address and pushed open the sagging gate. I rang the ground floor bell not sure of what to expect.

Genevieve Toussaint was very tall and older than she sounded on the telephone. She appeared to be in her late 70s or early 80s. Her jet-black hair, dyed no doubt, was pulled back severely and held in place with a silk scarf. A product of a bygone era, her makeup consisted of a thick layer of liquid foundation, covered with a very light, almost white face power.Her eyebrows were penciled in jet black, with matching mascara. Deep red lipstick drawn beyond her lip line attempted to make her lips fuller. On top of her black ankle length dress she wore a faded multi-colored cotton kimono.

"Mrs. Toussaint?"

"Yes.You must be Octavia Reid."

Nodding my head yes, I inquired, "Is the studio still available?"

"Yes, come in."

She smelled of talcum powder and liniment. Stepping carefully, Mrs. Toussaint led me up a dimly lit flight of stairs to the parlor floor. Behind closed French doors, in a room painted dark blue, trimmed in enamel white and gold sat a grand piano; on the floor a Persian rug in muted shades of cream, light blue and bits of gold. An elegant fireplace and mantle were directly opposite the French doors. On either side of the mantle gold candlesticks held thick white candles. There was no sheet music, metronome or other indications that the room was being actively used for lessons. Considering the disarray of the front yard, this room was a pleasant surprise.

A tall Chinese urn filled with pussy willows graced the turn of the next landing. I was led to the studio at the front of the building. It was a sun-filled room with a horseshoe shaped window around which were stained glass panels. Two side panels opened out. Below the windows was a cushioned window seat. The room had a working gas fireplace.

The sleeping area/bedroom was behind an open shelved bookcase. It was cozy, charming. The bathroom, which was in the hall, and the kitchen which was accessible through a door at the back of the studio, were to be shared. The rear studio was vacant.

I moved in that weekend.

After adding a sheer curtain to the back of the open bookcase and arranging books and knickknacks on the opposite side, the studio became my little cocoon. And the window seat quickly became my favorite spot in it. I found myself sitting in the window for hours, reading, communing with the huge tree that canopied my window and watching the people on the street below.

There was another tenant, Daniel Hare who lived in the back on the parlor floor. Mr. Hare was a long-distance truck driver who spent long periods on the road. When at home he pretty much kept to himself. On occasion he could be heard downstairs with Mrs. Toussaint holding long, lively conversations in her kitchen on the first floor.

Three months after I'd moved in, a slender, athletic looking man with curly blond hair and green eyes arrived. Bounding up the stairs two at a time, he propelled himself onto the top floor landing with a thud. The thud actually turned out to be a box of his possessions which he'd hurled to the floor. Seeing the startled look on my face he moved quickly in my direction, extending his hand.

"Hi, I'm Andrew Martinez, your new neighbor, and I'm not white."

Well, I thought to myself, the man clearly has a personal problem, but before I could respond to his unique introduction, he'd thrust himself back down the stairs to retrieve another box.

What had startled me was not the look of him, but the noisiness of him. With Mrs. Toussaint easing herself around noiselessly on felt slippers, and Mr. Hare away most of the time, the house had been comfortably quiet.

When Andrew settled down several hours later I introduced myself and broached the subject of how we would share the kitchen and bath. He worked long hours as an office equipment repairman so he would leave the house by 6:30 am – the time I was waking up. As for the kitchen, he didn't cook.

"I have a proposition for you," he ventured.

After the uniqueness of his initial introduction, I held my breath.

"I'll buy the food if you'll cook it. That way I'll be able to pack my lunch as well."

With my love of cooking and unpredictable income, it was an appealing arrangement to which I quickly agreed.

In addition to my temp work I typed manuscripts for grad and doctoral students. It was after one such late evening that Mr. Hare approached me as I climbed the stairs to my studio.

"Octavia, you got a minute?"

"Sure."

He followed me upstairs, but did not sit.

"Nice place, homey."

"Thanks Would you like some tea?" I asked as I dropped my bags onto a chair.

"No thanks. I need to ask a favor of you. When you come in late, Mrs. Toussaint worries. She actually stays up until she hears you come in. Did you know that?" He cocked his head to one side to emphasize his point.

While he waited for my response, his eyes scrutinized the place, paying particular attention to my myriad books and cheap prints by famous artists. I'd lived on my own since graduating from high school eight years before. "Mr. Hare, I'm 26 years old and..."

"Don't matter. She waits up, so do me a favor please. Give her a call when you're going to be late. It's not too much to ask, is it?"

Orphaned by the time I was 12 I'd learned to fend for myself from an early age. I bristled at the thought of having to report in like a child. I still missed my family, especially my mom. I tried to hide how I felt 'cause it wa no one's business but mine. Sometimes I was surprised to find tears drizzling down my face when I remembered...or the scent of the rosewater she liked to splash on her neck and shoulders...

But then again, Mrs. Toussaint had been so caring, especially when I was convalescing from a relapse of pneumonia. She cooked for me and carried the meals up two flights of stairs twice a day. She made sure I took my medications and even read to me on a few occasions. She never asked about the rent money. There was no way I could refuse.

"No, it's not Mr. Hare."

He nodded and without another word, left.

I wondered what made Mr. Hare feel he had to represent Mrs. Toussaint. Or had Mrs. Toussaint sent him? Was there a relationship between them other than tenant and landlady? I had mixed feelings about what had just transpired, but couldn't come up with a justifiable reason to feel put upon -- which is exactly how I felt. Or was I reading too much into the situation?

After I began phoning when I was going to be late, and sometimes to just ask if there was anything she needed on my way in, a bond began to form between me and Mrs. Toussaint. So much so that when she decided to visit her cousin Luna in Baton Rouge, she left me in charge of the house. What that really meant was keeping an eye on Mr. Hare, making sure he ate properly, and took his insulin.

After an exhausting Friday I put on my pajamas immediately upon getting home, opened a bottle of wine, selected some music and curled up in front of the fireplace to read. I must have fallen asleep. I awoke to a room full of smoke. My heart was pumping adrenalin. I ran barefooted into the hallway.

"Andrew, the house is on fire. Wake up!" I banged on his door several times before racing down to the parlor floor.

"Mr. Hare, wake up. The house is on fire!"

Suddenly, Andrew was at my elbow. We could hear Mr. Hare snoring. Andrew pushed past me into the room. Mr. Hare was not waking up. Andrew pulled him from the bed. Running down to the ground floor I found myself standing in the kitchen before I remembered that Mrs. Toussaint was away. Atop the stove was a skillet containing something that was completely charred. The flames had devoured whatever had been in the skillet and had moved to the dish towel hanging on the other side of a partition separating the stove from the sink area. It would only be a moment before the flames made a leap to the kitchen curtains! Andrew reappeared. Between us we put the fire out and opened the doors and windows.

"Where's Mr. Hare?"

"I put him up on the bench in the front yard."

"Is he awake?"

"He's drunk."

"Are you sure he's drunk? He's diabetic. "

"The man is drunk."

Andrew's tone was measured. He was struggling to contain both his anger and his elevated adrenalin. "He said he came in hungry and decided to cook. After putting whatever that was in the pan he went back upstairs to take a nap."

We made sure there were no smoldering embers before we both went back upstairs. It was only the sound of rain on the window that made me remember Mr. Hare was still outside.

The next day Andrew and I cleaned up the mess in the kitchen. "Pops," as we'd taken to calling Mr. Hare, stayed in his room. We figured he was embarrassed or perhaps trying to figure out what to tell Mrs. Toussaint.

The return of Mrs. Toussaint, soon dubbed "Ma'dear" by Andrew and I, was as traumatic as had been her time away. After hearing about the fire and scrutinizing our inadequate attempts to clean up the kitchen, Ma'dear went to speak to Pops. We had just made it up to the top floor when she called out. There was panic in her voice.

Ma'dear rode in the ambulance with Pops. We followed in Andrew's car. After a long wait we were told that he had pneumonia and some kind of kidney problem. He was admitted. She was visibly shaken.

During the following weeks, Ma'dear visited Pops daily. Fussing over "the paucity" of his hospital diet, what he ate or didn't eat and personally taking care of his feet, became her mission. Since she stayed at the hospital until late, Andrew began picking her up on his way home. By the time they arrived I'd have prepared supper which we ate together in the downstairs kitchen.

After several weeks, Pops was finally released. It was a very special occasion; not only was Pops home, but it was the first the time I'd seen the piano room doors open. Candles on the mantle and piano were lit. And Ma'dear played the elegant instrument with gusto.

Pops sat near the piano. There were tears in his eyes. Ma'dear watched him carefully; her happiness was evident in her frequent smiles. Andrew fussed over her, wrapping a shawl around her shoulders, handing her a glass of water. In short order we were all singing loudly, sometimes off tune but it didn't matter. My heart was happy. It was only in this moment I realized Mrs. Toussaint's house had become home and I'd found my family.

MIZ MIRANDA'S BOY

I never did know his name. In fact, it was a good while before I even recognized him except that he was the architect of my current dilemma.

All I knew was one minute my upstairs apartment was rented to a young, newly married couple and the next there was a U-Haul truck outside with Yvette Jordan and all the furniture pulling away from the curb. Her husband, Jonathan, was standing at the curb, hands plunged deep into his pants pockets, staring vaguely in the direction of the truck.

"What's going on?" I asked.

His red-rimmed eyes swiveled in my direction but there was no response. I guess it was a stupid question. I was annoyed by the course of events and the lack of courtesy of informing me in advance.

"When will you be leaving?" I asked since there was no way that he could manage the rent on his salary.

"I'm not going anywhere."

The first few nights were quiet. Then, in the middle of the night I was awakened by the sound of high-heeled shoes and what sounded like combat boots thundering up and down the stairs, sudden eruptions of loud laughter, and a constant, throbbing base. Since I had to go to work in the morning I was not pleased, and let Jonathan know exactly how I felt. He simply looked at me through glazed eyes, nodded his head and closed the door.

After a couple of weeks of this racket and calling the police, who never showed up, I knocked on Jonathan's door to let him know that he'd have to leave, that I was going to seek legal action. Instead, a very tall, clean-shaven, well-dressed man opened the door. I was surprised.

"Where's Jonathan?"

"He ain't here no more."

"And who are you?"

"You must be the landlady. Is it rent time already?"

"I don't know who you are, but I didn't rent this apartment to you. You have no legal right to be here. You have to leave."

The mildly amused look that had greeted me turned hard, sinister.

"Lady, I suggest you look out your window. I also suggest you take this money." He extended a well-manicured hand filled with cash. I gaped. Was that a gun tucked in his belt? This only happens in the movies, I tried to convince myself as I backed down the stairs empty-handed and frightened.

Outside were two robust, angry-looking men leaning on the fence in front of my house. They monitored everyone who entered. There was an endless stream of people and an ever-present pair of sentries, around the clock, seven days a week.

A week later I encountered my unwelcome tenant as he entered. I threatened to call the police. He laughed heartily then focused his cold eyes on me with such intensity, I fled to my apartment, slamming and locking the door as if that were protection. I was frightened into inaction. My home had been turned into some kind of drug den and I felt powerless to do anything about it. Weeks went by with no relief. I did not sleep well, was losing weight and felt drawn and tense.

Coming home from work one evening, Miss Green, my neighor. greeted me and invited me join her on her porch.

"Look like them thugs done took over your house too," she began quietly.

"And I'm scared to death. The police don't come and that boy has a gun," I blurted.

"A lot of these thug boys grew up around here but they lawless now." She rolled her head around indicating the two men in front of my house. "Some of 'em used to go to Sunday school at the church around the corner."

"That's hard to believe," I muttered.

"You remember Miz Miranda, the Sunday School teacher?"

I nodded.

"She still keeps her brood in check!"

We were quiet for a while, watching the traffic and people returning home from work.

"If the police don't come, what can we do?"

Miss Green raised an eyebrow and shrugged her shoulders. "I got my boy here with me now. He sleeps with a shotgun next to him."

Although the idea was tempting, I was too terrified of guns to even contemplate buying one let alone use it.

I often saw him around the neighborhood. Whenever I saw him I felt his name or his relationship to the neighborhood would come to me. But it didn't, not then.

He was always well groomed. If I didn't know better, I'd mistake him for a real gentleman. He was always courteous, nodding his greeting as if I were a willing neighbor. I tried to recall if he had been one of the boys I'd taught to read so many years before... The more I saw him, the more familiar he seemed, but still I couldn't place him, other than being the person traumatizing me.

One day I was coming out of the supermarket when I noticed Miz Miranda across the street with four of her five sons. It was an almost comic, but familiar sight. Miz Miranda was well shy of five feet tall, but she walked with absolute authority. Her sons, all at least six feet tall, marched behind her. Miz Miranda was known to take no guff from her boys, or anyone else. After siring five sons, Miz Miranda's husband had folded his arms and died peacefully in his sleep, leaving her to raise them alone. Known as Mother Miranda to her church community, she had raised her boys with a belt in one hand and the Holy Bible in the other. She was highly regarded in the neighborhood in general and by the church community in particular. A realization finally hit me!

I hurried home to await my unauthorized tenant. He didn't have to use his key; I swung wide the door to greet him.

"You're one of Miz Miranda's boys!" I yelled triumphantly. "And that's why you are going to leave my property and take all of your drugs and goons with you I'm not going to the police. I'm going to Miz Miranda and I'm going to your momma's church and tell them all about you!"

His eyes grew large and his body stiffened but he said nothing.

He and his crew disappeared from my home overnight the same way they had appeared.

Well, I've never been much of a churchgoer, but since then, I stop by Miz Miranda's church every so regular in gratitude to the good Lord. And of course, Miz Miranda's strop.

Amen.

BUSINESS WOMAN

No matter how often I travel to West Africa – Accra, Ghana specifically – I am always unprepared for the assault on my senses. First, there is the heat that engulfs me like a blanket at the height of summer. the humidity makes me think I will never again be able to breathe, but I do. And the crowded streets come alive with throngs of colorfully attired people going about their daily business. Perhaps the most welcoming thing to me is the huge billboard just outside the airport of an African man drinking a Coca Cola. There are no such images of black people stateside.

My business partner, Kwaku would meet me at the airport and take me to my lodgings at a small, inexpensive hotel in Kanishie, a suburb of Accra. The drive was accompanied by the constant honking of car horns and a light film of dust that rises up as we move along the narrow roads.

The next day, after I'd had time to rest from the long flight, he'd pick me up and take me to the carpenter who'd build a crate to my specifications for the items we'd purchase to be shipped back to the States. We'd then return to his home where his mother, daughter and niece would welcome me over dinner. His mother loved entertaining and would hover over us as we sat on low stools around one central bowl, which contained a ball of dough made from cassava (fufu) along with other vegetables in a fish sauce. Kwaku would break off pieces of fish and place it in front of each of us to make sure we each had enough protein. "Mama," I'd say after the meal, "you've outdone yourself. This meal has been wonderful, meda wo ase."

She spoke no English but my "thank you" was returned with a warm smile for my courtesy and attempting to speak Twi.

After a few days of planning the strategy for our buying trip and making contact with friends and business associates, we'd drive into upper Ghana where it was noticeably cooler. In the village we'd select a pattern for the kente cloth to be purchased and watch briefly as men at large looms weaved the narrow strips using silk thread.

We'd then drive across Togo, stopping at a large, outdoor market where the babel of languages sounded like avant garde jazz playing against a colorful collage of people buying and selling. Finally we'd drive into Benin where we would relax for a week or two. In all of the villages we visited, in either country, there was always the comforting sound of women pounding cassava or corn in large pestles and the acrid smell of charcoal from the outdoor cooking stoves.

The drive back would simply reverse our route, collecting and paying for goods ordered. Once back in Accra, the Ashanti stools, small wood carved tables and chairs, fabrics, carved statues, figurines and other items we'd purchased would be crated to await my departure.

This time was different. On a previous trip I'd heard about a merchant, called Obrisii, who was reputed to have the most exquisitely carved wood items including masks, finely carved stools, sculptures, furniture and other mysterious treasures.

Yaw, an acquaintance and businessman, took me with him on one of his buying trips to Obrisii's warehouse. The stipulation was that I was to be silent, to simply observe. (And, I gathered from Yaw's not so subtle remarks, to walk two steps behind him and "coo" appropriately at his "insightful" choices.) It was only later that the reason for this requirement, which I ignored, became clear.

Against Yaw's instruction, I gave my business card to Obrisii at the conclusion of the meeting. Obrisii's eyes looked over my head to glare at Yaw with an expression which said, "Didn't you teach this woman how things are done here?" Yaw shrugged. Obrisii's eyes then moved from my face to the card and back. He seemed amused. I wasn't. I was burning mad, but hoped my face didn't reveal it. From past experience I knew I needed to appear calm. If I wanted to succeed in what was perceived as a man's world, I'd need to be prepared to meet the challenges.

A day or so after this experience, I telephoned and made an appointment of my own. Kwaku could not accompany me; he was making final arrangements for our buying trip.

On the appointed day I took a taxi to the warehouse. I arrived promptly at my appointment time -- 2:30 pm. Mr. Obrisii had not yet returned from lunch. At 3:15 pm, I inquired if perhaps I should reschedule the appointment. The secretary was unable to look directly at me as she fumbled for an appropriate excuse. I left without making another appointment. Intuition, that lightbulb that often lights my way was aglow.

I returned to my hotel to retrieve something of interest to Obrisii and took another taxi to his residence. (I didn't know where he lived, but any taxi driver, for a nominal fee, could take me there.)

The servant who opened the door was pleasant enough but assured me in a firm tone that Mr. Obrisii did not have an appointment with me. At this I deliberately raised my voice, not in a hostile manner, but loud enough to be heard beyond the entryway.

"You are mistaken." I proclaimed. "My appointment was for 2:30 this afternoon, and since I depart tomorrow, I must see him, now."

There was no need for the servant to relay the message. Obrisii appeared, still in his wrapper, a brightly colored piece of fabric wrapped around his middle, to see what the commotion was about.

"Mistress, what are you doing here, at my home?" He was more than a little surprised.

Reaching into my purse I retrieved $5,000. U.S. currency. Fanning the bills in front of his face, I leaned in towards him. "This is five thousand dollars you will never see! Because I am a woman, you didn't feel the need to keep our appointment. You expected I would wait. I may be a woman, but I'm a businesswoman and I will not be treated with disrespect. Neither will I pay for such a 'privilege.'"

His beady eyes bulged and his lips were suddenly dry and moving, trying to frame a response.

I turned and was in the taxi before he could utter a word.

When I returned to my hotel, Yaw was already on the veranda. Word of my afternoon "antics" had traveled across town. Yaw rushed toward me with his arms flapping. He couldn't seem to stand still.

"Are you crazy? Everyone has heard about what you've done. Obrissi is a respected merchant..."

I brushed past Yaw and settled myself in the lounge to have a beer. Yaw slumped down opposite me. "Do you know what you've done?!"

"Yes, I take full responsibility," I smiled, sipping my beer.

The results were immediate. From that day onward, all appointments with businessmen were always extremely courteous – and above all, punctual.

And the women merchants looked at me with renewed curiosity and an obviously newfound respect. Perhaps I'll be invited to partner with one of them, or to form an international cooperative. After all, taking care of business is what we women do best.

DUTY AND EDUCATION

The people attending the art gallery opening in Accra were color-fully attired. The rich African fabrics in traditional styles and European inspired fashions were on regal display. Everyone wore their finest gold baubles: thick bangles, decorative rings, elegant ear-rings and large, shiny watches.

My friend Akua Lee, one of the featured artists, introduced me to a gentleman who stood off to the side surveying the gathering. The hair at his temples were greying and his twinkling eyes welcomed me warmly. Dr. Acheampong was a well-known physician, artist and beloved supporter of the arts. In fact he had sponsored several of the artists in the exhibit.

Dr. Acheampong was like a proud father at his child's graduation, eagerly informing me of the brilliance of Akua's work. Among other things he mentioned that he was working on a book comparing tradi-tional medicines with Western pharmaceuticals, but his project was on hold while his secretary took a two month holiday. After asking about his handwriting I volunteered to assist with the typing of the manuscript. He was delighted.

I cannot say I felt the same about the old manual Smith-Corona typewriter that greeted me, but I had volunteered. As for Dr.

Acheampong's handwriting, it was legible if you read elaborately looped European cursive. Being from the States, it was a bit of a challenge.

My desk, located near a window facing the front porch, gave me a nice breeze when there was one, and a magnificent view of the lush vegetation of the estate on which the clinic was housed. The long driveway was lined with coco palms. To the left of the clinic were colorful tulip trees with their crinkled red/orange tulip-like blossoms. In various places throughout the estate were large elephant eared taro plants in pots and fan palms in clusters. And of course there was the wafting scent of jasmine. Most pleasing of all was the fact that I could hear the patients' conversations as they waited on the porch. This helped improve my rudimentary textbook understanding of Twi and Ga, two of the local languages.

It was late in the afternoon and I was preparing to conclude my work for the day but it was so wonderfully beautiful and quiet that I lingered, taking a stroll through the garden. As I basked in the landscape and massaged my numb fingertips, two figures approached. I could see that one was an old man wearing a yellow and brown traditional style cloth wrapped around his thin frame leaving one shoulder bare. He was supported on one side by a walking stick. On the other side a younger man wearing a more contemporary blue and beige pin-tucked Fugu smock held him effortlessly.

Dr. Acheampong stepped out onto the porch just as the younger man gently settled the elder onto a cushioned chair. He greeted them both by name and seated himself so that he faced the older gentleman. I hurried back inside through the side door.

The doctor observed the patient but said nothing more, waiting. I served them cool water and retreated back into the building. The younger man moved to the side porch. The old man spoke softly in Twi. He said that he had come because he was having difficulty servicing his five wives and wanted some herbs to improve his performance. This could not be correct, I thought. The gentleman was of advanced years. Perhaps my understanding of the language was not as improved as I'd wanted to believe.

Dr. Acheampong explained, "Respected elder, the human body is like an automobile – when it's new everything runs smoothly. As it ages the performance slows and the parts do not always work as efficiently as when new."

The old man listened patiently, allowing the doctor to reiterate specific analogies to be sure he was understood. When the doctor had finished, the old man sipped his water, cleared his throat and repeated his initial request. It was clear from his manner and tone that he was not leaving without what he had come for.

I moved quietly but quickly through the side door and found the younger man. His name was Francis and he was the great grandson of the patient. He said his great grandfather was 102 years old. Since Francis was speaking in English I had no reason to doubt the accuracy of what he said. He was a college student at the University of Science and Technology at Kumasi, home on holiday. His grandmother, one of the five wives in question, was the mother of seven children. Francis didn't know the total number of children from all of the wives.

My inquiry was interrupted by the older gentleman calling for his great grandson. I hurried back inside in time to see the older gentleman tuck the packet of herbs into his robes.

Still in a state of disbelief, I approached Dr. Acheampong to ask if I'd heard the old man correctly. With a playful look, Dr. Acheampong asked what I thought I'd heard and chuckled impishly as he confirmed my understanding. His parting remark, delivered over his shoulder was, "A sense of duty is ingrained in African culture."

Did his wives share that same sense of duty? I wondered. And exactly how old were these women anyway?

Clearly, my education was just beginning.

SUNDAY MORNING IN THE OZONE

Friday is an absolutely sweet, gentle, lovable, well trained Golden Retriever. He can also be quite insistent when he takes a notion. Today, carrying his leash in his mouth, he nudges my knee. I look at the clock. Clearly my time schedule has no relationship to Friday's. I try to ignore him, at least until I finish my first cup of coffee.

Friday drops the leash and places a well-manicured paw on my knee. If I don't heed, he will begin pushing me from the chair. It's clear who is in charge here. Gulping one last swallow, I retrieve the leash, house keys and truncheon now used as dog-walking stick before heading for the door.

Leading the way my four-legged companion has chosen to take the long route through Ozone Park. It is a quiet neighborhood filled with tree-lined streets and single-family homes. My family has lived here for over forty years. We were one of the few African American families in the neighborhood.

According to my father, there were mostly Italians, although there was a Swede and his African wife across the street when dad first bought our house. Then a sprinkling of Africans from West Africa and a few Caribbean people moved in. It was a slow transition with no conflict. But Friday is not concerned with the shifting dynamics of

the community. He has friends to visit and business to take care of.
First, we visit with Daisy, the little non-descript pocket sized dog on
the corner, then Russell, a huge Doberman a few blocks away, and a
black mini poodle named Artemis. And of course there are favorite
trees and shrubs along the route to be consecrated. His final visit is
usually with Mr. and Mrs. Rizzo where a treat is guaranteed.

The Rizzos had come to the States from Italy 60 years before. They
told me stories of when they first arrived; the area was all farmland.
They'd point out some of the original farmhouses and show me the
milkman's route across the verdant fields of Queens to the Borden
milk plant in Brooklyn. Sometimes they would recall nostalgically
how they'd hitch a ride on the milk wagon.

From the Rizzo's Friday usually turned onto Leffert's Boulevard.
On this Sunday morning I drink in the dappled light filtering through
the horse chestnut trees. They are old and stately, centurions protecting the street. There is no traffic to speak of. The tranquility is suddenly disturbed by the sound of a squeaky shopping cart. An old man
is inching up the avenue tossing advertising circulars into each yard.
"Buongiorno" he calls. I return the greeting.

Almost at the corner of the block I notice the wide open door of a
house across the street. I can see light through to the back of the house.
I can see the profile of a man standing at a counter. The man turns,
spies me and Friday and does a double take. He points and shouts,
"Attack." A larger than life German Shepherd leaps into action.

I am unsure of what is happening; everything is flowing in slow
motion. "Sit," I say. Friday sits. The German Shephard races through
the open door, sails over the low picket fence and across the street. I
am terrified. He is still airborne when I hit him with the truncheon. I
strike with all my might. He falls to the pavement and is still. I wonder
if he's alive. Before I can check his owner is beside me screaming,
"You've killed my dog. You've killed my dog!"

"Be glad it isn't you," I say with an icy calm that frightens even
me.

I hear the old man before I see him; he is shaking his fist at the dog owner and screaming in Italian. I don't need to understand Italian to know that what he's saying is accusatory, threatening and not couched in polite language.

Mr. German Shephard lifts his dog, cradles it in his arms and walks slowly back across the street. There are tears in his eyes. "You and your kind should go back where you came from," he spits over his shoulder.

I'm still shaking. Friday is still sitting.

"Let's go home boy," I say in a voice choked by unchecked adrenalin, rage and indignation. Friday looks at me with sympathetic eyes, extends a paw. I shake his paw, bend and rub his ears. Out of the corner of my eye I see the shepherd raise its head to lick its owner's face.

With tail wagging joy, Friday leads the way.

WAITING FOR DALLAS AT THE TREE OF LIFE

Waiting for Dallas is almost like Waiting for Godot. But today I don't mind; it's beautifully sunny, the first warm day after a very bitter winter. Everyone seems to have decided to celebrate the onslaught of summer. Coats have been abandoned and folks are strolling 125th Street, stepping high and smiling. Street vendors happily line the curb with their wares. Even the Button Man is striding with vigor, covered from hat to pant leg hem with buttons proclaiming everything from Black Power! Free Assata, to the presidential campaign of Shirley Chisolm.

When I arrive in front of The Tree of Life Bookstore, I am dismayed to see that the display window on the right-hand side of the entryway is empty. Glass and all. The store is open although it looks dark. Boards have been placed at the back of the display case so that access to the store is blocked. What on earth has happened? Why? So much for killing time while waiting on Dallas.

As much as I'm enjoying the colorful parade of people on the streets, I'm now impatient. Dallas is already twenty minutes late. I love my cousin, and I know that he's holding down a full time teaching job, a part-time coaching job and tutoring as well. But today is supposed to be a break for him and an opportunity for both of us to hear some of the young neighborhood poets. It's also a chance for us to hang out in the energy of Harlem's illuminati, past and present: Malcolm selling copies of Mohammad Speaks out front; spiritual and cultural information lining the walls and shelves inside. The words of Amiri Baraka, The Last Poets, the insight of Drs. Ben and Van Sertima, young blood poets like Sekou Sundiata and Saundra Marie Esteves energize the place.

While I'm impatiently looking up and down the street, a man with three or four shopping bags brushes past me. He tosses the bags onto the platform of the empty showcase and climbs up behind them. Unlike everyone else, he is layered in clothing: cap, scarf, sweater, coat... As he removes each layer he folds the item neatly in a pile at his feet alongside his shopping bags. People passing by do not seem to notice.

I'm distracted by a disturbance a few feet away. Two young boys are tussling over a toy. No one seems particularly concerned and they continue around the boys. A very tall woman, with hip length locks, wearing a mud cloth poncho approaches them, snatches the toy and continues walking. The boys are stunned and stand mute in the middle of the sidewalk looking at one another before quietly following the woman down the street.

And then, as if by a magic wind, a giant of a man swoops across the street, shirttail flapping behind him, arms waving as he shouts, "John didn't I tell you to stop doing that? You know you can use the bathroom inside."

I turn. The man he referred to as John has been transformed. He is capless, hair glistening with pomade and brushed straight back; his face the recipient of Vaseline, lips smiling broadl,y emphasizing his perfect white teeth. He now sports a white shirt and houndstooth sport jacket, pressed trousers and shining black shoes. He pushes the container of Vaseline deep into one of the bags and hops down out of the window.

The giant feigns shock, "And where are you going all dressed up, John?"

"Lucas, I've got a date. In Brooklyn." He's grinning from ear to ear.

"And what are you going to do with those bags?"

"A locker at 42nd Street station!"

Lucas shakes his head, pats John on the shoulder and enters the bookstore.

Dallas finally arrives, wearing a sheepish grin. "Sorry, Cuz. Anything interesting going on?"

I open my mouth and close it. "Nah, just another day waiting for you, Dallas."

.

NONI

Wednesday, April 30, 1975

When will it end? Noni wondered as she glanced through the dining room windows and noticed that the streetlights had come on. The lights cast nothing but shadows and fear. *The shadows are worse than the darkness*, she thought as she rose from the dining room table, pulling down the shades and turning on the porch light.

Passing the hall mirror, Noni stopped abruptly as she caught a glimpse of herself. She was ashen, her plump face gaunt, and her large eyes lost in a sea of dark circles and deep lines. Shutting her eyes to block out the image of herself, she turned and walked quickly into the bedroom where she slammed the windows shut and fastened the shutters. She repeated this hasty ritual in all of the rooms. The living room window she left open but pulled the shade halfway down. This window was protected by a large fire thorn. She doubted anyone would challenge the thorns. *Besides*, she thought, *the front porch light is on.* Anyone attempting to enter could be seen.

Noni poured herself a glass of white wine, lit a cigarette and sat staring into space. Every few minutes she rose, went into the dining room, dimmed the lights and peered out into the night, checking each shadow, measuring and trying to identify each sound. Nervously, she turned on the stereo and tried to stretch out on the sofa. Each time she began to relax into the soothing rhythms, fear gripped her. She shuddered. It was as if someone was intentionally dripping ice water down her back. She lowered the volume of the stereo. Finally, she turned it off. The truth was she was afraid that the radio would hinder her from hearing outdoor sounds.

I'm being held hostage in my own home. And until he 'commits a crime' the police won't do anything. What constitutes a crime? What have I done to deserve this? she wondered.

The doorbell jarred Noni from her thoughts. She sprang forward, snapped off the light and crept to the dining room window. She eased the shade back and peered out. Aldo looked wild, psyched for a fight. His silver shirt, which glowed in the pale light, was unbuttoned, hanging out of his trousers; collar half in, half out. His hair was splayed about his head as if in protest.

"Open the damned door." His cold, bloodshot eyes glared at her from a distance of inches. Noni jumped away from the window.

At the sound of running feet, Noni again sprang to the window and peered out. He was sprinting down the walkway heading around the side of the house. Noni ran too – to close and lock the living room window. A chill moved up her spine, converging with the pulsating heat from her chest. Her palms were wet. She stood completely still, breathing heavily.

"Open the damned door Noni. One way or the other, I'm coming in. You can't get away from me," Aldo ranted as he ran. She saw him stumble, right himself and continue running around the back of the house.

With her head pounding, and dizziness overtaking her, Noni gripped the wall, moving slowly back to the kitchen. She checked the lock on the kitchen door and ever so quietly, picked up the telephone. The number to the local precinct was prominently posted, but her fingers dialed 911.

Aldo was running in the opposite direction now. Noni could hear his measured pace on the side steps and the clanging of something metal against the wrought iron fence.

Oh God, the lights on the side porch are out. No one will be able to see him from the street. Oh God... The thought died before it was fully formed. Something else was forming, propelling Noni forward. The phone kept ringing and she realized she was on her own.

She flung the receiver back into the cradle and ran into the bedroom. With one forceful movement she shoved the chest of drawers in front of one window, and swung the dresser to the other. She pushed the bed against the wall. From the closet she retrieved a baseball bat and a nightstick. These she dropped on the floor in the center of the room. From the linen closet she grabbed a hammer and a plank of wood. She sprinted back to the kitchen, collecting anything that could be used as a weapon. She was operating on pure instinct.

A plan unfolded as she scurried about the house rearranging furniture and turning off lights. She was momentarily stilled when Aldo began body slamming the front door.

"I'll break the mutha down. I'll burn your ass out, you hear me? Open the damned door!"

Noni again dialed 911 and set the phone down on the counter. Hopefully someone would answer, be a witness to her situation.

Her weapons were laid out in a staggered trail leading from the bedroom through the hallway, past the bathroom and stopping at the entrance to the living room. *I need a way out in case he gets in before... before what?* Noni's lips moved silently in prayer and the hope that someone would come to her rescue, even as her fear grew that they would not.

Noni took a deep breath, trying to slow her heartrate and still the terror that played like a mantra in her head:

I'm going to die.

Everyone dies.

What happens if I don't die and he just almost kills me?
Oh God, help me!
God helps those who help themselves.

Pausing to listen, Noni thought she could hear him breathing out side the window. *Or is that my own heartbeat: two competing drummers muffled in the closet of my chest?* Her groin was tense. Her stomach was a dense, tight fiber, encasing a hard, very hard rock.

Everybody's got to die sometime. And now is my time, that's all.

Noni crouched against the wall and reached into her pocket for a cigarette. She could hear Aldo shuffling around outside. It was no more than a background sound to her own rippling fear; a fear that seemed to soothe, like a blanket. She closed her eyes, exhaling. In her mind's eye, she saw her grandmother, arms akimbo waiting for her in the front yard.

"Oh no young lady. This is the last day you'll be chased home from school. Who's chasing you?"

"Timmy, Gilbert and…"

"Who's the ringleader?"

"Timmy, but …"

"Well you just turn around and go find Timmy. I don't care what the others do to you, you pummel him good! But whatever happens, don't let him go."

The knowledge that that was indeed the last day she'd been chased home from school was not comforting at the moment.

"What's different now, Noni?" She heard her grandmother's voice as clear as day.

"Aldo is bigger, stronger and meaner."

"The same principle applies, Noni. Are you going to spend the rest of your life running from Aldo or others like him?"

Noni watched the cigarette lighter slide upward and fly from her hand as the shutters blasted open, scattering glass and shattering the reverie in which she'd wrapped herself. The shutters smashed against the walls at the same instant Aldo's head burst through the hole that was once a window. A flaring crown of hair, extending as outstretched sculpted wire, moved slowly through mid-air, meeting the chest of drawers. The shock of hair disappeared into the wood that splintered. The head stopped momentarily, motionless, then slid, every so slowly downward. A shoulder angled gracefully into the barricade, followed by a knee which flew upward then bent over the windowsill, poised as if to run.

Noni inspected the dormant figure. A rush of breath escaped her lips. But the slumped figure moved, rolled to the right and opened a dazed eye. Their eyes met, locked. Noni reached for the bat, and rose slowly, majestically, from her squatting position. A smile formed on her lips. She was euphoric, ecstatic, high.

The foot which hung from the ledge began to move, as if searching for something on which to rest. Aldo's body followed the same awkward rhythm. Noni bent down and with her free hand grabbed the bedspread, flung it over the sagging form and swung. The bat connected, then left her hands and bounced off the window sill. She bent again searching the floor, but could not find the nightstick. Crawling now, Noni reached over her head and pulled several heavy objects from atop the dresser which she flung at the figure staggering towards her. It, he staggered blindly, trapped by furniture and struggling to free himself from the shroud covering his head.

Lunging forward, Noni reached the bedroom door at the same time as a hooded Aldo. Stepping deftly to one side, Noni escaped the outstretched arms of the massive body. He staggered, but regained his posture. With one hand he reached for her and with the other pulled the spread from his head.

Noni kicked his leg, dropping him to the floor. Her hands found the hammer. Hopping now on the balls of her feet and ducking under his arms, she managed to get behind him while wildly swinging. The impact slammed the stumbling figure into the bathroom door. He tried to protect his head with his arm, but the flying hammer caught him exposed. Blood splattered over the walls. He went down on one knee. Noni jumped over his slumped figure. Aldo propelled himself forward. His fist swung toward her stomach, but missed its mark and hit the wall. She tried to run, but couldn't move fast enough. He caught her around the legs, sending them both sprawling into the center of the living room. Noni's head exploded as a thundering blow caught her in the temple. Somewhere in the background she could feel a scream. The top of her head vibrated. His breath was on her neck. Her cold fear was greeted by Aldo's measured blows to her half-crouched body. She managed to tuck her head under her arms. I will not die here, doing nothing... It was a new chant playing and replaying in her head.

The rock that rested in the center of her being began to roll, swell, stretch. She saw herself huddled limply on the floor and an instrument, a sledge hammer, moving with the rhythm of pistons, pummeling her inert body. The force of the pistons raised her to full height, forced her to stand and face the fear that engulfed her.

She was atop him now, swinging a lamp. His chin shot forward and fell back. The next blow caught him on the forehead. Noni checked her next blow. She wondered if he was dead. *Suppose he gets up. I'm not going to let him get up.*

Noni studied the figure beneath her. His hair was aglitter with shards and splinters of glass. The blood streaming from the long snakelike gash on his forehead looked like a decorative ribbon. The shirt that had seemed so iridescently silver looked now like a shimmering Pollock painting.

Her fear was reshaping itself, honing in on the last time he had beaten her...being thrown across the room, spine cracking against the wall, head snapping, wondering if the snapping sound was the wall giving way or her back or her head... his wide-legged stance over her; the murderous mask of a face staring down at her. The violent spreading of her legs, the kick to her stomach. The sound of her clothes and flesh ripping as he penetrated her...

Afterwards he had bathed her, dressed her wounds, all the while crying and telling her that he hadn't meant to hurt her. But later in a calm voice he'd warned her: "If you tell anyone, you'll wish for death for a long time before it comes. You understand me?"

She did. She had walked with the fear until she could taste it, smell it, touch it. It crawled over her flesh like a rash. It was her constant companion.

She raised the lamp high above her head and swung with all of her might. No more. No more! The lamp shattered into a million pieces, blood and glass forming a halo around his head. Red splattered the wall, carpet, and chair. She was bathed in crimson and sparkling glass. Each shard that entered her flesh told her that she was alive. Her flesh tingled with the tiny slivers. Again she raised the lamp.

Something tugged at her arm. Turning, she saw that her wrist was being held by a large, black hand. Another thick, black arm encircled her waist, hoisting her into mid-air.

"Oh no, no, I will not die like this. I'm tired of being afraid. This is the last time you hurt me," she screamed. Noni's legs and arms flailed about, striking what felt like a tree trunk.

"Okay lady, calm down."

"Who the hell you calling Lady?"

"Calm down, I said."

Two mountain-tall policemen blocked her vision.

"You alright Miss?" the first officer asked.

"She don't look hurt to me," responded the other.

"Who the hell are you? Who do you think you are? Get out of my space."

Noni heard the scathing desperation of an alien voice issue from her throat, but it came from across the room, bouncing off the walls, ringing in her ears.

She twisted her head, trying to avoid the attack of words. Was this her voice? Was it? The officer made a move toward her, left hand moving to his gun.

"So you all are going to finish what he started," she ranted. "Go ahead, shoot! But I'm not going to take any more of this, do you hear? I'm ready to die."

The first officer, still holding her, moved between them and spoke over his shoulder.

"Get the medics Mac, the man needs attention, and so does she."

Noni heard the voice issuing instructions as a jumble of sound. She closed her eyes and shook her head violently trying to synchronize the images and the voices. Slowly she opened her eyes. Everything still spun in slow motion.

Two medics clad in white entered, maneuvering a long, flat board on wheels. Aldo's blood-splattered body was rolled and lifted onto the rolling gurney. One of the medics lifted the right eyelid of the lifeless prone body. Another produced a bullet-like pellet which he put under his bloody nose. Aldo moved as if to escape the smell. Noni involuntarily lunged toward the semi-conscious body, but was restrained. The two medics gripped the white board and in unison began rolling it forward, toward the door. Cherry lights swirled outside the open door. The whine of sirens filled the air.

"Stop! Stop!" screamed Noni, struggling against the grip of the officer holding her. "Where do you think you're going? Where are you taking him? Who's going to clean up this mess?" She tried to stop the flow of insane words. They blasted forth from somewhere deep inside the whirling mass in her stomach – a cord unraveling, uncontrolled, making no sense.

The officer held her, shook her, sputtering words she couldn't understand as he carried her into the kitchen and lowered her onto a chair. The police officer found a glass and filled it with water and handed it to her silently.

"Would you please tell me what's going on here? Are you dating this guy?"

It was some time before Noni responded. The officer waited patiently.

"He wasn't always like this." Noni sat back in her chair, and slowly recounted what had brought them to this night...

It was his walk that had caught her attention. He had moved through the office with the ease of a man who was walking barefoot down a country lane. He had teasing dark eyes and a quick, warm smile.

They were civilian employees at a Navy base in Brooklyn. While he sometimes joined her in the base's canteen, he quickly introduced her to some of the restaurants tucked in unexpected places along the docks. Stevedores, sailors, bartenders and waitresses all knew and greeted him by name. Soon they were going to movies, concerts, romantic dinners. And dances. He loved to dance, as did Noni.

But Aldo was also elusive. Sometimes he'd miss work for two or three days, calling in sick. When she attempted to check on him he didn't answer his telephone or his door. He never explained. And they'd been seeing each other for almost a year before he even mentioned that he had family in Brooklyn.

His Aunt Betty lived in an apartment on the second floor of a well-kept building on a quiet, tree lined street. The day they visited, Aldo was particularly animated. He bypassed the living room and headed straight to the kitchen where he immediately put the kettle on to boil. He placed tea cups before his aunt and Noni, while chatting about family members and events.

Aunt Betty had seemed amused by Aldo's activity. But then he set out a beer stein and a bottle of beer for himself. Looking from the glass to her nephew questioningly, Betty was clearly no longer amused. Noni was puzzled by the sudden tension between them.

"Aldo, I'd rather you did not drink that beer in my home."

Aldo glanced at his aunt briefly, picked up the beer and left the apartment. Noni was stunned. Aunt Betty looked at her wearily.

"I gather you've never seen Aldo drunk."

"No, actually, I was under the impression he didn't drink."

Betty studied Noni before speaking.

"Noni, I don't mean to interfere, but I do think you need to know, Aldo is an alcoholic. He may not drink for days, weeks even, but when he does he's a real mean drunk. Real mean."

Noni looked hesitantly at Police Officer Bowen. He waited for her to continue.

"Shortly after that I saw him drunk firsthand. I tried to break off the relationship. It's been downhill ever since."

Thursday, December 18, 1975

The mailman brought the usual assortment of bills and junk mail. Tucked in between, a letter in a small yellow envelope. Noni immediately recognized the cramped, almost illegible handwriting of Aldo. It had been mailed from a correctional facility in upstate New York. She stared at the envelope for a long time before tossing it unopened in the bookcase. It was the first of many letters she would receive over the next five years.

Friday, June 19, 1980

It was too hot to clean, yet Noni struggled from one room to the next, dragging the vacuum cleaner behind her. Sam, her German Shepherd, fled each room as Noni and the noisy machine entered.

In the living room Noni finally turned off the vac and gazed through the screen door. It was only the change in light that made her re-focus on the figure standing in the doorway. Sam stood at attention, but did not bark. The male figure observed the dog and stepped back. Noni could see the raised, three inch scar on his wide forehead. He was clean shaven, with a close haircut. He was still powerfully built. She gazed at Aldo with clear, unblinking eyes. She felt neither fear nor curiosity.

"Hi, Noni. I'm sorry I didn't call first," he said from outside the door.

Noni waited.

"I'm in New York to attend a family funeral and thought it would be a chance to come by and thank you."

Noni raised an eyebrow.

Aldo seemed hesitant as if not sure how to interpret Noni's stillness.

"I live in Ohio now, Noni, with my wife and daughter. I'm a foreman at the steel plant." He smiled nervously, "And I go to AA every day."

He waited for a response from Noni, but it was evident she was waiting for him to continue.

"Prison is a tough place Noni. It either hardens you or it makes you want to do whatever it takes to never return. I just wanted to let you know that I'm not the same person that treated you so badly."

Noni nodded, "Glad to hear that Aldo." Still she did not smile.

"I'm really sorry for what I put you through, Noni, I really am." He was serious now, almost boyish in his apology. Noni watched him for a few seconds before she responded.

"Thank you for telling me. Take good care."

He'd been dismissed. Aldo hesitated a moment before turning and walking down the steps. Noni watched until he was out of sight. She exhaled deeply.

With a solemnity associated with rites of passage, Noni walked to the bookcase, collected Aldo's letters and deposited them into the trash. As she made her way back into the living room she realized that she felt safe for the first time in years. It was even safe enough to smile.

REVEREND BRIGHT AND THE BUDDHA

Janine took pride in her well-maintained garden. Many weekends were spent in constructing raised boxes for her vegetables and preparing the flower beds. She loved the feel of the moist earth, the challenge of annuals vs. perennials, and the color and variety of the plants. She loved the cheerfulness of the forsythia planted along the boundaries and the privacy it created. Of special pride was a section of night blooming flowers.

Introducing herself and welcoming her new neighbors, she presented them with a fresh cut bouquet from her yard. The Newell family was a rambunctious lot with four young boys and a baby girl. Among the toys scattered about their yard, Janine noticed an item that seemed out of place – a large Buddha with an ashtray atop its head. When she first noticed it, it was between two lawn chairs in the back garden. Over time it made its way to the side yard where it stood abandoned. Not particularly religious, and certainly not a Buddhist, its use as an ashtray still struck Janine as sacrilegious. After several weeks she asked about it.

"The wife and I bought that ashtray at a yard sale several years ago. We've since quit smoking."

"Is your family Buddhist?"

"No, we're Catholic. Why?"

"That's a Buddha."

"Is it?"

"Yes. Can I have it?" Janine asked, hoping her question would not be misunderstood as rudeness.

"No problem, it's yours," Tom Newell said. He gladly brought the Buddha over and placed it in Janine's garage.

After sawing off the rod holding the offensive ashtray and spray-painting Buddha a deep, rich red, Janine placed the statue in her entry-way. To Janine, it seemed to exude a feeling of serenity.

***

Seminary had taught the Rev. Jasper Lee Bright what he needed to guide his flock. Any theology outside of Christianity was not part of his understanding although his job required interaction with religious leaders of many faiths.

Fortunately, he had opted to work in an administrative capacity rather than taking on a pastorate. And to ensure that he'd have an op-portunity to broaden his career options he'd taken classes to eliminate his deep southern accent. He now sounded like a New Englander. It was only on rare, very rare occasions, with very trusted people that he might lapse into a lazy accented way of speaking.

Although raised Baptist, he now presided over a very large minis-try of clergy and lay personnel in the head office of an Episcopalian organization. A hard working man, the Rev. Bright arrived each morning early so that he might walk through the offices and bask in his accomplishments. He enjoyed interacting with his employees, especially those he might not usually encounter during his work-days of meetings, luncheons, panel discussions and many speaking engagements.

Janine worked for the Rev. Bright, although not directly. She too came to work early so that she could catch up on anything that had not been completed the previous day and get a head start on those tasks requiring planning – without the noise of the full staff. She came to converse with Rev. Bright on a fairly regular basis. She learned a great deal about him though through these brief conversations.

One morning he'd found her in the conference room setting up for a meeting.

"You always arrive so early, do you live nearby?"

"No, I live out near the airport."

He nodded as if making a mental note of the information. "You and I are achievers," he'd said, "We make good use of every moment of every day."

Although Janine often received calls at home from her immediate supervisor about work related matters, she never heard from or expected to hear from Rev. Bright outside of work hours. She was stunned when he telephoned rather late one evening.

"Janine, this is the Rev. Bright. I'm at the airport and my flight has been delayed for a few hours. Since you live so near here would it be alright if I spent that time with you instead?"

"How did you get my number?"

"When I realized the delay, I called your supervisor."

Janine hesitated but finally agreed. Although he was a minister, life had taught her to be cautious. She also called the Newells and asked if they would check on her in an hour or so.

Rev. Bright arrived, overnight bag and briefcase in hand. He scanned the living room and seemed satisfied with the art work and size of her library. He stepped in and seated himself by the door.

"Lovely floral arrangement," he said. "I recognize the flower, but I've never seen red irises before."

"Would you care to see the garden? I have an entire section of night blooming flowers."

"Ah, perhaps another time."

Another time? Really? Not if I can help it. Janine offered spice cake and either coffee, tea or juice. He chose tea.

"I really appreciate your hospitality. I so dislike those lounges, even those for first class fliers like myself. They try to make it comfortable but it's never quite right, you know?"

"I'm afraid I don't, but I'll take your word for it."

Rev. Bright smiled apologetically and began talking about the meeting he would attend in Florida. He spoke about the prestigious hotel he would inhabit and the well-known clergy who would present alongside him. He had just begun to talk about his presentation when his vision shifted; he'd spotted the Buddha. Rev. Bright almost choked on the cake in his mouth.

"A Buddha!" He half rose, teacup still in hand. Janine rose too – perplexed but prepared to be of assistance. His eyes widened in disbelief. Janine followed his gaze. She attempted to explain how she'd come to have the statue, "My next door neighbors…." But the cleric seemed oblivious to her or her stuttering attempt to tell him about it. His hand shook, rattling the cup as it made contact with the saucer. Janine could see his mouth form the word 'heretic' as he snatched up his luggage and briefcase and bounded toward the door. In his eagerness to depart this place of sin, he stumbled, righted himself and scurried on.

Janine watched as he hurried away from her home. She shouted after him, "It's not your clerical collar but the collar of ignorance you wear that's choking your ability to recognize the oneness of creation. It's damned annoying."

She went back inside where she poured herself a glass of wine but changed her mind about sitting in the living room. She strode briskly into the back garden where she decided it was time to celebrate the might of the Buddha, the wonder of night blooming flowers and the soothing embrace of her garden.

A LEFT-HANDED AFFAIR*

Cleo's original travel to Accra, Ghana in West Africa was part of a research project for an anthropology course. She wanted to trace African cultural traditions that had been retained from Africa to the Americas. She hadn't expected it, but she'd been enamored –with the people, the languages, the food, dance traditions, the unique fabrics -- with just about everything. So much so, that when Kwaku, a friend suggested they start a business together, she'd eagerly agreed. She would, with his expertise, import items that African Americans were eager to acquire. It provided frequent opportunities to expand her knowledge of the West Africa and grow their business. During the ensuing four years, Kwaku moved to a suburb of Accra called Kanishie.

Unlike his traditional compound in Accra, his new home was built as a single house, in a European style but with the traditional wall surrounding it. Its lounge was furnished with Scandinavian-style furniture. Cleo loved the high ceilings, jalousie windows, ceiling fans and tiled floors that kept the house cool in spite of outdoor temperatures.

Cleo was amused by the kitchen. It was furnished with all the latest appliances including stove and refrigerator. Neither however was ever used. Food was purchased daily from the nearby outdoor market and prepared outdoors using a charcoal cook stove. But the modern kitchen spoke of the status of the family.

Cleo's travel to Ghana was focused on growing the business and visiting friends. He, on the other hand had other ideas. He wanted to bed the woman but was intimidated by her. Cleo had a sharp tongue and wasn't afraid to use it. And she was wild. She'd already slapped his British girlfriend, Beth. True, Beth had been disrespectful to his mother, Maame Esi, and had then been verbally aggressive towards Cleo. Besides all of that, Cleo had shown no interest in him outside of their business partnership in the four years he had known her. If she'd had an interest, she'd have said so. But that is not the point, is it? he mumbled to himself. So, he did what he always did when he didn't know what else to do – he went to his mother.

Maame Esi liked Cleo's assertiveness and self-confidence. In many ways she thought of the American as a younger version of herself. Not only had Maame Esi divorced her husband, but she had sent all five of her sons to college in England. As a very successful market woman she would have been known as Nana Benz had she purchased a Mercedes Benz (with driver). Enjoying her thoughts, she almost forgot why she had brought her grand-daughter, Awo into the sitting room. Seeing Cleo brought her back to her mission.

With Awo translating, Maame Esi asked, "Cleo, is your day going well?"

"Yes, MaMa, it is." Cleo bowed her head and moved across the room to sit where Maame Esi indicated.

"What is it that I can do to make your day easier MaMa?" asked Cleo.

Maame Esi liked this young woman. She was American but she was astute when it came to Akan etiquette. After a few minutes of more pleasantries, the older woman became serious.

"Cleo, we have many customs that are new to you, yes?"

"Yes MaMa."

"How do you feel about our custom of men having multiple wives?"

"Well," she began hesitantly, "I've read about it, but it would be arrogant of me to make a judgment about something I know so little about."

"But you don't object?" Maame Esi pressed.

Cleo could not understand the urgency of the question, but neither could she sense any ill will.

"Object? It seems to have worked for hundreds of years."

Maame Esi and Awo both smiled. Once again, the older woman turned the conversation to pleasantries. Finally, she asked if Cleo would accompany her to the market. Relieved, Cleo quickly retrieved the market basket from the kitchen and walked with her host to Kanishie Market.

A few days later Kwaku returned home from work in time for tea. Cleo was glad to see him. They needed to finalize plans for their buying trek across Ghana, Togo, and Benin to order new product. Their import business was doing well.

Kwaku sipped his tea and studied Cleo as she outlined some changes she wanted to make in their schedule. Apropos to nothing he said, "When we're married you will live in this house and open a shop in Accra."

"What?" Cleo was still talking shipping crates and antiques.

"Marriage? Although your wife is studying abroad, you are married, and you have a girlfriend. You need more? I'm as married to you as need be – we're business partners."

Kwaku frowned and half rose. Cleo looked up, "What's the matter with you?"

"My mother spoke with you, did she not?"

"We talked about a lot of things. What exactly are you referring to?" Cleo was studying him intently. She felt a cold breeze of hostility blowing in her direction but could not figure out its cause.

"Our marriage!" Kwaku was clearly upset.

Cleo tried to reflect on the last few conversations she'd had with Maame Esi.

"Kwaku, your mother did ask me what I thought about multiple marriage, and I told her that I could not argue with it since it has worked for hundreds of years. But I did not interpret that as a proposal, nor did I agree to be a partner in such a marriage. There's been a terrible misunderstanding. I am deeply sorry if I've caused confusion."

Kwaku seemed genuinely shocked. "But my mother said you'd agreed. What has changed your mind? Do you object to being a second wife? I will divorce my first wife if that is what you require."

"There must be some miscommunication; something misunderstood in translation" Cleo offered. But before she could get to the bottom of the confusion Kwaku stalked out of the room. She heard his bedroom door slam.

Cleo found her way to Labadi Beach. The sound of moving water always soothed her. And she needed to be soothed. Abena was waiting for her.

"You look upset."

"You're too polite, I look like hell!"

The friends sat watching and listening to the waves. Cleo told Abena what had happened.

"What are you going to do? Will you continue on the buying trip with him? Will you continue to stay in his home?" There was deep concern in Abena's voice.

"Good questions for which I have no answers. My first thought is to move out, to go to a hotel. But you know that I can't stay in a hotel without being viewed as a...." she struggled to find an appropriate word.

"A harlot?"

Cleo laughed. "That word is not used much anymore, but that's the general idea. To not go on the trip means that people who have placed orders will be disappointed and I'd have to return their money; money that's already been spent for my airfare."

"So, what you're saying is that you'll go on the trip and hope that the worst is over. You'll then figure out what comes next after you get home."

"You know me too well."

Cleo scanned the beach. Several horseback riders were heading their way. Usually, the sight would have brought pleasure to her. Today it reminded her of how far she was from home. Her ruminations were interrupted by Abena's voice.

"You are always welcome to our home Cleo."

"Thank you, but that might make you and Kojo targets of Kwaku's wrath as well." Cleo sighed.

"The offer still stands."

Not quite ready to return to Kwaku's home, Cleo agreed to have lunch with Abena.

When she returned to Kwaku's compound, he and his girlfriend Beth were deep in conversation, which ended abruptly when they heard her enter. He rushed towards her.

"Ah, you've returned in good time." He was all smiles.

"In good time for what?"

"Beth and I have decided that you will join us at the club...." It was not as much an invitation as it was a command.

"Thanks for the invite, but not this evening. You and Beth have a good time."

"But we've decided." His voice had become more insistent. She noticed that Beth kept at a safe distance.

"Kwaku, I am a full-grown woman. An American woman. I've tried to be accepting of some of our differences, but I cannot let this go." Cleo's voice escalated. "You and Beth will not tell me what to do or when to do it. As an adult I'm quite capable of making decisions for myself. I have no interest in going to the club this evening. But thank you anyway."

Kwaku extended his arm as if to grip her shoulder. She instinctively spun out of his reach and turned to face him. "No Kwaku, I am not an African woman who would stand still to be beaten because you think you have the right to do so. Maybe we need to rethink this entire relationship." She didn't know if his intent had been to be physical but two days before she'd seen two young women being beaten with a stick by a rather small man. They ran and screamed but made no attempt to join forces against him.

When she'd tried to come to their aid, she'd been stopped by two men who told her in no uncertain terms that the man had a right to beat them; they'd disobeyed him. The image and the acceptance of such treatment had remained with her.

Turning her attention back to Kwaku, she gave him a serious "Try me" look. He walked away.

Maame Esi had made a spicy fish stew served over fufu, which Cleo loved. In fact, it was her favorite meal. Afterwards she'd bathed and dressed and was about to walk to the main road to hail a taxi when Kwaku approached her.

"Cleo, have you changed your mind about accompanying me and Beth?"

"No, I'm going out with Abena and Kojo."

"You refuse me but you're going out with them?"

Kwaku was getting ready to work himself into a rage. Cleo softened her tone, trying to sound more conciliatory. "I'm sorry, but I have some business to discuss with them."

"What business? Aren't we business partners? Wouldn't I be included in that discussion?"

"No, this has nothing to do with our business Kwaku. Excuse me, I'll be late." She stepped around him.

Beth too saw Kwaku's agitation and attempted to calm him. Stroking his back and shoulders she reminded him that there would be other opportunities for them to work out a new business arrangement with Cleo. Or end the current one. Kwaku did not push her away, but he was not paying attention either.

Cleo had not intended to tell Kwaku about her plan to start a business with Abena and Kojo. She knew he would try to commandeer whatever it was, even if he had no knowledge or interest in the project. If money was to be made Kwaku was interested.

Abena, Kojo and Cleo planned to have an art exchange between African women and their African American counterparts. Abena already had a following in Europe. In Cleo's mind that would translate positively in establishing an arena in the States. When she had embarked on the import business with Kwaku it had not been a career choice. It was simply to enable her to afford continued trips to West Africa and perhaps even pay some of her college expenses. And the experiences would help her decide if she really wanted to get her master's in anthropology rather than join her family's auto dealerships. Partnering with Abena and Kojo in an art endeavor was much closer to her heart.

Kojo had chosen a hotel in Accra for dinner. He strutted grandly into the lobby with the two women walking behind him. Abena stage whispered, "Don't get used to this 'king' routine, Kojo."

"Why not?"

"Because I'm not agreeing to a second wife."

"And I'm going home soon" Cleo added.

They continued their banter as the waiter seated them at an outdoor table and brought menus. Only after finishing their appetizers did Abena change the tone of the conversation:

"I hope you don't mind Cleo, but I told Kojo what happened with you and Kwaku."

The concern in Abena's voice was evident. "No, of course not" Cleo answered.

Kojo chose his words carefully. "I know you've been in business with Kwaku for a few years. It's evident, he's been on his best behavior. But we know him as a very shrewd businessman, and we also know he can be vindictive when he doesn't get what he wants. You have refused him. He is not going to accept that gracefully."

"That's true enough, but I sense you're saying something more serious than his simply being displeased. What are you trying to say Kojo?"

"Kwaku and I are in the same businesses, beer distribution and restaurant provisions. He has had an intense hostility towards me ever since I outbid him on a contract. He tried to ruin my business by spreading rumors that we were padding our invoices. Fortunately, it didn't work. Once he found out that you and Abena were friends, well, I think, part of his anger with you has to do with your relationship with us."

"That's a stretch, don't you think? Maybe you're making more of this than you should."

"Maybe" added Abena, "but I have another theory."

They were interrupted by the arrival of their main courses and the refilling of their water glasses. Abena and Kojo's apprehension was contagious. Cleo toyed with her silverware as her mind wandered. *As a guest in Kwaku's home, I am at his mercy -- not a comforting thought. Women here have no legal protection other than that provided by their family, their male fam–*

Abena interrupted her trance. "Your business with Kwaku doesn't garner huge income, does it?"

Cleo smiled in spite of herself. "No. What's your point?"

"He wants something more financially rewarding from you. Think about it. His girlfriend, Beth, is useful to him because of her business connections in England and here too. You'd be valuable to him because of your family's business connections. And although he's not interested in art, he knows you have connections in that area as well. He knows he can't control you, but if you were his wife...."

Cleo was slow to respond. She sighed loudly, "Where does that leave us?" She pushed the food around on her plate.

Kwaku was still out when Cleo returned. She entered quietly not wanting to awaken Maame Esi and Awo. Once in bed she heard a knock at her door. Maame Esi and Awo entered carrying sleeping mats. Awo explained that they wanted to make sure she was safe. If Cleo had been disturbed by the conversation in the restaurant, this watch sent her into a tailspin. She couldn't sleep. She tossed and turned as her host snored not so gently. This has become a nightmare. How can I wake up when I can't even get to sleep?

The image of the two girls running and yelping replayed and re-played. They ran to the rhythm of Maame Esi's snoring. Everything synchronized with running and snoring.

And then the bedroom door burst open and Kwaku bellowed in a voice rife with anger, "You will do as I tell you to do!" The effect was heart stopping. As Kwaku advanced towards Cleo, Maame Esi spoke softly in Twi. Kwaku froze midstride, turned and slammed out of the house.

As soon as it was light Cleo headed to the airport. It didn't matter where the flight was going, she would be on the first flight out. Even after she'd been handed her ticket she was nervous. Kwaku had ears in many places. She sat in the waiting area with her back to the wall, vigilant. She was relieved only when she walked onto the tarmac to-ward the plane. As she was about to enter the aircraft, she heard a racket behind her. Kwaku was on the tarmac screaming something, but she couldn't make out what it was. Cleo turned to face him, raised her left hand, and gave a royal wave.

***

It had taken a few years but Cleo, Abena and Kojo estab-lished an art gallery and studio in Cobble Hill, Brooklyn. They called it Eve's Rib and their first exhibit featured Abena's work along with two of her protégés. By the second year the gallery had built an im-pressive international clientele and the art classes had a waiting list of students. At the end of that same year Cleo was approved for a bank loan to purchase a whitestone with attached coach house in the same neighborhood.

The first night Cleo slept in her new home she had a vivid dream: Kwaku was sitting on her back patio holding a glass of champagne. "My Love," he began, as he took a sip of his drink, "I will marry you and come live in your fine home."

Cleo woke up laughing.

In many African cultures, it is considered rude, even insulting, to give, receive, eat, drink or point with the left hand because that is the hand used when going to the toilet.

RITUALS

Lili and I approach the elegant wrought iron and glass door with appreciation. We have walked her favorite route; pass the Chinese
restaurant, and a few steps away where the Kosher meat and Kosher
dairy restaurants are next door to each other. In the next few blocks
there are barbecue, soul food and Caribbean eateries. We turn onto
the parkway where we take in the grandeur of a very old synagogue,
a Hassidic reading room, a converted movie theater, now a Seventh
Day Adventist house of prayer and St. Anna Catholic Church. We
make another turn at the yeshiva and back around past a small house
that has been converted into a synagogue.

I'm on speaking terms with the rabbi – at least as much as a female
of any stripe gets to have a conversation with him. On more than one
occasion he's asked me to turn off the lights in the synagogue. The
entire situation is odd. For a rabbi to speak to goyim (non-Jewish
person) is unusual enough, but to invite me into the synagogue is
downright unorthodox (pun intended). It turns out I don't have to enter the building to turn off the lights and there is no reason for me to
be unkind or unresponsive to his request. After all, we are neighbors.

Lili and I rest for a moment in the lobby, not so much to take in the
splendor of the marble walls, floor and stairs, but to gather our energy
for the four flights that still have to be climbed to reach home.

Lili, a 60-pound standard poodle, heads directly to her water bowl. after which she sprawls in the center of the living room. I claim the couch. This top floor apartment is always hot so all of the windows remain wide open, day and night.

The view from my living room is of the backs and roofs of the brownstones on the parkway. Sometimes I imagine myself in Italy gazing at colorful rooftops and elegant cathedrals.

In this neighborhood Friday is always special: the eagle flies on Friday (payday) and it is the beginning of the Sabbath.

I can see into one apartment; all of the lights are ablaze. The Shabbat table is set: an elegant white lace tablecloth, silver candlesticks, candles lit, challah bread and a decanter of wine among the other food offerings.

Below in one backyard lives an older couple. During the week they sit talking and laughing lovingly with one another. On Fridays though, a different custom is performed. They buy a bottle of something alcoholic. They sip and talk, but halfway through the bottle they begin to argue about who's drinking more than the other. The language gets salty and the woman begins smacking her mate on his head. He responds by snatching the bottle and staggering inside. From her stride I'd guess that he and the bottle don't have a chance.

On a rooftop a disheveled man walks around. He seems to be scanning the apartment windows across from him. He grins widely when he realizes he has an audience. He unzips his trousers and begins to masturbate. I drop the venetian blinds. By the time the police arrive, he has gone. A week later he's at it again. He grins at me, I grin back and point a borrowed BB gun. Before I can aim he disappears.

I work at Saint Anna's and I volunteer at its Exchange. This is where neighborhood people bring items they no longer need, like outgrown baby clothes, and swap for toddler shoes or some small household appliance. More than that though it's a gathering place for the community.

Most afternoons I play hand ball with the boys in the yard or shoot hoops. Ramon, Doug, Julio, Jason, and Butch make up the main crew although it varies with the day of the week or time of day. I've become adept at providing bandages for scrapped knees and hugs for bruised egos. Frequently, I'm given a ride home on the back of one of the boy's bikes. While this confers bragging rights to whoever gives me the most rides, it also renews my energy so I can climb the four flights of stairs, get Lili, walk down four flights, walk Lili and climb back up.

On this particular Friday, almost immediately after I sit down, there is a pounding on the door and a chorus of voices. About half a dozen boys are yelling at the same time; something about a baby and a windowsill. We run down four flights of stairs. My heart is racing. I don't know what I will find but instinct says, be afraid. Bikes are strewn helter-skelter across the sidewalk. I jump on the back of one of them. We race through the streets like a herd of thundering wild horses with the boys bellowing for people to get out of the way. We arrive in front of an apartment building where a throng of people are looking upward. I look up and shudder. On the top floor a toddler is dangling from the windowsill. My already elevated adrenalin escalates as I race in through the front door.

I hear the thud. Too afraid to turn back, I take the steps two at a time. In the apartment an old man stands at the window, looking dazed.

"What have you done? What the hell have you done?"

He shifts his eyes in my general direction. "He needed air. He needed some air." He continues repeating this, like a mantra. His voice is flat, low; his eyes moist and unfocused. In the distance the wail of a siren can be heard. One of the boys is holding onto me for dear life, we're both crying. Suddenly there are policemen everywhere. They are stoic as they try to figure out what happened. From their questioning it is revealed that the old man is the baby's grandfather. He was babysitting.

I walk the boys and their bikes to Saint Anna's. It is cool inside; peaceful. The faint scent of incense is calming. We light candles and pray. In silence I walk each boy home.

I feel like I've been holding my breath for eons as I turn into my block. The rebbe is exiting the synagogue. He looks at me, does a double take. "What has happened?" His face is sculpted with concern. I tell him. He rocks and begins what sounds like a prayer chant. I don't know the language, but I know the feeling and it's comforting.

I sleepwalk myself up four flights. I'm greeted by Lili, holding her leash.

THE UNDERTAKER'S ABODE

Mr. Braithwaite is a friend of my family. He and my uncle attended primary school together and stayed in touch over the years. And because Mr. Braithwaite is quite wealthy, my family members often consult with him when considering any major financial investment. I remember meeting him in 1997 at a family reunion when I was just 16-years-old. He was in New York City on one of his frequent business trips. Five or six years later Mr. Braithwaite invited me to his home on St. James Island in the Caribbean.

Mr. Braithwaite is a charming, agile, older gentleman who I seldom think of as a funeral director. He's more like an uncle. He has retained his slender figure and dresses in designer suits or English gentry style sports jackets. At parties he dances almost every dance – when he's not flirting with the ladies. I was quite flattered when he invited me to his home. Actually, what he said was, "When you visit St. James Island, you must stay in my home."

At the time, I had not thought seriously about Mr. Braithwaite's invitation, but winter, with its icy pavements, bone-chilling winds blowing off the Hudson River, and the termination of my thirteen-month long relationship with my lover sent me rushing to the airline office to book a week on St. James Island.

"You don't talk. I don't know what you're thinking or feeling," is what Raymond, my lover had said. I, on the other hand, had been so happy to have found someone I felt comfortable around while being quiet. I thought he too enjoyed the silence. Besides, our other nonverbal communications seemed to go exceedingly well.

I needed time to reflect – to reassess...

It would be my first trip to the Caribbean. I consoled myself with the notion that at least I'd not be alone while navigating this new emptiness I was feeling.

Mr. Braithwaite met me at the airport and drove us up winding roads into the hills. In the distance I could see a grand, white house atop a hill. It turned out to be the abode of Mr. Braithwaite. The house was in a large compound surrounded by a high white wall entered through an elaborate ironwork gate. I commented on the elegance and beauty of the gate. A satisfied smile spread across his face. He noted that for the most part, it always remained open. The garden was awash with hibiscus and other colorful plants. In the back garden there were more flowering shrubs and a dog run for his two German Shepherds. Behind that, entered through a smaller, less ornate gate, a grove of fruit trees. All of this Mr. Braithwaite proudly showed me before we entered the house.

I found myself in a modern but dark kitchen. The dining and living rooms were filled with large, heavy, hand-carved mahogany furniture. For some reason, I was surprised by this. Perhaps I'd seen too many television commercials in which island dwellings were filled with abundant light, rattan or wicker furnishings, and translucent, airy curtains blowing in the breeze.

The room that I would occupy was a bit closer to my envisioned image; there was a sun-filled window that looked out onto the back garden. It was furnished simply. It also had its own bath.

After I'd gotten settled, Mr. Braithwaite served cocktails on the terrace from where we could see almost the entire island, including the sailboats in the bay. I began to appreciate his great love for the house.

The terrace was quite large. Mr. Braithwaite sat across from me. As time went on he maneuvered himself next to me on the loveseat He began punctuating his conversation with gentle strokes to my thigh, or with his arm over the back of the chair cradling my shoulder. I smiled nervously and moved to an adjacent chair. I found his actions forward, but since he was at least 40 years my senior and a family friend, I was sure I misunderstood his intentions. He was probably just lonely I told myself. I made a mental note though to check the availability of a hotel in town.

From colonial mansions, elaborate floral gardens, local handcraft shops, fried fish vendors, dances on schooners to evening swims at one of many beaches, Mr. Braithwaite took as much pride in showing off his island as he did his home. Sometimes, I felt he was showing me off too. But perhaps that was my imagination.

Mr. Braithwaite talked incessantly. He spoke cricket and soccer, weddings and funerals, and who was connected to whom through blood or marriage, but never about himself or his family, if he had any. Even though there were photographs of himself in his youth, there were no current ones. Neither were there pictures of any other family members, alive or dead.

He spoke of business opportunities on the island for a woman of my intellect and worldliness. He spoke of the wisdom and great income one could acquire from investments in the funerary business. "After all," he reasoned, "everyone must die."

On occasion, he'd have business to attend. Since I was not the least bit interested in funerary matters, I'd use these times to shop or explore town on my own. But I was naturally curious by some of what Mr. Braithwaite was suggesting. So, while in town, I took the opportunity to research many of the investments Mr. Braithwaite had suggesting. And since everyone –especially the island's womenfolk–

seemed to be interested in the mansion at the top of the hill, I investigated that too.

Whenever we went out together, though, the women would give me icy glances and focus their full attention on Mr. Braithwaite. Although I found this rude, he never seemed to notice these slights.

One evening Mr. Braithwaite had to go to a meeting. Feeling uncomfortable at the prospect of being left alone in such a large, isolated residence, I asked him to lock the gate when he left. I retired to the living room to listen to music and read. Within minutes, the doorbell rang. Since I thought the gate was locked and there was no intercom, I had to physically go out to the gate. I was already in the courtyard before I realized that the gate had been left open. A rather ample, squat woman wearing a green uniform was moving slowly but steadily towards me. She carried a brown paper bag. Her eyes were intently focused on my face.

"You Hilma?" she scowled. From my review of real estate holdings on the island, I knew that the house was owned by a Hilma Braithwaite, but I wasn't going to tell that to this stranger. Thinking that she had a package to deliver to Mr. Braithwaite, I reached out to receive it. Instead, she reached into the bag and drew out a small cutlass which she raised over her head. She moved swiftly toward me.

"I gonna kill you! You tell he, I gonna kill you!" With that she was upon me.

I struggled mightily, all the while screaming at the top of my lungs with the hope that someone would come to my aid. No one came. The dogs did not bark. I don't know how long we struggled, but I managed to force the blade from my would-be assailant's hand. In one deft movement she scooped up the blade and ran out of the courtyard. I chased after her but only to close and bolt the gate.

The police did not come either – at least not for another hour and a half. They were lost! Lost? The island is only twenty miles by eight, and both officers admitted they were born and raised there. I'm not sure if I was more incensed by their bumbling or their admission of it.

In either case, the police report could not be taken because I had no key for the gate and no idea where Mr. Braithwaite had gone or when he would return. The police and I spoke through the gate.

It was well after midnight when Mr. Braithwaite returned. He was surprised to find the gate locked and all the lights in the house ablaze and me anxiously pacing from room to room. He listened carefully and was very apologetic for the terrible event. He had no idea who the woman was or why she had chosen his home for her insane actions, but it would not happen again. The more he tried to reassure me that there would be no further incidents, the more I disbelieved him. How could he make such assurances if he didn't know who the woman was?

My anger was a slow burn on the way to full flame. It was not enough to be in a strange country, in a strange house, attacked by a strange, possibly mad woman; but to be lied to, played with as if I were a mindless, ignorant child was more than I could abide. I was shaking with rage. I backed away from Mr. Braithwaite and locked myself in my room, but I dared not close my eyes.

The police returned very early the next morning. I explained what had happened, providing a description of the woman, including the uniform she wore and what she'd said. Again, Mr. Braithwaite claimed not to recognize the woman I described nor anyone named Hilma. I knew that was not true. After all, Hilma Braithwaite was the owner of the business and property. "So, you don't know anyone named Hilma?" I asked boldly. He glared at me with such brash daring that I was frightened to say more.

The police were intense in their questioning of Mr. Braithwaite. They asked where he had been the night before and what time he'd left the house. They asked if there were any spurned lovers, dissatisfied clients, creditors. From where I sat, Mr. Braithwaite looked like a man trying to sell a mahogany casket to someone who'd come to purchase a pine box. Mr. Braithwaite poured himself a tall glass of scotch that he swallowed in two gulps. The police were not buying it either. But he did not waiver in his denials.

I was anxious, afraid. While the police were still there, I called a taxi and fled to the airport.

I did not hear from Mr. Braithwaite after that. Embarrassed by the experience and my naiveté and unsure how they would react, I made a point not to tell my family what had happened – at least not until I had a plan of action.

Back at home some months later, my uncle, who never missed a copy of the St. James Courier, called and mentioned in passing that there was a lively scandal surrounding the disappearance of Mr. Braithwaite.

"What happened Uncle?" I asked. Uncle's voice became animated. It seems Mr. Braithwaite had bilked a number of women from several different countries out of their hard-earned financial resources. The women ranged in ages from their early 20s to late 70s. The rumor mill had it that Mr. Braithwaite was somewhere in South America. There were also several women claiming to be Mrs. Braithwaite and all claiming ownership of the large house at the top of the hill. I found this intriguing yet consistent with my experience of the island women and their relationships with him. Still, I could not reveal what had happened to me.

A few days later. Uncle called again. This time he asked if I knew anything about Mr. Braithwaite's funeral business. I thought his interest odd, but was pleased to tell him what I knew:

"Uncle, that funeral parlor that everyone thinks belongs to Mr. Braithwaite is owned by a Hilma Braithwaite." Uncle was quiet but eventually, with trembling voice, demanded to know why I believed this. I didn't get the import of Uncle's tone so plunged ahead.

"Mr. Braithwaite tried to interest me in investing in his funeral business, but I had absolutely no interest. Then he tried to encourage me to invest in real estate, pointing out that tourism was growing and that owning property, a well positioned house, or guesthouse could be quite advantageous."

Because I tend to be a quiet person, people assume I am either not paying attention, not understanding what's being said, or that I'm in agreement. Mr. Braithwaite had taken my silence for acquiescence.

Uncle was quiet on the phone so I continued. "One day, while in town I decided to get more information about the properties he was promoting. At the library I discovered that the Braithwaite Funeral Home is actually owned by a Hilma Braithwaite, as is the house on the hill. Hilma resides in Venezuela and visits St. James rarely."

Uncle was extraordinarily quiet. "Uncle, are you still there?" I could hear him breathing heavily. "Uncle, you didn't give Mr. Braithwaite any money, did you?"

"Not exactly."

"What do you mean, 'not exactly'?"

"His agent, a woman named Hilma Braithwaite, accompanied me to the bank…"

"Uncle, tell me you did not give her any money."

"Cash," is all he could utter into the phone before the line went dead.

.

NAUTICAL MANEUVERS

Lenny and I were running buddies. We worked together at the naval base and partied together. He seemed to know every party within a 50-mile radius of the base – and possibly beyond. He was discreet and seldom partied or hung out with other sailors from the base. How he knew who he knew was indeed a "military" secret.

Marva, a civilian like me, befriended me almost from my first day on the job. She was a tall, dark, big boned beauty. I remember the first time she saw Lenny. We were at a party. Marva looked across the room and declared the equally tall, broad-shouldered, rust brown sailor, "Yummy!" She walked across the dance floor and introduced herself. I glanced up from the drink that was keeping me company and re-thought my intention to tell her that Lenny was off-limits. He was full grown and didn't need me to run interference. They spent the rest of evening together dancing, drinking and laughing. I noticed though, they did not leave together. In the weeks and months that followed, neither of them mentioned the other to me.

My first encounter with Lenny had been an accident trying to happen. I was in the cafeteria food line deciding on what to have for lunch when I heard a barking command from the MP on duty, "Simmons, hit the deck!" I immediately dropped and rolled under a nearby table.

Lenny, sitting nearby leaped the railing and brought down the man behind me who had raised his food tray to attack me. The MPs took the man away. Lenny helped me to my feet.

"What was that all about?" he asked.

"Your guess is as good as mine," I stated, dusting off my skirt.

"Well what did he say to you?"

"He was mumbling something but I was focused on food. I didn't even realize he was talking to me."

A small group gathered to find out what happened. A civilian who had been in the line spoke up. "He was agitated by your hair. He said your Afro was a disgrace to the race."

Lenny ushered me to the table at which he'd been sitting and introduced me to a civilian named Maurice, who looked me up and down with unmasked disdain. Lenny gave him a withering look and he seemed to adjust his face, if not his attitude. Although off-putting, I was not concerned with Maurice; I was extremely appreciative of Lenny's quick response to a situation that could have turned ugly at my expense.

Over time I encountered Maurice often. He was a barrel-chested man who always dressed as if going to meet the queen. He wore everything brown: Brown turtlenecks with brown plaid sport jackets, brown three-piece suits, and designer shirts. Everything matched his complexion. Although he always dressed with elegance and flourish, far more elegantly than was required at a military installation, none of it made him appealing. Noticeable perhaps, but not appealing.

Lenny began stopping by my office regularly – regularly enough for the Commanding Officer to inquire. I was advised that fraternization between military personnel and civilians was frowned upon.

We still hung out together. What we did off base was our business.

Even though the military offered housing when the barracks were being renovated, Lenny asked if he could stay with me temporarily. I lived in a studio but agreed if he would provide his own air mattress or sleeping bag. Everything was working well until the day Maurice called wanting to speak to Lenny. I said that Lenny wasn't there but before I could inquire if I could take a message, Maurice went into a rant:

"Don't tell me he's not there. I haven't heard from him in days and I know he's staying with you. I don't know what you think you're doing, but let me tell you one thing, I'm the one keeping him in fine clothes, it's my car he's driving all over town in, with you in it. I'm the one–"

I hung up. He called back several times until I took the phone off the hook. There was no place in my experience to file this information or situation, but there it was.

When Lenny came in, I told him what happened. He cocked his head to one side, but made no comment. Later that evening he went out and did not return. At the base the next day he smiled when he saw me and winked but made no attempt to explain the call from Maurice.

Several days later we were snowed in. We had planned to go to a party, but the roads had not been cleared and it was anyone's guess when they would be. I cooked while Lenny played records and made drinks. We were festive – it was the first snow of the season. We raised the blinds, lit candles, ate dinner and watched the snow fall.

Lenny's voice was soft, as if talking to himself: "After two tours I mustered out. I'd been sending money to my mom the whole time. I sent a certain amount for her needs, the rest she was putting in a bank account for me. I wanted to have my own business --- a restaurant and bar or a liquor store. When I got home there was no money. She'd never put any money in the bank. All my money was gone."

There was a long pause before he spoke again. "I stayed in a drunken stupor for a couple of weeks. Then I re-upped. I wanted money – a lot of money. And I knew that I could depend only on myself. The only thing I had was my body."

His large doe eyes rose to meet mine. His hurt, disappointment and pain was palpable – even now. I felt ill equipped to counsel him, but he was my friend and it hurt me to see him in distress.

"Have you been home since then?" I asked.

"No." He continued to peer intently at me, waiting for a judgement, or a pronouncement of some kind.

"Well, that explains why Maurice hated me on sight."

Lenny smiled vaguely. "Yeah, he has a lot invested in me."

That night we slept in the same bed, with me holding him tightly; offering comfort, not judgement.

When the renovations were completed Lenny moved back to the barracks and life continued as before. At the end of his tour he moved to Tennessee – somewhere near Memphis. We exchanged a few letters, but over time lost track of each other. I left civil service, moved to Maryland and was selling real estate. Marva came to visit several times. On her last visit she asked if I still heard from Lenny. Before my brain engaged, my mouth wondered aloud if Lenny was still sleeping with men. Marva's drink hit the table with such force that it bounced, spilling onto the floor. Marva was trying not to let go of the liquid still in her mouth.

"Men? Are you saying Lenny's gay?"

"Well, I don't know if he'd classify himself as such, but he was sexually involved with men," I offered with some trepidation.

"Bull," she spat out. "Wasn't nothing gay about him!"

With my foot firmly planted in my mouth, I took a sip of my drink and tried to control my urge to be right. "I'm sorry. I didn't know you were seeing Lenny. He never said anything. Neither did you," I said with sarcasm.

Marva glared at me with the same look of disdain that Maurice had given me on my first encounter with him. She was clearly angry – and hurt.

"Why didn't you say something to me about Lenny?" she demanded.

"And how was I supposed to know you were dating him?" I yelled right back.

Marva stormed out.

I drained my glass. If Marva was angry with me she would probably hold onto it for a while. Or longer. If she was angry with herself, well, she'd just have to get over it. And herself.

I made myself another drink and put some music on the record player. I wondered if I should change my hairstyle – maybe grow some locks. After all, it was my 'fro that had started this mess... And clearly it was time to move on.

PROMISE

The community did not need another philanderer in the pulpit so I was glad that after delivering his trial sermon Drake opted not to be ordained. But I'm ahead of myself. It all began ten or twelve years ago.

Andrew and I had been married for only a few months when we met Drake and his wife Grace. We were all in our early to mid-twenties and pleased with ourselves and the lives we were living. We were strivers – believing that education and real estate were our passports to success.

Andy and I had both attended City College. His Master's was from Columbia University. Mine would come from New York University. We had just moved into our new, sunny, one-bedroom apartment in Crown Heights. Everything was near at hand; the subway, buses, movie theatres, churches, temples and a mosque. And it was a culinary bonanza, from street food: knishes and Jamaican meat patties, kabobs and samosas; to sit-down restaurants. It was all just a few steps away.

***

We met Drake and Grace at a party. Andy and I were still in the "can't get enough of each other" phase, always touching, kissing, hugging -- newlyweds. Everyone at the party seemed to fit into the same category although some couples had been married longer and were less demonstrative in their affections.

And then there was Drake, who arrived with with his wife Grace quietly behind him. Attractive, charming, well dressed, a brilliant wordsmith with a hearty, contagious laugh were all descriptors of Drake Evans but there was a worrisome aspect of the man that I would, in time, find trying.

Drake made no attempt to camouflage his attraction to me. His wife's shy glances and soft brown eyes followed his every move. If Drake looked in her direction her lids lowered, studying the carpet. My husband, however, was not so passive. After several gentle but unsuccessful attempts to let Drake know that his attentions towards me were not appreciated, Andy propelled Drake into a corner where he delivered what appeared to be a serious come-to-Jesus sermon. The women paused in their conversations, and tried not to be obvious as they stared. The men paid rapt attention with raised eyebrows and nods of approval. But no one said anything. And then it was over.

Grace sat through it all alone as the other women gathered in small groups chatting, moving in and out of the kitchen refilling trays of appetizers and drinks. I brought her a small plate of cheese, crackers, some kind of sausage and a glass of soda. She smiled appreciatively.

She sniffed the soda. "Ah, non-alcoholic." She began to nibble the snacks. Although she did not look at me, she did offer a soft-spoken, "Thank you."

"I guess you don't drink," I said by way of starting a conversation.

"Actually, I love wine, but I'm pregnant. Again."

"Congratulations."

The look she gave me was that of a wounded puppy. "Sorry" I whispered, not sure of what line I'd crossed. She smiled the saddest smile I'd ever seen.

"No, I'm sorry. It's not you. It's just that I have a two-month old son and I'm pregnant again -- not what I'd had in mind when we got married." She paused. When she again spoke it was softly. "We didn't socialize much when we were dating. I had no idea he was a drinking man." She looked across the room at her husband, who was nursing a bottle of Johnnie Walker Black and delivering a very lively, if somewhat garbled diatribe on the sins of mankind.

"Sometimes," he preached, "you have to go within; step away from your earthly concerns, focus on the lessons found in the Good Book..."

By the time Andy and I were ready to leave, Drake had passed out holding a now empty liquor bottle. Our hosts had confiscated his car keys and tossed a blanket over him. We drove Grace to her mother's home where she picked up her son. We then drove her home to the Brevoort Projects in Bed-Stuy, walked her to her apartment and made sure it was locked before we left. During the drive we'd learned that Drake Evans worked full time driving a bus, part-time in a bookstore and took college classes at night. We were in awe of his ambition, but not at all pleased with the way he treated his wife.

I tried to befriend Grace, but she was always very busy or tired, or both. With one small child and another on the way, I didn't question her lack of free time.

The next time we saw Drake and Grace, the "crew" had gathered to watch a football game. She looked like she was going to have the baby at any given moment. She was quite different from our earlier encounter: Her eyes sparkled and she no longer studied the floor. He on the other hand was subdued; watching her every move, nursing his one drink. He still made sneaking glances at me when Andy wasn't watching and then he'd slowly undress me with his eyes. If anyone noticed they said nothing. Grace periodically surveyed his movements with disinterest. She was more relaxed with herself and with us.

My curiosity got the better of me. I corralled her at the far end of the dining room when everyone else was in the living room cheering on their team.

"Grace, it's amazing that you are so effervescent so late in your pregnancy. And what's going on with Drake – he seems so... subdued?"

Without missing a beat, she looped her arm in mine and walked us back toward the living room. With a conspiratorial wink, she said, "One day I'll tell you all about it."

Several years passed. Andy was an associate for a high-tech electronics firm and I taught linguistics at City College. And we had our first child, a girl we named Tiffany. We purchased a brownstone in Brooklyn's Carroll Gardens neighborhood on a quiet, tree-lined street. Unlike most brownstones it had a small, but well-appointed front garden featuring large rebloomer daylilies.

***

On this Saturday afternoon in July, our four-year-old daughter was spending the weekend with her grandparents. Andy had gone to buy some wine in anticipation of a quiet, romantic evening together. I was creating a sensuous ambiance including candlelight in the backyard and selecting appropriate music when the telephone rang.

"Hey babe, you won't believe who I ran into on the way to the liquor store. Why don't you come join us at The Lounge. You know, the bar that has live music on weekends."

I groaned. "Love, I was looking forward to spending some quiet time together. Who have you run into?"

"It' a surprise. Come on, Hon."

I hated when he called me "Hon." We'd been married long enough for me to recognize the word and the tone. It meant he was feeling trapped and wanted me to extricate him.

I heard the voice before my eyes adjusted to the darkened room; the contagious laughter punctuated almost incomprehensible speech. Drake Evans. He and Andy were seated at the bar with an empty stool wedged between them. It was too early for live music but the jukebox was pumping out a steady beat of base infused blues. Andy and Drake both seemed elated to see me.

I turned the stool so that when I sat I was cradled between Andy's knees. He leaned forward, wrapping himself around me in a classic posture of possession. It was not lost on Drake. He emptied his glass and poured himself another from an open bottle at his elbow.

"You two seem very happy," his mouth said while his eyes were suddenly sad.

"We are." I said smugly. "Aren't you?"

There was a pause of several beats before he responded. "Yeah. I've finished my undergrad studies and I'm enrolled in a low residency school for my MFA." He paused again, looking directly at me this time. "Grace and I are estranged, even though we live in the same house."

I was silent. Andy made soft humming sounds deep in his throat.

"The boys are enrolled in a private school and Grace works from home. She's become a fairly successful artist. Sells her work on the internet." His hunched shoulders indicated that he did not take pleasure in her success. "We've moved to a larger apartment in Bed-Stuy." By this time the Bedford-Stuyvesant neighborhood was being quietly gentrified by a few realtors who recognized the value of its brownstones, many of which had never been chopped up into smaller units like some of their Manhattan counterparts.

After we'd talked about nothing in particular for a while, I announced that we had to pick up our daughter. Andy went to the men's room. Drake took the opportunity to whisper in my ear, "I still want you, you know." There was a smirk on his face which quickly evaporated when Andy returned. I was too stunned to respond. We left him with his half empty bottle.

"I'm sorry Lori. I didn't want to bring him to our home and for some reason I didn't want to just leave him. He makes happy noises, but it's obvious he's very unhappy." After a few moments Andy's face went from relaxed to a tense jaw and pulsing temples. I could see he was caught between his instinct, which wanted to do physical harm to the abrasive man, and his upbringing which instructed that he should always be cordial.

I too had "feelings" about the encounter. On one hand I was happy to support my husband, but on the other I was annoyed to once again be face-to-face with the likes of Drake Evans. I was eager to reach the safety of home and ran ahead. Andy called after me to say that he was stopping at the liquor store. With great effort, mainly on Andy's part, we managed to salvage the rest of the evening, never once mentioning Drake Evans.

***

We had planned to spend the weekend buying furniture for our summer cottage in the Black mecca of Oak Bluffs on Martha's Vineyard. Grace's invitation to attend her first one woman exhibit at a gallery in Greenwich Village had arrived a few days earlier. We were both surprised but excited for her and eagerly altered our plans.

The gallery was small but awash with vibrant color and movement. There was a faux wall in the center of the space that held one dark, broodingly commanding abstract oil painting. It was of unusual size and disposition. The vertical canvas was narrow. The top was painted a light teal with dark blue veins running through it. A third of the way down the color burst into bright red that looked as if it had been vigorously applied in thick globs with a butter knife. The red bled into burnt sienna before darkening into a shiny black lacquer. The entire canvas was slashed and gouged. It was entitled, "Promise" and was not for sale. Something about it was disconcerting, violent. I shuddered and backed away. It seemed so unlike Grace and any of her other work.

Most of the paintings on the left side of the gallery were bold and brightly colored with small geometric shapes dotting the canvases. On the right wall the pieces were more subtle, with flowing color cascading and melding into other colors. Each canvas on this wall felt like a different view of an underwater paradise containing unexpected treasures within each. On the back wall were landscapes and portraits. Many of the paintings had already been sold, I assume to the many Louis Vuitton and Givenchy attired patrons. They moved gracefully around the room intently studying each canvas.

On the back side of the faux wall was a table filled with champagne and appetizers. To the right was a single rattan peacock chair occupied by Grace Evans, champagne glass in hand, warmly greeting her guests. In quiet moments, she looked much as she had on our first meeting – alone and shy.

She was glad to see us. She rose, arms spread wide to embrace us as we approached.

"I am so glad you could come. The invitations were so late going out, I was afraid you might have made other plans."

"We wouldn't have missed this for the world," I said.

"Your work is amazing, seductive, it pulls the viewer in..." smiled Andy as his eyes panned the room. He seemed to be trying to determine which piece he, we, would purchase. As he wandered off, Grace and I played catch up. It had been at least eight or nine years since we'd seen each other. Eager to get reacquainted, Grace invited me to have lunch with her in her recently purchased art studio in the Williamsburg section of Brooklyn. This neighborhood had once been a manufacturing center with many factories and small mom and pop shops. The factories had been converted into pricey lofts and the small shops into up-scale boutiques and restaurants.

Grace's studio was in an old factory building that had been converted into artist lofts. There was an entire wall of windows, giving the space amazing light. Two easels held incomplete canvases. Large completed pieces were stacked along the walls. In a corner was a small kitchenette and a seating area containing a sofa and chairs surrounding a low, round coffee table. It is here that Grace invited me to join her. The tea service was something from a long gone era – ornate silver with matching sugar bowl and creamer. As I sank into the down cushions, Grace poured tea into dainty bone china cups.

Grace sat cross-legged on the oversized armchair opposite me. Although we'd never gotten to know each other well, she chatted as if we'd been best friends for years. She said that the boys, ages nine and ten, attended private schools; that her mother picked them up from school and cared for them until she arrived to take them home. She talked about the various venues where her work would be showcased and ideas for future pieces. As she spoke I realized she was still a very private person, but something had changed. She was excited about her work and the future for herself and her family. Her eyes were bright, focused. She was much more confident and comfortable with herself than I remembered.

In turn, I told her about my teaching job, about the summer home we'd purchased and that six-year-old Tiffany was finally losing her baby fat and really enjoying school. During a brief lull in the conversation my curiosity kicked in. "Grace, that piece entitled "Promise" was quite... striking. May I ask what's behind its title?"

A schoolgirl grin spread across her face. "I remember telling you at a party that one day I'd explain about why our 'energy' as you called it was so different. Well, the painting is part of it.

"I was so naïve when I got married. All my mother ever told me was that as a wife my role was to make sure my husband was happy. I had no model for what that meant since my dad died when I was very young. I was 18 when I met Drake at a church function. He swept me off my feet. He was 21. We were married on my 19th birthday. Pregnancy followed shortly after that. And that's when I realized that Drake was a womanizer. Actually I wasn't sure, but I suspected that there were other women because often I'd smell perfume on his clothes."

Grace paused to pour herself more tea, then continued.

"Too shy to confront him, I took my frustration out on canvas. One day I was changing the bed linen and found a pair of woman's underwear. I was devastated. I cried until there were no more tears. Then I realized that I had one child and another on the way. My pride would not let me go home to my mother. My anger would not let me forgive him. So, I painted."

She paused for a few seconds before continuing. "That was the disturbing painting you saw. When it was finished, I stood it up in the bedroom. When he came home I explained to him that I'd found the underwear, which I threw at him. Then I promised him that there would be no next time because if so, I would calmly remove the instrument of joy from his body in such a way that it could not be reattached. I also promised him that if he wished to eat or sleep in this house without fear, he'd better show great respect for his marriage and family. That was the change you saw at the party."

Glancing over her teacup, Grace laughed aloud at the expression on my face.

"Now you know why I couldn't tell you my story at the party."

"Clearly not," I managed.

We became fast friends, as did Raphael and Gordon, her sons, with Tiffany. Although younger than the boys, Tiffany gave them orders like a field marshal. They in turn were very protective of her. And she wanted no part of Oak Bluffs unless they were there too. Drake was never invited.

Grace, the boys, Tiffany, Andy and I were lounging in the backyard of our Martha's Vineyard home when Grace announced with a wide roguish grin that Drake was going to deliver his trial sermon at a large church in Brooklyn in about a month's time. Andy and I exchanged questioning glances. When had Drake gone to seminary? We'd heard him in his drunken rants quoting scripture on more than one occasion without seriously considering it might be a career choice for him. Although we prodded her with questions, Grace, with her usual smile and good humor, did not elaborate.

***

On a blustery afternoon, Andy and I sat with rapt attention waiting for Drake's sermon. It was noteworthy that Raphael and Gordon were seated up front but without Grace. The sermon, delivered with energy and clear references to biblical and contemporary texts, was enthusiastically received by a largely female congregation. I noticed throughout Drake's delivery his eyes favored the mini-skirted women in the front pews. To be inclusive, he managed to undress several buxom women in the audience as well. Drake moistened his lips frequently with his tongue and wiped his sweaty brow with a large white handkerchief. Near the end of his sermon his eyes fixed on something at the back of the sanctuary. His demeanor changed. I turned to see Grace standing arms akimbo, head cocked to one side and an eyebrow raised as if to say, "Really?"

Weeks later I ran into Drake coming out of a liquor store. Without preamble I blurted out, "What made you decline ordination?"

He scrutinized me leisurely before replying. "I realized while delivering my sermon that I was plotting the seduction of more than one of the women in the congregation. Even I knew that wasn't right." Was this remorse, I wondered, or was he baiting me?

"Well, good for you. I'm glad to know that you managed to hang onto at least one scruple" I said, perhaps too cheerfully.

I wasn't sure I could trust the sincerity of his statement, so, I played to his religiosity. "You know, God's promise to…."

Drake's reaction to the word "promise" was immediate. His eyes riveted to my face, as if seeing me for the first time. The look he gave me was one of intense distain. Drake Evans brushed past me and disappeared around the corner. He did not look back.

.

THE 11TH COMMANDMENT

The chemicals that had burned through her body rendered her weak and sometimes violently ill. Elaina had survived by learning to live with pain – the dull throb in her underarm, the elongated ripple of pain that went through her right side whenever she tried to raise her right arm; the taut pain in her neck and left shoulder from trying to change her handiness from right to left. She'd grown used to pain. It was a reminder that she was alive.

After surgery and chemotherapy treatments she had been given a so-called miracle drug – a drug to be taken for five years – a drug that intensified her menopausal hot flashes and sent hammering pain to her chest. The miracle drug that made her rush to Urgent Care sure she was having a heart attack. A drug that had side effects including internal bleeding and death. (In spite of what the label said, she was sure death was not a side effect!)

The doctor said that in six months or so, the horrid side effects would subside. Six months?

She was deep in conversation with Deborah, her best friend, when out of the corner of her eye she saw a city bus bearing down on two young boys who were crossing the street.

"Get back!" Elaina shouted. The package in her hand flew up into the air as she snatched the smaller of the boys from in front of the swerving bus. The taller of the two boys scampered to the other side of the street. Elaina clutched the boy tightly. The bus driver slumped forward from the momentum of slamming on the brakes. The same momentum pressed a female passenger's face and hands against the window of the bus, her soundless scream blending with the screech of the brakes. Passengers were flung forward, then back. On the curb Deborah's hands covered her chest as if protecting herself from all danger, and by extension, everyone else. Elaina's entire body shook, but the adrenalin pumping through her would not allow her to release the boy. She shook him hard. "Don't you know you could've been killed?"

He looked to be about seven or eight years old, but the little boy's ashy face stretched into open hostility as he attempted to wiggle free from her grip. When he finally got loose, he sprinted out of her reach and spit back over his shoulder, "So what? Everybody dies."

"He has a point" snapped Deborah, who was annoyed by the boy's rude response. "So, where's the thank you?" She directed her question to the young boy who made no attempt to respond.

Elaina was incredulous. How could Deborah be so cavalier about death? She knows I'm still in treatment for breast cancer. Does she think so little of my struggle? Littleman may not know better about life, but... Her thoughts were interrupted.

"If I die, my momma'll collect a lotta money."

"Money! You think your mother would rather have money than you, her son? Do you think money could replace you?"

He was not impressed. "That's whatcha do, you die. My father and my Uncle Tony, they died in 'Nam and my baby sister, she dead too. Everybody dies, dontcha know that?"

Elaina chose to ignore the question. My God, she thought, he's seen so much death in his young life. Instead, she asked, "What do you know about war?"

"I know." His voice and sagging shoulders were that of an old man. "You go to war, and you die."

Elaina's voice softened, "Everyone that goes to war does not die. Some...."

Deborah cut her off. She could tell from the clouds gathered in Deborah's face that she was back in a time and place she didn't want to be. "What you mean Elaina, is if you survive these streets with gang and drug wars, you might get to go to Vietnam."

Elaina tried another tack. Pointing at Deborah she said, "She was a nurse in Vietnam. She's not dead."

Littleman scrutinized Deborah from head to toe. "Ain't nobody got no money for her neither."

"But if you live long enough, you can earn more money than your mother can make by your dying" Elaina reasoned. She could almost read his mind as his face wrinkled in concentrated thought.

"You mean I don't have to die to get big money?"

"That's exactly what I mean." She smiled at him. He returned the smile somewhat tentatively. She knew she'd given him something new to think about but before she could follow up, his friend skipped towards them from the other side of the street. Littleman brightened. He turned back to wave as they ran down the block. Littleman and I have a lot in common, Elaina thought, we are survivors.

She watched them depart as she fingered the tiny pill bottle in her pocket. She turned to Deborah, "Do you know what the 11th Commandment says?" She didn't wait for a response. "Thou shalt not die before one's time." She took the pills from her pocket. "These pills are an experiment and I'm the guinea pig."

With a celebratory three-point toss, Elaina pitched the miracle drug into the trash can at the corner. "Two points for life and another one for Littleman" she said aloud.

She hadn't felt this good in weeks.

IN THE VILLAGE OF ELMINA

K ofi Dapo is old, weathered, yet there is a timelessness about his face. His hands are fluid movement as he mends his fishing nets. It is his eyes which plumb my very being as he waits for my response.

His wife, tall, willowy and serene, is watchful as she stands off to the side. She has brought me to the village. She found me at Elmina Castle. I'd been outside, alone, trying to assuage the pain that was radiating through my body from having been inside the castle sensing the pain of my ancestors. They'd been held captive in the dark dank bowels of this fortress before being shipped as chattel slaves to the Americas.

Although it was quite warm outside, inside the Castle was damp, bone chilling. Just standing at the Door of No Return sent a bolt of panic and fear through me. It was as if I'd been gutted. Was this what my ancestors felt as our captors warehoused us in the cells to await a ship which would take us into the unknown? I envisioned myself wondering if the sea would eat me. How would my parents find me? Would I be returned? Would they forget me? Would I remember the sweet comforting face of my mother? The alert, wise face of my hunter father? My siblings?

This assault of ancestral memory propelled me back outside to the entryway where I escaped onto the concrete space to warm my body, to stop the cold sweat that had formed on my brow and underarms. I listened to the gentle lapping of the sea at the edge of Elmina Castle; the serenity which it purports. This "castle" belies the horrors that took place in it – the brutality of villagers being snatched from all they'd ever known, chained, beaten, malnourished, and raped. The false sense of hope after delivering a baby and being left in the village. Only to be loaded on the next ship after delivery. Stripped of all humanity, perceived as merchandise to be bartered, sold, used, and disposed of.

It was in this state that I heard her voice: "Come, I will take you where people look like you." I stumbled after her. At what seemed to be the center of the village there was a very large wood sculpture of a ship, including the Caucasian captain staring for all eternity out to sea. I was confused by it. Was it a tribute to the slavers? A reminder of their unfortunate history? How long had it been here? There was no time to question the purpose of this structure -- my host was still moving steadily through the village. I ran to make sure I didn't lose sight of her. The smell of salt in the air, the warmth of the sun on my skin and the sight of brightly painted fishing boats resting on the shore lifted my spirits.

The people of Elmina look different from the many tribes I've encountered in the rest of Ghana. Many are honey-brown, red headed and freckled. It is the first time in the months I've been in West Africa that I do not stand out – where market women do not snicker behind their hands and ask one another, "What kind of Oburoni (European) is she?"

Kofi Dapo is wiry of frame, relaxed, his movements focused, eyes intense. I'm offered cool water by his wife and made comfortable under the coco palm tree. After a polite silence during which I am scrutinized from head to foot, Kofi Dapo asks simply, "What became of you when you left here?" It is not rhetorical.

Several times I begin and several times I realize the inadequacy of what I'm about to say. After what seems an eternity, I stop trying to encapsulate four hundred years of history. Instead I ask, "Do you know why the people of this village look like me?" His hands slow their mending, his forehead furrows, his eyes meet mine. Slowly, he nods his head, yes, acknowledging what I already know is the answer to my question. But I see his bigger question to me in his eyes. And so I begin:

"It was the same, except the enslavement did not end after a pre-scribed period of time, as was the custom in antiquity – this was for life. Our families were separated, language and customs stripped from us. We were property to be bought, sold and raped at the whim of the slave master. Sometimes we were branded like cattle. We labored for a lifetime with no pay, no acknowledgement of our intellect or skills. We could be killed with no consequence."

Kofi Dapo's hands come to a complete halt. The fishing net is put aside.

This conversation is too painful. I don't want to accuse or blame but that is exactly how I am feeling. Until I see the incredulousness in Kofi Dapo's eyes. His mouth forms an "O" and his voice issues a long low moan. His understanding of the word "slave" has a different meaning. It was not a lifetime sentence It was a period of time in which you were enslaved as spoils of tribal warfare. But it was not permanent. After the time was served the formerly enslaved might even marry into the tribe to which he'd been enslaved. He could and was expected to prosper. The formerly enslaved were not dishonored, discredited or shamed. Kofi Dapo is aghast, horrified at what I've told him. He seems suddenly frail, whipped into weakness by this information.

There is nothing more to say. There is only a shared, remembered ancestral anguish and an enduring ache. We are silent as the sun fades from the sky; each hoping to be enveloped and comforted by the night. A cover for his shame, my blame.

But it has been dark for four hundred years. We both wonder if or when the sun will rise again.

JOURNEY TO ACCRA

Marcus searched Tina's face as if a great mystery resided there. At the same time his arms wrapped gently around her, pulling her to him for a long, passionate kiss. The lovers always raised eyebrows and smiles, especially in airports. This time was no exception. They were older than most lovers of the demonstrative type. His tawny complexion, salt and pepper hair and slightly receding hairline gave him a look of distinction. Tina's dewy dark complexion, mischievous brown eyes, and long slender legs gave her an air of youthfulness. After seventeen years, they were still playful. They held hands as they descended the escalator to the parking lot.

In the car Tina selected a CD, slid it into the player, eased her seat back, extending her legs, and settled herself into the leather upholstery. Marcus knew her rhythm as well as he knew his own. After a few minutes she would uncoil her solitary braid, slide one foot under her and rest a hand on his thigh. His desire for her would escalate, as his foot on the accelerator would move them at high speed to their destination. Tina would take in the lush foliage and the refreshing mountains, allowing the stresses of New York City to evaporate. North Carolina, Asheville in particular, had its pluses. She drifted off into the scent of his cologne – a new scent, somewhat floral.

While Marcus loaded the dishwasher Tina carried the coffee and cognac into the living room. She loved the room's floor-to-ceiling windows and the fat overstuffed furniture. She paused to look at the portraits of Big Mama and Persephony, also known as Sweet Sweetpea. The paintings were in matching antique gold frames and mounted side by side above the mantle.

She'd never met his grandmother or mother or any of his family members. Marcus almost never spoke about them or his youth. When he did it was with reverence. Persephony had raised him in what Big Mama called a "bardella" somewhere near Baton Rouge. He always eased into a strangely affected voice and a somewhat distant, dreamy look when he spoke of his days in Baton Rouge.

It had never been clear to Tina whether Sweetpea tended laundry and kept the rooms refreshed or had other employment there. Whatever her role, Marcus seemed to have fond memories of his mother and the many women who worked there and who gave him money to run errands for them.

He was unceremoniously snatched from this environment when Big Mama took him back to Pensacola with her, all the while lamenting the evils of sin and improper places for raising children. Marcus never saw Sweetpea again until he was grown – in college in fact. But he loved his mother. That was very clear to Tina.

Marcus looked like neither of these women. Perhaps he resembled the father he never knew. At the same time he was devoted to Tina's children, her family. He'd helped her children with their research papers, took them on trips during Easter and summer breaks, even bought a car for Brianna, her daughter, when she went away to college. He'd steered Jason away from a military career. And he never missed a birthday or one of her family reunions.

Marcus eased up behind her kissing her ear. "Ready to check calendars?"

She hated this particular ritual – having to arrange to be together.

"I have a meeting with the English department tomorrow morning to… Tina the meeting will only take two hours, really." Marcus tried to ease Tina's dismay.

She groaned, reaching for her planner. "I'll be shooting in Scotland and Ireland next month after which I'll be between New York and DC for about three months or so. What about you?" she asked.

"London, but not more than a week or two. I need to find an apartment for my sabbatical."

"How come you never invite me to London with you? This is your third trip to sequester yourself in London to write."

"The book is almost finished Tina. Be patient."

Tina said nothing but a thin veil of sadness crept into her eyes.

"Besides, we have a date in Accra, remember?" Marcus said. Tina brightened.

They had fallen in love with Ghana and had taken several trips there. For Marcus each trip convinced him that he had found his spiritual homeland. For both of them this trip would be special because they had decided to look for a home, or land on which to build a home.

Marcus had already left when she awoke, but he'd remembered to open the shutters knowing how she loved to feel the sun on her bare skin. Fifteen minutes lapsed before Tina finally slid from the bed, easing herself into her yoga routine, in the buff.

Her suitcase lay open like a sacked treasure chest on the floor. Marcus completely spoiled her when she visited him, doing everything for her, as she did for him when he visited her in New York; unpacking was not one of those luxuries. Flinging open the closet door she reached for a hanger but stopped abruptly. A long pink and purple flowery print robe with a ruffle running around the neck, down the front and around the hemline hung like an abandoned afterthought on her side of the closet. It wasn't hers. It wasn't her size or style. Anger swelled from her stomach, expanding and exploding in her chest and head.

An hour later Marcus found her still in the bedroom fully clothed and her suitcase shut as if she'd just arrived. Her face was a closed, dry, hard knot. He followed her eyes to the closet. He seemed as surprised as she was when he saw the robe.

"Love, I can explain."

"Take me to the airport, Marcus."

"Tina, wait. I can explain." His arms extended outward as if trying to stop her, although she was still seated.

"Explain? Yes, please do Marcus, explain!"

"The robe is mine."

"Yours? Really Marcus…"

Marcus reached into the closet and put on the robe. It was a perfect fit, ending at his ankles.

"Why do you have a woman's robe, Marcus?"

Marcus' shoulders sagged and he took a deep breath. "Just wait Tina, a moment."

When Marcus re-entered the room his eyes were tentative, pleading. The deep auburn wig complemented his fair, freckled skin perfectly, as did the simple pageboy hairstyling. His makeup had been applied flawlessly. The high-neck ivory silk blouse covered his neck elegantly; the matching wide-legged raw silk slacks flattered his tall frame. He wore brown patent leather pumps.

He looked at her with a sad, expectant gaze.

Tina's thoughts came to a standstill. Her shock and confusion were evident; there was no order to the myriad questions that arose. Who is this stranger? How long had he led this double life? Does he have partners? Could she bear to know? She could not stop feeling the burning hurt, shame, and absurdity of the situation. She wanted to run, but her feet were anchored to the floor and her mouth remained open with no words forming. She was numb.

Marcus sat on the edge of the bed facing her. "Don't leave Tina, please. I need you now more than ever."

"For what?" is all that she could whisper.

"Tina, we've been more than lovers, we've been friends, family. I need you."

"How could you do this? I want to go home. I've got to go home." The tears finally began to form. "I want to go home." With tears streaming down her cheeks, she ran downstairs and onto the back porch.

Sometime later, when she'd spent her tears and came inside Marcus was seated at the dining room table, his back to her.

"Talk to me Marcus." She sat down opposite him.

"Are you all right?" he asked.

"All right? No Marcus, I am not all right. I'm hurt, angry, confused, and unsure of what I'm supposed to feel or what I'm supposed to do next. When were you going to tell me? Were you going to tell me?"

Marcus took a long time to respond. "I've often thought of telling you, but then I'd decide that it would be too painful. But sooner or later I knew I'd have to tell you."

"Why?"

"Come with me to meet my counselor."

"Counselor? We've been together seventeen years – and it's all evaporated in a few minutes. I don't want to speak to your counselor. I need you to talk to me. What is happening?"

"Tina, stop." Marcus struggled to find the right words. "I can't tell you when this began, simply that I have always felt there was a female inside of me. Except that I wasn't. I was taunted in school and even in Sunday school because my behavior and interests were not like that of most boys my age. I remember wanting to take ballet lessons, but my mother would only agree to tap dancing class. I liked jumping rope, not cops and robbers. I didn't understand why I was being teased, just that it hurt.

"And I remember my mother's distress when she found me experimenting with her makeup. After that I stopped talking, stopped interacting, and kept to myself. I watched people, learned the separate roles and the expectations of each. But I was both. Not like two separate parts, simply as…me."

Marcus's attention drifted, as if in another time and place. Tina waited.

"I had to make a choice then and I did. I'm making a different one now."

"What's different now Marcus?" Tina's voice was cautious.

"The balance has been tipped. The truth is I'm beginning to think about becoming female, being physically female."

The words struck like a tidal wave against her already besieged emotions. Tina rose slowly and slapped him with all of her might. And again. She slapped at the vulnerability she felt washing over her. She fought having been deceived; she fought the unspoken and unknown. She railed against the raging sea that was sucking her down into its undertow.

The pain in his eyes haunted her. They had pleaded for her empathy, her care, her love. But there was something else too; something else that she could not identify, something daunting. She had turned away afraid of what her eyes would reveal. In a blink she had lost her lover, friend, and soul mate. What would her children say, her friends? Who else knows? Had he been discreet? Was she being laughed at behind her back? Had her health, her life been compromised? Jesus God, how do I deal with this?

And then she'd been angry with herself. Had there been signs of something amiss? She could think of nothing. Bitterly she realized that their long distance relationship had enabled the situation. And just as suddenly Tina realized she would need to tell her children. She was rocked with another wave of self-pity and grief.

***

Although there was a difference of two years in their ages, Brianna, 23 and Jason 25 could have been twins. Both had their mother's smooth dark complexion, dark eyes and long legs.

Brianna did not handle the news well. She burst into tears and clung to her mother. Jason was stoic, seeming not to have heard. But two weeks later, it was Jason who called a family meeting.

"Mom, we can't act as if Marcus is not part of our lives. Brianna and I think we need to get counseling as a family."

Tina raised an eyebrow but said nothing.

Brianna added, "Mom, we're Marcus's family. Would you be angry if we visited him?"

Tina was surprised at the ease with which they seemed to have accepted the situation. Hurt still held her in its grip. And yet she too had to acknowledge that Marcus had held her close through many crises: the car accident that put Jason in the hospital for weeks; when racism and sexism kept her from a well-earned promotion and through subsequent unemployment when she'd quit. Through thick and thin Marcus had been there for her. "Stay in the moment, trust love, Tina" is what he'd always say whenever she felt less than positive.

"Mom?" Brianna's voice brought Tina back to the conversation. "Mom, we're scared and hurt too. We don't know what to expect either. The only thing we do know is that Marcus is still our family." Brianna's eyes brimmed with tears but she stood firm, not looking at Jason for support.

At that moment Tina was still angry and unsure of where this journey was taking them, but she also knew that this was something Jason and Brianna had to do regardless of how she felt. She nodded her assent.

Tina felt as if each day were an endless savanna with no destination on the horizon. With scripts stacked high awaiting her attention, she was drawn into fitful sleep. In spite of endless pots of coffee, she slept. In spite of everything, she slept. And dreamed of what had been. She missed him. Even though they were not always in the same city or continent she had always felt his presence. Now something had died, but she couldn't identify the "it."

***

Brianna and Jason sat in the family room in separate side chairs facing one another, sharing a single footrest.

"Jason, this is more complicated than I thought. Between the hormones, the surgery to reduce his Adam's apple, learning to adjust his voice a few octaves higher, not to mention counseling, it's too much. And what about his man parts!"

Jason bristled. "Come on Brianna, you're a full grown, educated woman, 'man parts!?'"

Brianna rolled her eyes, ignoring his comment. "We need Mom. We can't do this alone."

"I don't think Mom's ready yet."

"Nobody's 'ready' Jason, but here we are!"

Jason found his mother in her study, staring into space.

"You can't think your way out of everything Mom. Sometimes you have to let your heart take the lead."

"You sound like Marcus."

"Yeah, I do, don't I," he said, looking pleased. "We need you Mom. Me and Brianna and Marcus. This is new territory for all of us. And we need each other."

With her children leading the way, Tina began with baby steps: asking questions, being brought up to date on medical procedures and whatever else was happening. Telephone conference calls between them with counselors or doctors helped but it was the eventual face-to-face with Marcus that Tina feared.

Sensing her mother's discomfort Brianna arranged a family weekend visit. Jason, anticipating any possible problems, rented a car at the airport in North Carolina and rented a room at a nearby hotel as well – just in case.

Marcus was seated in front of the fireplace reading when they arrived. To Tina he looked the same – almost. His hair and fingernails were longer and his eyebrows more contoured, although not severely so. He'd also changed his name from Marcus to Femi.

"Tina, you look well. I've missed you."

In spite of herself Tina had to admit that she'd missed Marcus – now known as Femi– too. Tina's eyes searched Femi's, whose gaze did not waver. There was the same warm, loving look that had always engulfed her. Tina's shoulders relaxed.

Later that evening Tina found Femi on the porch looking painfully androgynous and forlorn. Tina slid into the swing next to Femi. They clung to each other, aware that this was just the beginning of an arduous journey.

***

In time Tina went with Femi to her counselor and even met some of her transgender friends. And she came to see the vulnerable, sometimes frightened person. With a strangely affected voice and a somewhat distant look, Femi sought her strength to navigate difficult physical and emotional times. And Tina saw her resolve as well.

Sometimes Tina felt heavy hearted; sometimes she felt drained by what seemed an absurd situation. Sometimes the feeling of betrayal crept over her. Most often she felt stretched and pulled beyond the bounds of possibility. Yet she came to believe that no matter the circumstance they as a family would figure it out.

***

With the sound of women pounding cassava and the smell of palm oil thick in the air, Tina boarded the small boat. The fishermen rowed in silence. After some time Nana Nyarko, the Akan priestess, touched her indicating that the boat had reached its destination.

The nana began to chant as Tina opened the funerary urn, allowing the ashes to catch in the wind. Femi had died unexpectedly, quietly of a heart attack – seven years after the process began. There had been no warning signs.

As the boat turned back to Accra Tina pulled the well-worn handwritten note from her pocket.

My Dearest Tina,

If you are reading this then I have departed this mortal coil. Know that I have only shed my tortured body. Know that we are bound in love, we are and have always been Love

It was dusk when the boat reached the shore where Jason, Brianna and some of Femi's friends waited. As Tina's feet touched the sand, the drummers began to play. At first she simply listened, not aware of the tears that flowed from her eyes. She began to dance; her feet pounded the earth as if uncertainty and pain were underfoot. She danced with intensity and release. She danced until there was no sound other than her own heartbeat. She was free of regret. She held tightly to Femi's words: "Stay in the moment and trust love."

It was all there was to hold onto.

CRACKED

Movement I: Adagio
The Fool balances himself on the double yellow line in the middle of the street. One foot is placed squarely on the line, the other raised as if to find a place to perch. His arms are spread wide like an eagle landing. And so the dance begins. Or continues. He lowers his body slowly toward the ground, pauses, twists to the right, right arm lowering but his left foot is still staked to the line – his anchor. The slow-motion dance continues as he soars upward, both hands coming together momentarily in a pose of prayer. In spite of the traffic. In spite of car horns blaring a warning. In spite of children mocking him as they return home from school. The dance continues, with a variety of poses; all with focus and always with fluid grace.

Until he falls off of the line, staggers between moving cars and disappears down the street. I offer a prayer for his safety. To pray for his sobriety would be asking too much.

Movement II: Timestep
Tony, young, tall, slender with big brown eyes, is the newest mail-room hire. He has a warm smile and friendly banter for all. Mail has never been so anticipated by more secretaries, married or single. He evokes only camaraderie and goodwill for all who encounter him.

More wide than tall and duck-toed, Ming, another mailroom employee, speaks only when addressed. I know his name only because it's embroidered on his uniform. On this most routine day, Ming runs into my office, "Come quick" he whispers. I follow intuitively, questions of where and why lodged in my throat.

In the men's room, slumped over in a stall, a syringe hanging from his exposed thigh, Tony's trousers hang around his knees. Ming asks if he's alive. "Yes," I answer, but I recognize this is no medical syringe and street drugs have a way of ending too many lives too soon. Instinct rather than any profound medical knowledge kicks in. "Ice, get me some ice," I demand. Several other men are now crowding the space. To no one in particular, I order them to prop him up. With the bag of ice held firmly in both hands, I not so gently press the coldness to his genitals. And pray.

By the time the police and EMS attendants arrive Tony is coming around. The syringe has disappeared. I am the only one willing to accompany him to the hospital. I don't judge his way of life. I simply hold his hand and ask if there is anyone he'd like me to call. There isn't.

Movement III: Moonwalk

It is the only house on the block without a fence. The house, and the waist high shrubs, are untended. There is an unusual ritual performed here each morning. An attractive, well-dressed couple, each carrying an attaché case, enters the house but stay only a few minutes. They proceed to the bus stop. The ritual is repeated in reverse each evening on their way home.

Most mornings there is an old battered blue car parked on the opposite side of the street. Near the corner. Under the low hanging limbs of a half dead horse chestnut tree. The driver always slumps low.

One evening in autumn everything changes. A dozen or so police cars, marked and unmarked, including the battered blue one, descend on the little house, pulling out a horde of disheveled people. It is an older woman who catches my attention. With one hand she clings tightly to her blond wig; her matted gray hair pokes out on one side. With the other hand she tries to close the long white shirt that fails to cover her nakedness. Her eyes open only to half-mast. She quivers in place like a sick bird. Listing to one side she tries to steady herself. I recognize Deaconess Johnson, mother of four, grandmother of three – exposed, addicted. Arrested for drug use and prostitution.

I linger, waiting to see if they pull the Fool from the house. It seems hours before the last occupant is removed. And once again the Fool, my son, has escaped arrest. But there is no arrest or intervention for this tormented mother who continues to witness the dance with an anguished, cracked heart.

.

EDUCATING TEACHER OLIVIA

Melanie was not pleased. From the way she paced the floor and wrung her hands one would think I was her child. Actually, she's my best friend, but instead of being elated that I had landed the job I'd been seeking, she's in panic mode.

"Have you lost your last mind? Nobody goes to work in that part of Williamsburg. There are treacherous gangs there. Crime is rampant! Everyone who can gets out. No one goes in willingly. Who will protect you?"

"From what Melanie? I've survived three brothers. I have a Ph.D. from the School of Hard Knocks."

"This is not funny, Olivia."

"It wasn't meant to be. 'Those people' you keep referring to are indeed, people. They are some mother's children; people interested in learning. I've already signed the contract so there's nothing else to discuss. Besides, since you claim I'm a witch, there should be nothing for me to fear."

Melanie grunted and dropped the subject although she rolled her eyes whenever the thought resurrected in her mind.

Even now, in retirement, I remember that first teaching job with fondness. I remember being excited and eager to prove myself. And in spite of what I'd said to Melanie, there was a bit of trepidation too.

The community high school was housed in an old red brick fortress with bars on all of the windows and a tall Cyclone fence completely surrounding it. The schoolyard consisted of battered concrete disturbed only by the basketball hoops flanking each end. Picturesque it was not.

In the classroom it was hard not to notice him. He commanded attention without even trying. The young man was tall with dark wavy hair, long eyelashes, large, clear, hazel eyes and a bodybuilder's physique. He didn't walk – he sauntered. I can't say if he was a gang leader, but he moved with the confidence of a genuine kingpin or ex-offender. And tiny Esmeralda was always tucked gently under his arm where she fit perfectly. All of the other students deferred to him. The female students clearly envied Esmerelda.

From the first day of class Ricco sat with Esmerelda the same way they walked the corridors – together. Even seated they held hands. Midway into the second week of class, I walked over to their table, stood behind them and asked if they would each take my hand. To do so meant they had to disengage. Still holding their hands, I continued to instruct the class. After a few minutes, Ricco looked up at me, puzzled. "Yo Teach, whatcha doin'?"

I gave him my own look of puzzlement. "Ricco, do you really think all of this 'love' can fill my classroom and I not get some?" He smiled broadly, showing off his beautiful, perfectly straight white teeth.

One day while teaching, I happened to glance out of the window. Against school rules, Therese, a very attractive petite student, had gone off school grounds and was heading toward the corner bodega. Before she could reach it, she was surrounded by five or six young thugs wearing gang colors. Although she tried to put on a brave face, her rigid body language and wide eyes said she was frightened. The young men seemed determined to force her to accompany them, but they also seemed to enjoy the cat and mouse game they were playing.

I tried to keep my voice calm. "Ricco, would you please come here?" I positioned myself with my back to the window so that he would have a full view of the scene outside.

"Please don't react, just look out the window. We have to get Therese away from those guys. What can we do?"

Ricco turned to the class and spoke authoritatively in Spanish. The only sentence I understood was the last, which he spoke in English, "You don't have to come – it's up to you."

With that the entire class stood. Ricco instructed the boys to follow him, the girls fell in behind them. I brought up the rear.

We moved quickly and quietly through the corridor. Just as they reached the door, the principal came out of his office. "Ms. Gilbert, what's going on?"

I assured him that I'd explain when we returned and sprinted to catch up with my students. Oh hell, I'm going to be fired before I even begin, I thought. But my adrenalin was already elevated and it was too late to rethink it.

Ricco signaled and the boys formed a circle around the group holding Therese. The girls formed a second circle behind the boys. Ricco spoke softly but firmly, then took Therese by the arm and gently propelled her toward the girls. They formed a protective flank around her, turned and walked back to the school. The boys waited until the gang left before returning to class. It gave me a chance to calm down; to slow the quaking of my body. This could have turned into a gang war, with me Miss New Teacher smack dab in the midst of it -- endangering my students. That was the first semester in my ongoing higher education.

As I waited for Melanie to meet me for lunch, I continued to enjoy the spring weather and to reminisce:

I was late. My car was being repaired and I'd taken the bus. Rushing to get into the classroom and get started, I was surprised to find Marisol standing outside the Life Skills class with her three-year old daughter.

"Miss Gilbert, I can't come to class today because the nursery is full and the administrator says that Ana can't come into class with me."

"Is that right?" I replied. "Tell you what, you take your seat and I'll take care of Ana."

"Really?" Marisol beamed.

Ana took my hand and followed me into the classroom like she'd known me all of her young life. As the class progressed I noticed that Ana made sounds, not quite words, yet she was clearly pleased with the syllables she produced.

After class Marisol told me that her daughter had recently received a cochlear implant and was just learning to speak. By the end of the class, Ana had adopted me and was not happy about having to go home without me.

A few weeks later Marisol came to class with a black eye. My gut instinct was to ask what happened, but something in her manner stopped me. The other students acted as if this was a normal situation. I seemed to be the only one perturbed. At the end of the class I reminded Marisol that she had my home and cell numbers (as did all of my students) and that she was free to use them if ever she wanted to talk.

Marisol called later that afternoon. Her voice was choked, a stammering gush of words, "Ana, Ana, he's got Ana...in room...locked in the room..."

"I'll be right there." I had come to understood that calling the police was not an acceptable first response in this community -- as an absolute last resort... maybe.

I called Ricco, explained the situation and asked his advice. He said he'd would meet me at Marisol's. I donned my jeans, a cap and grabbed a baseball bat before heading out. There wasn't much traffic. Ricco and Esmeralda were already outside the apartment building when I arrived. For some naïve reason I was surprised to see Esmeralda.

When Marisol opened the door her eyes were swollen and red. "He's trying to keep me from leaving," she said as she pointed to the bedroom door. Esmeralda put her arm around Marisol and led her into the kitchen. Ricco and I approached the bedroom. Ricco knocked on the door.

"Yo Tony, open up. Me and teacher Olivia are here. What you doin' ain't cool man."

The shuffle of feet could be heard. "This ain't your business Ricco. Teacher Olivia's neither."

"It is now Tony. Open the door." Ricco's voice was deadly calm, sending a chill up my spine. Tony must have felt the arctic foreboding -- the door opened. Ana ran out, arms outstretched, in search of her mother. During the entire ordeal she'd not made a single sound. Ricco entered the bedroom and closed the door.

I can't say that I knew exactly what happened that day but afterwards I did notice that Marisol and Esmeralda had become friends. And for the rest of that term, Marisol seemed more at ease and free of any visible bruises.

I must have looked like a dotty old woman, sitting at the outdoor table chuckling to myself. But I didn't care, I was enjoying the memories:

In preparation for writing their employment resumes I asked each student to identify a potential career choice. Most had the usual responses, teacher, nurse, model, mechanic or cosmetologist. Rosalie however, stood up and pronounced rather smugly, "I want to be a prostitute." The other students snickered and waited expectantly for my response.

"Well, what kind of prostitute do you want to be?" I asked without missing a beat. The class went quiet. "Well, do you want to be a three-dollar trick in the back of a parked car? A street walker working for a pimp, or a call girl, an escort? What do you have in mind?"

Rosalie was not prepared for my response. Her intention had been to shock me and earn some brownie points with her fellow students. She blushed and sat down.

The rest of the assignment was for students to find classified ads in the newspaper that matched their career goals and then to write a targeted resume. Rosalie's revised choice was to open a daycare center.

I looked up and down the street to see if Melanie was in sight. Not yet. No matter. My reminiscences continued. Family Day was fast approaching. It would afford an opportunity for teachers to meet the parents as well as to share with family members the goals and aspirations the school had for its students. And a time for the community to celebrate the achievements of its future leaders.

The mood was festive as the refreshment table was set up and teachers established their stations for parent/student consultations. I'd just finished with one family and stood to stretch my legs and back. My attention was drawn to a short, stocky gentleman who was moving through the crowd. He stopped every few feet to ask a question. As he got closer I realized he was on a mission, looking for someone specific. I couldn't tell if he was confused or angry; his eyebrows were raised and he seemed intense. When he spotted me, he moved more purposefully in my direction. There was no escape; I was stationed in a corner with no exit. I put on a calm face while developing a survival strategy, like drop and roll under the table.

Boldly invading my personal space, he asked, "Are you Teacher Olivia?"

"Yes, I am," I said in what I hoped was a poised, respectful manner. I prayed silently.

The man wrapped his short, muscular arms around me in a bear hug. "You are the best thing that has ever happened to my son, Julio. He actually looks forward to coming to school. At least to your class." It was only when he released me that I realized I'd been lifted off the floor. Thank you was all I could whisper. I was addressing the Creator, but Mr. Lopez was elated to be so appreciated.

I was beginning to wonder if Melanie had forgotten our lunch date. But then again, she was always late. I went back to my musings:

Students and staff were preparing for the graduation ceremony and party. On one hand I was saddened that my students would be moving on. On the other, I was pleased that they had successfully completed their work and could enter the world with confidence. The students were excited and playful. I was informed by the Student Council that I'd been selected as the featured speaker for the commencement ceremony. I was flattered but thought that one of the students should speak for the class. (I did not win that battle.) And I was further informed that I had to learn the Electric Slide. (Now that was truly a memorable feat!)

I was becoming impatient. Where was Melanie? I began to think about the fifty plus year journey she and I have been on. We're both working on second marriages. And we've both moved around the country with enough frequency to write a best-selling travel guide! Through it all we've managed to stay in touch and remain friends. But now she's pushing it… I reach for my cellphone to see if she's is on her way. There's no answer. I order a carafe of wine, perusing the street both ways for my friend. A couple with flecks of gray in their hair move slowly past, pushing a baby carriage. It's probably a grandchild I decide absently. I like the affectionate way the man wraps his arm around the shoulder of the woman as they engage in playful banter. There was something in the way the woman fits 'just so' under his arm, his sauntering walk, and hazel eyes…

"Ricco, Esmeralda?" I stammer.

They turn in unison. "Teacher Olivia?"

We rush to embrace one another. Somewhere in the back of my head I hear Melanie swearing I conjured Ricco and Esmeralda up out of thin air. Well, maybe I have. It sounds like something I would do, if I could. Maybe I can 'materialize' Melanie while I'm at it. But no matter, I have the feeling I'm about to embark on another level in my education.

ALTERATIONS

Situated in a strip mall anchored on one end by a drug store and on the other a bank, the shop offered fabric, dressmaking services, patterns, and notions. Alterations were not offered. It had been a deliberate decision by the co-owners, Cynthia and Greer. It was too time consuming and didn't pay well. But people walking by often inquired.

The two women had been friends from childhood. Since both were only children they had become protective of one another. The shorter of the two, Greer, was the one with the mouth; Cynthia was more of a silent observer. When she did offer a thought or idea, it was like E.F. Hutton speaking: everyone stopped to listen. Most of the time though, her body language spoke what was on her mind.

A customer entered the shop, nodded at the two women and began cruising the shelves, fingering the fabrics as she went.

"I can get this cheaper on Main Street," she said as she stroked a colorful silk blend. She repeated this ritual several times before Greer approached and pointed outside.

"Do you see that sign? It's the bus stop. The #12 bus will take you to Main Street in no time."

The woman looked Greer up and down, then laughed. "But I'd have to pay the bus fare in both directions."

Greer gave her a quizzical look. "Yeah, and?"

"I wouldn't be saving very much and the travel time would kill my day."

Greer nodded smugly.

Cynthia made a mental note to speak to Greer about her customer service skills in spite of the fact that the woman bought fabric and was fitted for two dresses.

Cynthia watched as a florist truck entered the parking lot. It drove past. "By the way, how was your date with Whatsits?"

"His name's Tyrell and it was weird," Greer answered. "I couldn't get a word in edgewise. The man talked ad nauseam about his two kids. When he'd tired of that he began lambasting his ex-wife; talked about her like a dog. When I reminded him that she was the mother of his children he didn't take kindly to it. Said they were his kids, and I should butt out." Greer laughed. "I followed instructions and left."

"You okay?" Cynthia leaned in to get a closer look at her friend.

"Damn Skippy I am."

Cynthia answered the ringing phone, listened briefly and handed it to Greer. The voice was loud and insistent: "You will babysit my kids on Saturday."

"No I will not, Tyrell." Greer tried to speak calmly. "You don't get to tell me what I will do. I don't know you or your kids. I've been on one disastrous date with you and that's enough for me." She hung up.

"Your guy sounds like he has some issues."

Greer rolled her eyes, "Ya think!"

Less than an hour later Greer looked up from cutting fabric and saw Tyrell steamrolling across the parking lot. He was built like a bulldog. His arms bowed out from his body, his hands fisted. His eyes lasered in on her as he burst through the door, "You will do what I told you to do, or else!"

"Or else what?" she shot back, dressmaker's shears in hand. "And before you say anything else, I suggest you look behind you."

He turned. Cynthia towered over him, with yet another pair of shears poised for action. He jumped aside and ran from the shop.

"The need for alterations seems clear," Greer mumbled sarcastically as she watched Tyrell speed out of the parking lot

"Maybe we should add it to our price list," Cynthia mused as the two women returned to their dressmaking.

.

DREAMS AND T'ING

Once again Rodrick found himself twisting uncomfortably, entrapped in another dreadful nightmare; a reminder that he'd escaped but had left his mother behind.

In the distance it looked like the leaning Tower of Pisa but as it drew nearer, the tottering building was a four-story brownstone, and not just any brownstone, but his mother's Brooklyn home, lumbering down the beach on cinder blocks, heading for the sea. He could see his mother in the parlor floor window. She screamed and flailed her arms but could not escape even though the window was open. "Mama, Mama," Rodrick called, "I'm coming, hold on!" He ran to the front of the building but could not scale the cinder blocks to reach the entrance. The building continued moving toward the sea. Stumbling backwards into the water he shouted, "Jump, Mama, jump!"

Rodrick awoke with a start. He was clammy and cold. Pulling himself upright, he scanned the beach. In the distance a boy and his dog played with a ball. A group of children ran noisily back and forth, in and out of the water.

The dreams were increasing in frequency and intensity. Each dream heightened his concern for his mother. He had tried repeatedly to get her to return home to St. James Island.

"Mum, why can't you sell that house, come back home and forget that place…" he'd asked, more than once.

His mother had winced, "Are ya mad? I work two jobs fa years to buy dis house. You t'ink I gon'ta walk away ta let your worthless fatha have it? He never put a dime in dis place."

"But Mum, is all the grief you suffer worth it? How much longer do you plan to tip around him? How much longer will you sleep with your clothes and shoes on not knowing when, or if, he'll come in, and in what condition?"

It was to no avail.

Rodrick loathed the pomp and false ritual his father demanded: waiting in his room to be called to dinner; having to be "properly" attired in shirt and tie. What a charade, a horrid charade, always was – having to dress for dinner, keeping silent unless addressed, no music unless Poppa ordained it. He remembered vividly his father swaying in his chair at the dinner table, trying to act as if he were sober; examining the table settings to make sure everything and everyone was in its proper place.

Not even the rich aroma of curry goat could mask the scent of cheap women's perfume that clung to the handkerchief his father used to wipe his brow. Or worse, his father slapping his mother because dinner was not what he wanted or the kitchen wasn't clean enough. When Rodrick had protested his father had pinned him to the wall, "Only one man in this house. Remember dat boy! Dis a warning, ya hear?" His father had stopped beating him only when Rodrick grew taller than his father and had fought back.

Rodrick and his mother sat in silence through most meals, listening to the rant and drunken discourse. They listened to the sound of the oven crackling as it cooled, the tick of the grandfather clock, the rustle of dried leaves and twigs in the backyard. From habit they listened, especially for the sound of his father's key in the gate and the scrape of staggering feet.

Warmed by the sun, which was now high in the sky, Rodrick shifted himself into a comfortable position, and slipped once again into a
sound sleep.

*It was pitch black, but he could hear the squeak of the heavy
front gate slowly opening and even more slowly closing. Rodrick
raised his head to hear better, but there was only silence. He
went back to sleep, pulling the covers up over his head. Just when
he had drifted back into a deep slumber an explosion shook him
awake and then another. His feet hit the floor, running toward
the sound. Halfway down the stairs he saw his father racing out
through the front door. Rodrick ran in the direction from which
his father had come. At the kitchen door he stopped. His mother
was crumpled on the floor, bleeding from head and chest, the
telephone clutched in her hand.*

Rodrick's own screams awakened him. With his heart pounding,
he ran up the beach toward his house. He slowed to a brisk walk as he
realized that he had been dreaming; that he needed to calm himself. He
didn't want to alarm his mother when he phoned her. He stopped in the
front yard to catch his breath. In spite of himself he had to admire his
handiwork. He had repositioned the family chattel house so that it faced
the sea. He had painted it blue, to remind him of the sky and water. The
windows he trimmed in yellow, the color of the sun. The cinder block
front steps and window boxes he painted white. Yes, he thought, Mum
would like this. A smile relaxed his face as he stepped into the house.
He was confident he could convince her to visit, at least for a while.

"Hello Mum, how goes it?" Rodrick tried to sound composed,
carefree.

"So-so, your fatha is causing me grief, as usual. But he's to come
today to fix the kitchen faucet. But what about you, you don't sound
too perky."

"Mum, why can't you just call a plumber?"

"Plumbers come free now? Roddy, we have had this conversation a'ready and we don't need to have it again. Why you sound so down?"

"The dreams, I've had another dream." He wiped perspiration from his face and neck.

"Roddy, ya put too much store in dreams and t'ing..."

"Mum, why can't you just come home for a while?" he pleaded. "I've painted the house, moved it so it faces the sea. You'd love it."

"You fret so...here comes ya fatha now...Oh, my God, no..."

Two shots rang out. "Mum," Rodrick shouted into the phone. "Mum!"

He could hear his mother gasp. He could hear the hollow thud as her head hit the tiled floor. He heard the sound of feet shuffling away, drunken feet, their shuffle growing faint. Slam! He recognized the scraping sound the front gate always made, as it slammed to.

Rodrick prayed he was dreaming.

DIVA WALKING

Sadie rushed into the room, pushing her I-V pole. "Olympia, you've got to see this!"

Olympia looked up from the magazine she was reading, "See what?"

"Diva walking!"

Olympia raised herself on her elbow in time to see a tall, erect, elegant, baldheaded woman on crutches in the hallway. The woman held her head high. Large, bright, red, dangling hoop earrings danced energetically with each step. Luminous red lipstick accentuated her full lips. Her gray print dress stopped at the knee, revealing one long, very shapely leg on which she wore a bright red, 6-inch stiletto heeled shoe. The woman moved deftly down the corridor, maneuvering the crutches as if they were high-end accessories rather than necessities.

"Now that's hutzpa!" beamed Sadie.

Olympia smiled her agreement.

"Sadie, how was your session today?"

"All the way live. After walking our fingers up the wall, Laura started talking about a positive attitude being helpful to healing. That's when the stuff hit the fan. Miriam, with fists balled and tears streaming down her face screamed, 'A positive attitude will not make me whole!'"

Sadie paused reflectively before continuing: "Everyone was silenced by the outburst, except seventy-year-old Mrs. Singh, who never speaks in these sessions. 'You can have reconstructive surgery,' she said. 'I did.' I was surprised. It didn't occur to me that someone her age would have opted for reconstructive surgery."

"Why shouldn't Mrs. Singh have reconstructive surgery? Are you saying that older people shouldn't…?"

"No, I guess I wasn't really thinking."

The women were quiet for a time.

"How do you measure wholeness, Sadie?"

Sadie realized that the question Olympia posed was one she had been asking herself daily, hourly since her surgery. Physically and emotionally she felt gutted, neutered; her confidence shaken. A breast implant might address the physical emptiness, but they were not reliable. Sometimes they detached, floated around in a woman's body. Sometimes the replacements looked like bowling balls instead of natural breasts. And what man would want a woman with a gash across her chest where a breast should be? She was not comfortable discussing any of this. But the question remained…

While Sadie continued to ponder this, an orderly arrived to take Olympia for her own surgical procedure.

Unlike most breast cancer patients who were released within a week of surgery, Sadie was still hospitalized after two and a half weeks because her body continued to produce fluid. She would be released only when the flow stopped and her drain was clear. In the meantime, she spent her days visiting other patients, making jewelry in the craft workshop, choosing flowers for an arrangement in another offered class and whatever other activity the hospital provided. Sometimes she wondered if she'd ever be sexually active again. But, at the moment, her focus was on getting well – getting out of the hospital. But that had not been Olympia's question.

***

Sadie awoke to the sound of a very rhythmic, lilting, baritone voice. She turned toward the melody but the curtain between the beds had been drawn. The voice was familiar, although she could put neither a face nor a name to it. Whoever he was, he was assisting Olympia back to her bed and assuring her that she'd feel less groggy in short order.

Not wanting to seem impertinent, Sadie tried to figure out how to interject into the conversation. Before she could develop a plan, a powerfully built man in blue scrubs stepped from behind the curtain. He was all smiles.

"And how are you today, Sadie?"

"You have me at a disadvantage; I don't know your name."

"Joseph Barrington Prince, at your service." He bent low in an exaggerated bow. "J.B. to my friends."

Sadie smiled sheepishly. "Why does your voice seem so familiar?" she asked.

"I attended you in the recovery room. I'm surprised you're still here, but pleased to have a chance to talk to you when you're not anesthetized."

Sadie blushed, but held his gaze. "Do you flirt with all your patients?"

J.B. flashed a broad, mischievous grin. "No, not all."

The next day was traumatic. First, Olympia was taken for an experimental procedure. Metal rods would be irradiated and surgically placed around the tumor in her liver. This was supposed to shrink the tumor. Olympia would then be placed in isolation for a number of days. Sadie couldn't imagine not having Olympia as her roommate. And worse of all, she would not be able to visit, other than to wave through a glass partition. If that were not enough, that afternoon she was thrown out of the group counseling sessions.

It had seemed to Sadie that the topic of the day had been what am I afraid of? Ida Mae said that since her breast cancer her husband no longer wanted her – he didn't call or visit. Luz equated having a mastectomy to having been raped – she would no longer be considered marriageable. Her life as a woman and as a member of her community would just about end. Tatiana was afraid her cancer would spread, so she was thinking about having her healthy breast removed.

As the women continued their group discussion Sadie wondered if she would ever have the self-assurance of the woman with one red shoe. Laura, the counselor, turned to Sadie, who had not spoken during the entire session, "Would you like to weigh in on this discussion?"

Sadie spoke hesitantly, not wanting to offend anyone. "I don't want to negate anyone's experience but somehow everything seems negative—to be based in fear or on what someone else thinks about us; not how we should feel about ourselves. I don't have a husband so my perception may be a little different. I just want to get well; I want to figure out how to get groceries from the store to my kitchen, how to cook or do laundry when I'm not supposed to lift anything heavy. I want to get back to work. How and when I relate to the next man in my life is of concern, but it's just not at the top of my 'to do' list right now." And remembering Olympia's question, she thought, but did not say aloud, and figuring out what it is that will make me whole.

The session had wrangled Sadie's emotions more than she let on. She'd taken her physical body for granted. Her body was altered, she was altered. How people responded to her would be different.

"I hope I didn't put you on the spot Sadie." Laura offered Sadie a chair.

"You're pretty well adjusted," Laura continued. "And you've spent more time in our sessions than most. If you choose not to come, it would make room for someone who really needs the sessions."

"Laura, you don't have a clue about my 'adjustment.' Do you see me, us? Can you feel or begin to understand our hurt, our pain? And I'm not just talking about physical pain. And please don't advise me to not take this conversation personally. I'm not in the right state of mind for that right now. Am I being invited out?"

"Why no, of course not. It's just that you've been attending for quite some time and I thought you might be getting bored with the sessions. But, it's your choice."

Laura left hurriedly, apologizing for the misunderstanding. Until that moment Sadie had not realized how angry she was, but not at

Laura. It wasn't death that frightened her now; it was living. Cancer had shaken her to her core.

The only bright spot in the day was a visit from J.B.

✝✝✝

Upon her release from the hospital the staff put Sadie in a taxi. The driver, an attractive young man, made Sadie self-conscious. The empty half of her bra had been stuffed with cotton, but it was uneven, and unweighted, making her hold one shoulder higher than the other in an effort to feel balanced. She feigned interest in the passing landscape but began to wonder how, if she ever met an interesting man, she would introduce the subject of her surgery. Sadie pushed these thoughts aside; there were more immediate matters to address like restocking her re-frigerator, letting friends and family know that she was home, buying a breast form, and scheduling follow-up medical appointments.

Even though they had exchanged telephone numbers, Sadie was sur-prised and delighted to hear from J.B. He invited her to dinner, but she was still too uncomfortable with her body for a public outing. Instead, she invited him to her home for lunch.

J.B. arrived, carrying a large bouquet of peonies, a bottle of wine and a small bag of gauze pads and bandages. While Sadie found a vase and arranged the flowers, J.B. noticed Sadie's music collection and se-lected Johnny Mathis's "I'm Coming Home" album to accompany their lunch. After she'd placed the flowers on the end table, J.B. reached out, encircling her in his arms.

"I can't remember the last time I've danced," Sadie offered.

"Why is that?"

"Oh, I don't know. I guess I've become addicted to work."

"Bad idea. One always needs to take time to smell the roses."

J.B. stepped away from Sadie, looking down at her. Taking her by the hand he led her to the dining room window. "What do you see?"

"Houses, cars, trees..."

"Closer."

"Grass, shrubs, a squirrel, birds."

"What kind of shrubs, what kind of birds?"

"I don't know."

"See? You're missing half the fun!"

"Are you a bird watcher?"

"Not officially, but I try to observe and enjoy whatever the environment has to offer."

"Well, in that case, you're standing in the dining room. Let's enjoy this food environment, shall we?"

During the course of lunch, they discovered that they both loved soccer, modern dance and all kinds of food. As their visit came to a close, J.B. offered to change her bandage. Sadie was hesitant. "Are you trying to get to my body?" she asked playfully.

"Yes, but for now, just to clean your wound." And he did, with great gentleness. Sadie wasn't quite sure how to respond to a man caring for her so intimately yet making no overt sexual overtures. She was turned on, especially after he kissed her chest wall before putting the bandage in place. Then he was gone.

***

"I think that phone number you gave me is connected to a p.o. box!" Sadie said when J.B. finally returned her call a few days later.

"A what?"

"A post office box."

"What makes you think that?"

"You're never there. And you never return my calls the same day."

"I'm sorry. I've been working long hours. When I get home, I'm not too sociable. But, I've got a day off tomorrow. Would you like to meet me for lunch in Chinatown?"

"You're on!"

"That's how our ritual got started," Sadie told Olympia, who was lounging on a divan in her backyard.

"Ritual? That implies something ceremonial, maybe even sacred."

"Sacred, sanctified, indeed. That's how our lovemaking makes me feel."

Olympia sat up in the chair, opening her eyes wide. "Is this something an old, married, terminally-ill woman can bear to hear?"

Sadie winced at the mention of Olympia's terminal illness, but as Olympia had explained to her, she treasured this 'extra' time with her husband and family. There would be no regrets.

"Do tell me about your ritual," Olympia prodded.

"We always meet for lunch in different restaurants, in different parts of the city. No matter what kind of food we have, he always eats slowly, savoring the aroma, the taste, texture and color of the food; the ambiance of the place. It doesn't have to be a fancy place, but, whatever it is, he takes it all in.

"We always walk afterwards. He takes that in, too. Sometimes he comments on a specific floral scent in the air or the feel of the sun on his skin, the scent of approaching rain or the meow of a stray cat. Now I'm beginning to notice things -- to take pleasure in the experiences. I feel so alive. And we make love the same way, slowly, savoring..." Sadie's words trailed off as her body relaxed into the chair, her face aglow.

Olympia interrupted her reverie. "Are you falling in love Sadie?"

Sadie thought for a moment before responding. "No, but I'm so grateful that he came into my life."

"I'm sorry Sadie, I didn't mean to interrupt you. Please continue."

"One day I was walking in the park. I saw a family walking toward me. The man reminded me of J.B. A woman was holding his arm loosely. Her face was turned toward him, sharing something that made them both laugh. They were so comfortable with one another, like a couple who'd been together for a very long time, yet they were still enthralled with each other. The teenage girls walking with them were clearly their children. As I got closer my heart stopped. It was J.B. I wanted to feel anger, but what I felt was wonderment. I felt like I was looking at a picture, as if I were not in the frame. At that moment, he looked up, catching my eye. For one instant he seemed to stand absolutely still, poised and vulnerable. I mouthed a 'thank you.' J.B. nodded ever so slightly. I can't explain it, Olympia. In that moment I knew our relationship was over, but I wasn't angry or sad. There was nothing to mourn."

Sadie leaned back in her chair, closing her eyes to the late afternoon sun. She felt serene. Olympia waited a few moments before asking, "What will you do now?"

"Do? There's nothing to do."

Realizing that Olympia was still waiting, she opened her eyes, and flashed a broad grin. "I'm doing what needs to be done." She extended her bare feet. "Can't you see? I'm wearing the hell out of these red shoes!"

IF ONLY FOR THIS MOMENT

My mother thought my next-door neighbor, Nigel Cumberbatch, an ideal guy for me to date. Of course she had not asked my opinion. As usual. Needless to say, I had absolutely no interest in Nigel.

Four years my senior, a college graduate, Nigel was already working in his field of chemistry. He was tall, well groomed, and well-dressed at all times. Even though his luscious black skin was pleasing and his wide eyes appealing I didn't like him. On the few occasions when I tried to talk with him he seemed to be bored or uninterested in what I had to say. If I spoke to him on the street he looked down his nose and grunted something undecipherable as he rushed past me. He was always in too big of a hurry for "idle chit chat." He acted as if he was too good to interact with me or my friends. He didn't play stick ball or basketball. He told the guys who did that they should spend more time getting educated.

More to the point, I found him conceited, arrogant and overbearing, which is why I was surprised one afternoon when my mother interrupted my house cleaning to inform me that he was in the living room waiting to see me.

"Take that rag off your head and give me that dust cloth!" Mom instructed. I stepped around her and entered the living room to find Nigel comfortably seated, scanning the back of a record album.

"Nigel, what are you doing here?"

"Well Piper, I thought I'd introduce you to two albums you might enjoy." He extended two record albums. One was Nat 'King' Cole's "Love is the Thing" and the other was Miles Davis's "Porgy and Bess." I thought he was just too smug in his presentation; sure that he was exposing me to something new, something beyond my realm of knowledge.

While he was cueing up the records, I rummaged through my album collection. When I returned he was again scanning the album cover. He wanted to show me something in the liner notes. I moved directly in front of him and extended the very same two albums.

"By the way, have you heard of Eric Dolphy? I can introduce you to his music if you like."

My sarcasm was not lost on him. He rose to leave.

"Be careful on your way out -- don't trip over your ego," I shot over my shoulder as I returned to my chores.

I was most annoyed when I discovered that my mother had invited him. It was not the first time that mom had tried to set me up with someone she thought would be a good date for me, but I resented it. I wasn't ready for a serious relationship. I felt badly for the way I'd treated Nigel, but not badly enough to apologize.

After that I didn't see much of Nigel although he still lived next door, but then again his work and social circle and mine had no reason to intersect. Since his sister and I still studied together, I often heard about his activities. Nigel did this, or Nigel did that. Nigel, Nigel, Nigel. It was annoying but I said nothing. It was some time though, before my mother stopped mentioning "the wonderful chances you'll surely miss by running Nigel away."

In my senior year of high school I'd already completed the required credits for graduation but wouldn't graduate until the spring. So I took an elective Spanish class and began courses at Brooklyn College. I also took a part time job working in an auto insurance firm. That's where I met Sunny.

Sunny was stunning – all 5' 8" of her part Cherokee self, possessing a thick mane of jet-black hair that reached her waist. She was elegant and poised. Whatever she wore seemed like a designer piece. Sunny appeared to be more experienced than her 19 years.

Sometime between Thanksgiving and Christmas Sunny asked about my boyfriend. I didn't have one.

"Well, what are your plans for celebrating the holidays?" she asked.

I stared at her blankly. I didn't have plans. It wasn't clear to me if her incredulousness was because I didn't have a boyfriend or that I didn't have plans in place. Perhaps both. Besides, I usually celebrated Christmas in church with my family.

"Would you like to double date?"

I was flattered, but skeptical about going out with someone I didn't know. Actually, I was shy. It took time for me to feel comfortable enough with people to talk about anything that really mattered. "I've never been on a blind date and I'm uncomfortable around people I don't know. But thanks anyway."

"Listen, Doug, my boyfriend, is going to borrow his father's car Saturday night so we can go to the drive-in. We'll introduce you to his friend, Jackson. Y'all can come with us to the movies. That way, you won't be alone with a person you don't know and you'll have a chance to see if you like him."

By the end of the day I'd agreed. It was almost the end of the week though before my mother did the same. Mom didn't know Sunny and didn't like not being in control of the situation. The bottom line was that Mom never liked anyone I liked.

Jackson was prize-fighter muscular, and moved with an easy gait. If he was at all uncomfortable it was not evident. My father shook his hand and indicated that he should be seated.

"Is Jackson your first or last name?"

"Last, sir."

"And your first name is?"

"Everyone calls me Jackson."

"Why is that?" My father was toying with him now, peering over his reading glasses.

Jackson hesitated a moment, taking a deep breath. "Sometimes I use my initials, H.T."

My father laughed. "Oh, you have one of those biblical names too? I know about that. I got stuck with Titus. You're probably Hezekiah." Both men laughed. That would have been the launch into a very long conversation had my mother not reminded my father that Jackson had come to see me, not him.

The ride to the drive-in gave us a chance to get acquainted. Originally from Elyria, Ohio he had been in New York for two years and worked in a steel plant in Brooklyn, as he had done in Ohio.

Once the sodas and popcorn were delivered, the speaker attached to the window and the movie begun, Doug and Sunny began heavy necking in the front seat, sound effects included. Jackson, obviously inspired by the front seat activity, began trying to do the same. I tried to hold his hands – to stop his attempt to touch me all over. Finally, on the verge of hysteria, I insisted he stop, and maneuvered his hands into his own lap.

"Look, we don't even know each other," I offered as gently as possible.

Jackson looked at me somewhat quizzically, but sat back draping his arm around my shoulder. I was embarrassed by the bold making out in the front seat but pleased that Jackson at least didn't press the issue.

Jackson phoned the following week and invited me to attend a Christmas Eve party with them. The party would be in Harlem. Doug would again drive his father's car. I hesitated, but decided that Jackson had ultimately honored my request and acted accordingly. Besides, it was Christmas Eve.

Mom went with me shopping. The dress was a deep green, double knit trapeze stunner, belted in the front, swinging away from the body in the back. It fit me perfectly, accentuating my small waist. Black suede heels with a small rhinestone clasp on the front of the shoe and a matching black clutch purse completed the outfit. Although nervous, I looked forward to the Christmas Eve party and my date with Jackson.

After climbing a flight of stairs, we entered a long narrow hallway in need of paint. The rug was shabby. The room we entered was a drab, non-descript color containing two large beds, a naked light bulb suspended in the center of the room and an odd-looking radio. Tattered shades were raised, allowing a view of Lenox Avenue. I was shocked. And I felt angry, vulnerable, trapped and betrayed, all at the same time.

"I thought we were going to a party"? I mumbled weakly.

Jackson smiled wickedly. "It will be, shortly."

Doug and Sunny were already undressing each other in full view of the window and us.

Jackson pulled me down onto the bed and began unbuttoning my coat, which I clutched tightly. I was in absolute panic, but realizing that I could not fight him physically, tried another tack.

"If it's a party, where's the music?"

He stood, reached into his pocket, took out some coins and began inserting them into the radio. As he did so I made a dash for the door, running as fast as I could in high-heeled shoes, down the stairs and out onto the street. It was snowing. The only place open was a pharmacy on the corner. The pharmacist was at the door preparing to close. I pushed past him.

"Help me, please!"

I ran into the phone booth, peeking out to see if Jackson had followed me. The startled pharmacist locked the door, searching my face and the street to try to determine what was going on. I managed to find a dime but was too ashamed to call my parents. The only other person that came to mind was Nigel – he had a car.

Nigel listened quietly. I'm not sure what he thought from my disorganized rambling other than that I was upset and somewhere in Harlem. He spoke to the pharmacist who agreed to stay with me until he arrived.

It was the first time I'd ever been happy to see Nigel. He was gentle as he led me, still trembling, to the car. A very attractive woman was in the front seat. I was truly embarrassed and kept apologizing to both of them.

Elizabeth was even more gracious than Nigel had been. She suggested that I come to a party with them. Nigel thought it an excellent idea. I felt like a third wheel, but they convinced me that it was the best way to salvage Christmas Eve. Besides, Elizabeth reasoned, my parents would wonder why I was home so early.

Elizabeth repaired my tear-stained face with fresh powder and rouge and rearranged my hair. Nigel introduced me to everyone and made a point to dance with me too. It was a delightful party with great music, friendly people and really good food. One young man was particularly entertaining and attentive. He volunteered to take me home, but Nigel would have none of it.

I was anxious about returning to work and having to deal with Sunny but she was way ahead of me and ignored me completely.

Watch Night Service on New Year's Eve was different from previous years. In addition to the choir, there was a guest musician playing guitar. Carlos Reyes played everything from classical to Gypsy flamenco to foot stomping gospel and blues. I was engulfed in the wash of sounds; completely engrossed. At the conclusion of the service, I made my way to the front of the church to speak with the guitarist. He was in conversation with Nigel, who I'd not noticed in the congregation. Nigel introduced us.

"Piper, we're going to The East. Care to join us? Pharoah Sanders is playing."

"Piper is an unusual name," Carlos said as he extended his hand.

"It's a nickname. My name is Julie. Julie Bernard."

"And she plays a mean flute."

I was surprised that Nigel knew I played flute, but then again, he did live right next door.

Carlos smiled broadly. "You must join us."

"Are you sure Sanders is playing?" I directed my question to Nigel, but it was Carolos who responded.

"Does it matter? The East always has memorable music, and color-ful patrons." Cradling my elbow, Carlos propelled me toward the door with Nigel, bringing up the rear.

Carlos and I became fast friends. Enrolled in the post graduate program at the Manhattan School of Music he had already begun per-forming regularly around the city. Nigel often joined us as we traipsed around town reveling in the music of Sun Ra at Slug's, Max Roach at the Blue Coronet, Miles at Town Hill, Julian Bream at Lincoln Center. A few of Carlos's music buddies even found a second home in my living room, listening to records of Eric Dolphy, Yusef Lateef, and Ricardo Ballardo, better known as Manitas de Plata, a French Gypsy flamenco guitarist. There were frequently impromptu jam sessions. My parents seemed to enjoy having a houseload of musicians underfoot. For me it was like having the sisters and brothers I always wanted.

I was getting ready for graduation and becoming a full-time college student when out of the blue my mother asked, "Whatever happened to that Jackson fellow?"

"Who?"

"The young man you went out with on Christmas Eve?"

"What made you think of him, Mom?"

"I don't know exactly, perhaps because you haven't spoken of him since."

"I have no idea," was all I managed to mumble. It was, mercifully, the truth.

"Well, something must have happened."

Mom was watching me closely. I opened my mouth to give her a revised version of what happened, but realized she would see through it just as she had known something had happened.

"Thank God for Nigel!" is all she said before returning to the kitchen.

Indeed, I thought.

As I approached his gate Nigel was coming out.

"Oh, Piper, just the person I wanted to talk to."

"I was coming to talk to you too."

"Really? Will the park be okay with you?"

Nigel was quiet as we walked to the park. He'd always been quiet. Perhaps quiet was not the right word, but it was the first time I consciously realized how safe and calm I felt in his company, in his state of quietude. I was still pondering that thought as Nigel guided me to a bench overlooking a field of wildflowers. We sat taking in the spring greenery.

"I owe you an apology Nigel. I thought you were stuck up; but I was wrong. What I thought was conceit I see now as confidence. The fact that you never retaliated when I was really ugly and mean towards you – well, I took that for weakness. You've been nothing but caring. I am so sorry for the way I've treated you."

I was prepared to ramble on, but Nigel stopped me.

"Apology accepted."

He seemed pleased, but tentative.

"What were you going to talk to me about, Nigel?"

"I've accepted a position with a perfume company. In France."

"France? As in Paris? When will you come back? Will you come back? When will you have to leave?"

I was as unprepared for the tears which suddenly began rolling down my cheeks as I was for Nigel's news. Why was I feeling so confused, abandoned? The tears would not stop.

"I've signed a two-year contract. I leave in a few days."

Days? Two years? I wasn't sure what came over me, except that I didn't want him to leave me. Nigel put his arm around me and I clung to him while my thoughts raced. Would he write? Could I visit? Would he want me to? Nigel held me, kissing my forehead, cheeks, and finally my lips. My thoughts were stilled, comforted by his embrace -- if only for this moment.

REQUIEM FOR JOLENE

The first time I lost Jolene was two years after her bitter divorce, the loss of her home and an unsuccessful custody battle for her young son. She'd had a breakdown and her recovery, such as it was, had been slow. She'd shown up at my job, disheveled, shoeless, hair spiked about her head as if in protest. The shouting racket she caused as she ran through the corridor brought people out of their offices, including me. To say that I was embarrassed would be an understatement. But this was my friend, so I ignored my coworkers, harnessed Jolene, escorted her back into the elevator, and once on the street, hailed a cab. When we reached my home, I called her shrink and scheduled an emergency appointment. She stayed with me for several weeks until she could return to her work as a nurse and to her own apartment.

The next time Jolene disappeared was after Norman.

The wedding was going to be small, private. Norman, a professor at Columbia University, had given her a stunning antique ruby and diamond engagement ring, a family heirloom. They were searching for a home in upscale Larchmont but agreed to occupy her apartment in upper Manhattan until one could be found.

Jolene was happy but was agitated too. She claimed Norman was dragging his feet when it came to introducing her to his family. As the days went by her behavior became erratic. She was unable to focus. Or she'd focus but not on the subject at hand. And her moods would go from jovial to hostile within seconds.

I was surprised by their marriage plans. "How long have you known him? Have you met his family?" I asked. None of our friends had even met him. I'd envisioned a long engagement. In my mind, a wedding was premature.

"Lauren why can't you just be happy for me?" she whined as she began twisting a lock of her hair.

"I'm not sure what I'm supposed to be happy about. You only mentioned him two months ago and now you're planning a wedding."

Granted, this was Jolene's business and of course she had a right to seek happiness, but I was bewildered by the situation. I'd known Jolene almost all of my life – we'd gone to elementary school together. Maybe I was being overprotective.

But happiness was elusive. Jolene never met Norman's family. Within a month of the engagement it was over. From what I could glean from her sob-choked conversation, Norman had told his parents about her previous marriage and divorce. His parents were extremely "saddened" that Norman had selected someone not of their choosing. After all, they had a family name to protect. They were blunt about their desire that he retrieve the ring and terminate the relationship with "whomever it is that you've entangled yourself." Norman had complied with his family's directives.

Jolene ran. All the way to relatives in New Orleans. She never mentioned her pregnancy to Norman.

After a few months she called to say that she was living with family and was doing fine. During the following months communication became spotty. I had the telephone number of a cousin but her number was soon disconnected. I heard nothing more for a couple of years.

It was about 1987 when I attended a meeting in New Orleans. I was excited about going because it would be an excellent opportunity to look for Jolene. She was not listed in the telephone directory. Neither was her cousin. I was pondering my next move as I walked back to my hotel when I noticed a bit of blue ribbon braided into the hair of a woman walking ahead of me. Jolene always wore a blue ribbon in her hair. "Jolene?" I called tentatively. It was her!

We reconnected as if it were old home week. We had lunch at an outdoor restaurant in the Quarter. She mentioned only in response to my question that she'd had the baby, a girl and named her Juliette. She seemed more interested in telling me about Etienne – her new beau. He was at least 15 years her senior. "He's handsome, kind and treats me well. He's a house painter by day, but sometimes he 'sits in' on piano at a few of the local clubs around the city." This she said in one long excited breath. She beamed with happiness.

"Does Juliette live with you?" I asked, but she either didn't hear or chose to ignore my question. The way she began twisting her hair around her finger told me that she was becoming agitated. I obtained contact information and decided to save the questions for another time.

I tried to reach her using the phone number she'd provided without success.

Another couple of years passed before I heard from her again. She sounded distressed. No, she was bordering on hysteria. I thought a change of scenery might help and suggested she and Juliette come for a visit. She agreed.

Brantley, my husband, and I were sprucing up the place as part of our usual spring routine. I'd already finished painting the front fence, and since Brandley had repaired the porch railings, I'd painted those, too. Although I liked painting and was pretty handy with a hammer, the truth was that I was painting everything in sight to keep from worrying. In our last phone conversation Jolene had not sounded like herself. Her normal sprightliness was absent, and I couldn't get a feel for this man she was still living with. She'd said he was older but he'd sounded like an energetic person. Now she described him as "sickly." But my antenna really went up when she said she was taking a bus from New

Orleans to New York. When I pressed her she said that she didn't have money for airfare. I offered to pay for the flight but she refused. Why didn't she have money? She was a registered nurse. It made no sense to me. "Are you still working as a nurse?" I asked. She was still on the line, but all I heard were mumbled, incoherent sounds. Was she having another breakdown? I wondered. "How is Juliette, is she well? Is she with you and Etienne?" I ventured. "She's doing fine." Jolene replied tersely.

By the time Jolene was to arrive I was such a nervous wreck that Brantley volunteered to drive me to the bus terminal. It was a good thing. Jolene rolled off the bus as if in another world. She was disheveled, eyes wide and frantically rotating around, but not focusing on anything in particular. Other passengers gave her wide berth as they looked back over their shoulders anxiously. Clearly she had not taken her meds. And where was Juliette? I asked the driver to double check the bus. No Juliette.

The drive from Port Authority to the Bronx seemed to take an eternity with Jolene ranting on about Mr. Millett having beaten her, taken her money and house keys. Mr. Millett? On the telephone the relationship sounded much more intimate. Whenever she'd uttered his name, "Etienne," it was always with affection and sometimes a bit of naughtiness. Now she referred to him as Mister? Brantley signaled for me to be still, to let her rant.

Once at home Brantley brewed chamomile tea while I dumped her purse in search of her meds. She wanted scotch.

Our bedroom door almost always remained open. This night Brantley closed and locked the door when we retired. Even with the chamomile tea, I couldn't sleep. I kept remembering how Jolene and I used to go to the movies on 42nd Street as teenagers, moving from one movie house to the next. How we often had to ask passers-by the time, lest we miss our home curfews. Or her finding wicked humor in my non-existent dancing ability. But mostly I fretted over the recollection of what had driven Jolene from the Bronx to New Orleans in the first place and how nothing seemed to have been resolved. Curling myself into Brantley spoon fashion, I decided to have a real heart to heart talk with Jolene the next day.

In the morning I was surprised that Brantley had not gone to work. His elbows were propped against the kitchen counter listening to Jolene with a completely unreadable expression on his face. When I entered, she quickly changed the subject. I looked at Brantley for direction. His response was to inform me that he'd decided to take a few days off.

"Good morning," I offered trying to sound as if all was well. Jolene mumbled an undecipherable greeting while simultaneously sipping coffee and avoiding eye contact.

"Jolene, where is Juliette? I thought you were bringing her?"

Turning slightly, Jolene positioned her back to me and offered no response.

Brantley, who was usually animated and playful in the mornings, offered a tense smile as he turned to pour a cup of coffee, which he handed to me. There was frustration etched in the rigidity of his back. I felt like an intruder in my own home.

"What's going on? I asked. Brantley nodded for me to go out to the back porch. As I moved past her, I notice she was wearing a bit of blue ribbon in her hair. As miniscule as this was, I found the consistency reassuring since I'd never known her to be without it.   "What's going on, babe?" I asked again. He held my elbow gently as he guided me toward the door. He draped his arm over my shoulder as we moved deeper into the yard.

"Sweetheart, she's not who you remember," Brantley stated sadly. He watched me carefully before continuing. "She's plotting demonic retaliatory actions against Etienne."

"What?" I couldn't even grasp the idea of Jolene doing or being involved in anything demonic – nutsy perhaps – but not demonic. The escalating intensity of Brantley's voice was making me nervous.

"When I came into the kitchen this morning, before I could even say 'good morning' she began telling me how she sometimes hid Etienne's medicines and his cane. From what she was saying I gathered that he's diabetic and losing his eyesight. In fact, she said that he attends a special school for the blind to learn how to care for himself when he loses his sight completely. Why would a nurse, of all people, hide the man's meds? Lauren, you had to see her face – her eyes were glazed over. She was gleeful in a sadistic way." He paused and looked at me with dismay. "And I'm not leaving you alone with her."

"Brantley, you're reading her wrong. I know she's not quite herself, but what you're describing is just not Jolene."

"That's what I said," Brantley answered with finality. He turned and went back into the house.

That afternoon I sat in my bedroom thumbing through one of my old telephone books, trying to find the name of Jolene's former shrink. I could hear Jolene whispering in the next room. I moved closer to the bedroom door. Her voice was soft, seductive.

"I'll be home soon Love, as soon as I get my bus ticket from Lauren. I'll call you when I leave here."

There was a long pause.

"Ok. When you send the money for a plane ticket, I'll do just that!"

The rest of her conversation was very affectionate -- lots of sexual innuendo. I was floored. Just the night before she'd held us captive with tales of the man's mean ways, including taking all of her hard-earned money and beating her with his cane. I didn't see any bruises or other physical indications of these beatings but that was not to negate them either. She was emphatic that she would never return to him or to New Orleans. What about Juliette? I almost shouted, but caught myself.

When Brantley came into the bedroom I told him about the conversation I'd overheard.

"I'm not surprised," he said. "In fact, last night, actually it was about two this morning, heard her on the phone. She said we'd brought her here under false pretenses, she was being held under duress and that we were hiding her bus ticket. When I entered the kitchen and went to the sink to get water, she hung up quickly and ran out of the room."

After all of our years of friendship, I felt betrayed and used. I went to find Jolene.

"Jolene, let me get this straight: Etienne is beating you and taking your money; we brought you here under false pretenses, we're preventing you from returning to New Orleans and Etienne. Didn't you say you didn't intend to return to him? Have I misunderstood something? And by the way, where is Juliette? Did you really have the baby, Jolene?"

Jolene's face contorted and she began to spit out a string of curses. It began as barely audible and grew in volume. I was called all kinds of names and I could see that she was working herself into a complete frenzy.

Brantley appeared and stepped in front of Jolene. She rose up as if to strike him. He didn't move. In a level voice he said simply, "I am not Etienne."

Jolene sat down and her rage disappeared as suddenly as it had arisen. Brantley spoke firmly. "Jolene, you need to figure out where you want to go right now because you are not spending another night in this house. You can pack while you think."

Jolene chose to return to New Orleans. We drove her to the airport.

That was a couple of years before Hurricane Katrina hit New Orleans in 2005. The levee system failed, causing devastating death and destruction. The traumatic events were documented on national television.

Since then I've been unable to find Jolene. Or Juliette. Neither Jolene nor Etienne could drive. Was it possible they could have escaped? Had they been relocated?

Have you seen her? She's only five feet tall but walks in a very erect manner, like the dancer she always wanted to be. She has a scattering of freckles dancing across the bridge of her nose. And while her eyes are sometimes sad, there's usually a devilish glint of mischief flirting around the edges.

Have you seen her? Even though many years have passed, I'm sure you'd recognize her – she always has a bit of blue ribbon threaded through her hair.

Have you seen my friend Jolene?

CHANGE

I've been black all my life. And I've lived in this same neighborhood for the past forty-two years of that life. So I was surprised, and not the least bit annoyed, at what happened when I frequented my local pharmacy.

Perhaps I should backtrack and tell you that the neighborhood has changed over those years. When I first moved here there were still a few white folk. In fact, a few of those few are still here. There were some folk from Puerto Rico and the Dominican Republic. Then came the Africans. Nigerians mostly. The most recent neighbors are Guyanese and Trinidadian Indians. And I'd noticed a few Sikhs too. Some Caribbean folk of Indian descent came next. But many of these folk were aloof. This mix of brown and black people could potentially make for a rich cultural exchange, provide an eclectic assortment of produce in the supermarket and an interesting variety of restaurant choices. But I digress.

The pharmacy is not new. The owners are. Caribbean Indian folk have replaced the black owners. But that is not a surprise. What was, was the uniformed security guard. Since the store is within an indoor mall which is on the lower level of a huge middle class housing development, I was mildly concerned. Was there a need, I wondered since the mall was already patrolled.

With a shopping basket over my arm and my list in hand, I ambled through the aisles, checking out sales and all manner of new products. After a short while, I noticed that the security guard appeared to be following me. So, I did what any self-respecting middle-aged black woman would do; I called him over.

"Yes?" he said as he approached. I simply smiled and placed the basket over his arm and continued shopping.

"Ma'am, what do you want me to do with this basket?"

"Well young man," I said, peering over my bifocals, "since you're following me around the store, I thought you could make yourself useful and carry my basket. That way you can do your job and not have to try to look inconspicuous."

Somehow, he managed to look sheepish, embarrassed and angry simultaneously. But he did place the basket gently on my arm before disappearing.

When I visit the pharmacy now I never see a security guard. I don't know if the store no longer has a need or if the young man makes himself scarce when he sees me. All I can say is that change can be a wonderful thing. My neighborhood continues to evolve, as do I.

EVA-JEAN

I'd never seen such a sad little girl. Each day she walked slowly toward South Ozone Park Elementary, the school at the end of the street. She dragged her feet. And her eyes were always cast downward. Her clothing was unusual too. Unlike most of her schoolmates who wore jeans, she always wore a dress. And she carried herself as if weighted by ancient burdens.

It was months later that my seven-year-old daughter, Jemma told me about a girl in her class named Eva-Jean who never spoke or interacted with her classmates. My extraverted child had tried to several times to befriend Eva-Jean without success.

"Everyone is not like you Sweetheart. Some people are shy." Jemma had heard this so often she simply gave me a hesitant look, made a grunting sound, and went to her room to play.

Like most of my neighbors, we grew accustomed to Eva-Jean's slow drag to school. On her return home, she seemed to walk even slower. Her father, Royce, was usually waiting for her. He'd open the gate and usher her inside. She remained inside until the next school day. By the time she was eleven, I began to be concerned. he was still wearing little girl dresses. They were so snug that the back closure couldn't be fastened and so short she had to feel self-conscious. I was embarrassed for her.

Thinking that I might be of help, I rang the Reid's doorbell. Mrs. Reid opened the door with a scowl.

"What do you want?"

I was caught off guard and it took a moment for me to remember why I'd come.

"I'm your neighbor – three doors down and Eva-Jean goes to school with my daughter," I said, pointing toward my home.

"Yeah, and?"

"Well, I've noticed that Eva-Jean's dresses are a bit snug, and she's quite developed for her years. I'm a seamstress. I make most of my family's clothing. I'm offering to make some clothes for your daughter, for free, of course." I offered a smile.

"You need to mind your own business." She slammed the door.

Eva-Jean's father went to work every day but was back home by mid-afternoon. He was also the resident drunk and could usually be found in or outside the local bar or stumbling up the street hanging onto some bedraggled young woman.

One afternoon I heard my front gate slam. Royce staggered up my walkway. "Hey now!" he slurred. "My daughter here?" He undressed me with his eyes and smiled, probably thinking he was being seductive.

"You know very well she isn't. Whatever it is you think you want, you'd better rethink it."

Royce swayed in place for a few seconds before he managed to turn around and wobble out of my yard.

My husband and I were planning a 13th birthday party for Jemma. So, paper and pen in hand, I sat in our dining room fleshing out our ideas. I glanced up in time to see Eva-Jean walk by. She wasn't showing yet, but it was obvious to me she was pregnant. I wondered if she even knew.

Several months later I was completely taken aback to find Mrs. Reid at my door. She had a black eye and her lip was split. "My God! What happened?"

She looked sheepish but said nothing.

"Come in, come in." Everyone in the neighborhood knew that her husband beat her, and several people had called the police, but each time Mrs. Reid refused to press charges.

She moved slowly and seated herself gingerly. I left briefly to get an icepack.

"Thanks, but I didn't come for me. I came because of Eva-Jean." She placed the pack on her eye. "I think she's pregnant."

"She should be about six months pregnant, Mrs. Reid" I said. She sat up straight.

"How do you know that?"

"I see her every day on her way to school. How is it that you live in the same house with your daughter and haven't noticed? Are you seriously telling me that you didn't know?"

She hung her head.

"Mrs. Reid, why are you here? What exactly do you expect from me?"

"I thought you'd know what to do?"

I was slow to get her meaning. "It's far too late for abortion if that's what you had in mind." My empathy was fading fast. We sat for several minutes in silence.

"How old is Eva-Jean?"

"Thirteen."

I groaned. "Do you know who the father is?" Mrs. Reid's body went limp, she hugged herself and began to rock from side to side.

"Mrs. Reid?"

She looked up. "My name is Elyria." She continued rocking.

"Elyria, do you know who the father is?"

"Royce," she said ever so softly as tears cascaded down her face.

***

One day Royce didn't return from work. Elyria did not attempt to find him. She and Eva-Jean had to figure out how to order their lives. Elyria asked me where her daughter could get medical attention. I drove them to Booth Memorial Hospital. Eva-Jean was seven months pregnant.

When Elyria and I finally had a chance to talk she said that Eva-Jean was distressed, not by the pregnancy, but about the whereabouts of her father. She continually asked, "When is Daddy coming back?"

Elyria shifted in her chair, clearly uncomfortable. Her eyes moistened but the tears did not fall. "Eva-Jean keeps asking, 'What did I do to make daddy leave?' It don't matter how I explain it, she just don't believe me."

I gave her a moment to collect herself.

"Have you heard from him?" I asked with a measure of hesitancy.

"No."

"Any idea why he left?"

Elyria rolled her eyes. "Who knows? Maybe he figured out incest was a felony. Maybe he didn't want another mouth to feed. Maybe he found some young girl who.... Whatever the reason, I'm not looking for him."

The infant was born with severe debilitating abnormalities. Eva-Jean wheeled him around in a special stroller which allowed for easier handling by his caregiver, who I assumed was Elyria. Eva-Jean didn't often touch or speak to him, that I ever noticed, but her eyes were always on him. It was as if she were trying to figure out how he'd come to be.

Eva-Jean's baby died before he was two years old. Eva-Jean withdrew, becoming more taciturn than ever.

It was not a new question in my mind, but after the death of the baby I truly couldn't fathom what Eva-Jean was feeling. Other than her usual reticence, her facial expressions and body language gave little indication. *How much can one little girl bear?* I wondered.

Eva-Jean was 16 when she left home. The police said it wasn't all that uncommon for kids her age to run away. "She's still just a kid... she's my baby. My only child...." Elyria pleaded with the officer to find Eva-Jean. She cried, threatened, and cried some more but the officer had nothing to offer except that they "would do their best." Elyria didn't care what they called it, her daughter was missing, possibly abducted… She was duly distraught.

***

It was Jemma's junior year at Howard University and she and a few of her sorority sisters decided to go to New Orleans on spring break. Her calls home were loud events with her screaming over the sound of music and people yelling. She was excited by the sights, sounds and food. She'd never had blackened fish before but loved it. The many wrought iron balconies in the French Quarter fascinated her as did the horse-drawn carriage and band parading through the streets in a "second line" funeral parade. And she was intrigued, and a little frightened, by the stories of the legendary voodoo queen, Madame Laveaux.

"Mom, you and Dad have to visit 'Nawlins'. It's really different."

Her next call was sobering. "Mom, I saw Eva-Jean."

"Where? Is she okay? What did she have to say?"

"I didn't speak with her." There was a long pause.

"Mom, she had on a really short, tight red dress. As short as it was it had a slit up the front and the top didn't cover very much, and she was holding up a man who was drunk. His hands were all over her." Another pause. "Mom, it was Mr. Reid."

Even before I hung up the phone, I felt sick.

.

A MATTER FOR FAITH

Niecy's death wasn't a surprise to the family. She'd been mis-treating herself for years. In fact, the doctor had advised her just three months ago that if she didn't change her ways she'd be hospitalized, or worse. She paid him no heed. She often said, "I'm too young to die!" There was no reasoning with her. And yet I was un-prepared for her passing. Even during the drive from Florida to New Jersey I tried to make sense of her early demise.

All through the funeral I tried to reframe a life taken too soon. To wish her back into life.

Lingering at the gravesite, I looked up and recognized the young man approaching. He was wearing a bright red sweatsuit. Jeffrey, her brother.

Why that boy come to his sister's funeral wearing gang colors? I wondered. Sad. Just plain sad.

I cried inwardly as the limo sped back into the city to the repast. It had been twenty years since I last visited. This town never was prosperous or pretty. At least not during my memory. And I got long memory. Now it's worse. Like after a war. Boarded up storefronts. Boarded up houses. Vacant lots full of candy wrappers, abandoned shoes, windowless window frames, abandoned supermarket carts –

discarded pieces of people's lives. In between all these vacant spaces people struggle to live normally.

On the corner a bunch of boy-men shoot craps. Right out in the open. Another group conducts drug business. They're not even trying to hide. The corruption's so bad, the state is planning to remove regular cops from street duty, replace them with state cops.

Been knowing Jeffrey since before he was born. I remember helping Niecy change his diapers and make formula; their mama was so sick. It's hard to think of him as a criminal. Maybe he didn't have a whole lot of options. No, that's not true. I'm making excuses. None of his brothers made that choice. Or maybe they did but I didn't know about it. Or they outgrew the street life. Or maybe some other family member snatched them out of the mire without making a lot of noise about it.

When I see Jeffrey with his little boy though, I don't see a criminal. Just a devoted dad. Gentle and caring. Eyes filled with pride, love. For a brief moment I forget all that street stuff. I enjoy watching Jeffrey with his son.

Still, my mind tries to picture what kind of life baby Jeff might have. I shudder at the possibilities. I force myself to not think – to focus on the good feeling of being with Niecy's family -- catching up with all the new marriages, babies, graduations and plans for their first family reunion.

When I leave the repast, I see Jeff on the street surrounded by a bunch of rough looking men. They're conducting their street business. Diagonally across the street is a police car. The officers must see them but it obviously does not concern them.

Shaking my head in frustration, I remember a Bible passage:

I have cried until the tears no longer come; my heart is broken. My spirit is poured out in agony as I see the desperate plight of my people. Little children and tiny babies are fainting and dying in the streets. **–Lamentations 2:11** *

It's sad that it takes a funeral for me to see this but I am a woman of faith. Faith's not the same as magic though. Faith's like a flower. Flowers need dirt, sun and water. Flowers come through the dirt, but they're not the dirt.

I've been focusing on the dirt and not seeing the flower. In the end it's a matter for faith – a flower requiring continuous tending.

I will try to remember that as I mourn my friend.

*Holy Bible: New Living Translation, Tyndale House Publisher

OBADIAH WASHINGTON

Obadiah Washington was ashen, unconscious; almost unidentifiable – a man with a tube taped into his mouth and a bevy of additional tubes and wires protruding from his chest and arms. He was surrounded by beeping, blinking, LED-lit machines. Mariah's breath caught, *Hail Mary full of grace...*

"Mr. Washington is in extremely critical condition. If he has any chance at all we must move him to ICU at Main Hospital. Quickly."

Mariah tried to comprehend what the doctor was saying while being acutely aware of the chaos of gurneys and EMT staff scurrying about under a cacophony of moans and screams of people in pain.

Mariah nodded as she signed the authorization form the doctor held out.

"But what happened?" she asked.

"He was eating at the barbecue shack, when he collapsed."

"Barbecue?" Mariah was puzzled -- Obadiah Washington had sworn that because of his high cholesterol and weak heart, he'd given up pork, beef, and shrimp. Mariah looked again at the waxen man in the bed. His large, cocker spaniel eyes were half-closed, unseeing. He seemed so very small.

"Miss Thompson?"

Mariah faced the doctor. "Will you ride with him in the ambulance?"

"No, I drove. I'll meet them at Main."

Mariah paused, "Doctor, do you know why I was called?"

The doctor seemed surprised, but looked at the clipboard she carried, flipping through several sheets. "You're listed as the emergency contact person." By the time the doctor asked, "But aren't you his wife?" Mariah was already halfway down the corridor.

While Obadiah Washington was being situated in Main's intensive care unit, the doctor asked about his medical history. Mariah clearly recalled how he told her that he'd retired at the age of 43 because of a severe heart condition. Obadiah had been animated. It was as if he wanted to engage her in an intriguing drama. And a few months later he'd called her from a hospital on Long Island to say that his rent would be late because of his hospitalization. "They had to put in a stent," he said groggily. And as an afterthought and with much more energy, "Yeah and my kidneys aren't functioning at full capacity either; only 20 percent."

He'd sounded rather pleased with himself for being able to report this information. She now told the doctor what she knew. As she reflected back on the way he shared information, she thought it cavalier, but being a landlord had taught her to listen and not necessarily to react or make a quick judgement.

It was dark, cold and raining when she reached the street. It matched the way she felt. She wondered what she would do if Obadiah's business partner, Leonard James, didn't have any information about Washington's family. Driving home, her mind wandered back to when Obadiah Washington first came to look at the vacant apartment. He wasn't someone you'd remember if you passed him on the street, but once he flashed that broad, crooked-toothed smile and focused his large puppy dog eyes on her, he reminded Mariah of a charming, but delinquent schoolboy. Once he'd moved into the upstairs apartment, however, she'd begun to wonder if she'd rented to a drug dealer. He came and went at odd hours, usually at night. And he entertained a lot of women. The only thing that didn't match his drug dealer profile was his car – a black Suburban truck. But what, she asked herself, did she know about what drug dealers drove? She began to wonder if she had made a mistake in renting the apartment to Obadiah Washington.

Then one afternoon while Obadiah was out, a man and woman had entered the apartment with a key. Mariah confronted Obadiah Washington the next day.

"Mr. Washington, we need to talk."

He was in a hurry and annoyed at the imposition. "Can this wait until I get back?"

"No, it cannot!"

Obadiah reluctantly entered the apartment of his landlady, but did not sit down.

"Yesterday, a gentleman who I do not know entered your apartment with a key. A woman was with him. They were loud enough for me not to have to use my imagination to know what was going on. I need to make it crystal clear to you that this is not a brothel. This is my home."

"Hold on, Little Bit."

"I beg your pardon! Don't get familiar with me, Mr. Washington!"

Obadiah had stepped back, away from Mariah. "That was my partner, Leonard James. He's married, so I let him use my place," he said, frowning.

"His marital status is not a concern of mine," Mariah answered. "I suggest he take his friend to a hotel. He's not included in your lease." She was becoming more uneasy about her tenant. "You say he's your partner?"

"Yes, he is."

"Partner in what? I thought you were retired."

"Technically, I am retired, but I have a little business on the side." He gave a conspiratorial wink. "We provide services to funeral homes. We pick up bodies, embalm them, and return them to funeral homes, which is what I need to do right now, so, if you'll excuse me..."

Leonard James returned her call the next morning. He'd be right over. Before she could dissuade him, he'd hung up. Unlike his partner, who was always grinning, Leonard James was serious of bearing, his brow a permanent furrow of concern. He greeted Mariah with a nod of his head.

"I'm sorry I couldn't get back to you last night. It was a busy night and when I couldn't get hold of Obie, I had to scramble to get back-up help. How's he doing?"

Mariah shook her head. "He's in a coma, on a respirator. His chances of regaining consciousness are slim, which is why I need to get in contact with his family."

If Leonard was upset by the news, it was not evident. He provided the telephone number of Obie's sister without comment.

Obie's sister was nonchalant about her brother's hospitalization. She said their mother was in poor health, and since she was the only one providing care, she'd visit her brother when she could. Once off the telephone, Mariah asked Leonard if there was anyone else they needed to call.

"Yeah, his wife, Luetta, and Delilah, his adult daughter from another union. I don't know where to begin to look for any of his other children."

"Other children?"

Leonard gave her a cautionary look. Mariah let the subject drop.

"Will you contact them?"

Leonard nodded.

"Doesn't he have a girlfriend?" Mariah ventured.

Leonard didn't respond, but continued drinking his coffee while studying her over the top of his cup, which made her uncomfortable.

"Miss Thompson, I owe you an apology. Obie told me how upset you were when I brought my lady friend here. This is not an excuse, but an explanation. My wife will never get out of her wheelchair, other than to move into a hospital bed. She's aware of my activities, but I try not to rub it in her face."

Mariah was embarrassed. "I'm sorry about your wife. The rest is none of my business." She wondered, though, why he didn't visit his friend at her home, but that was not her business either.

On the way to work the next morning Mariah stopped at the hospital. She donned the requisite protective gown and rubber gloves before entering. Obie's eyes were more open than the day before. And his hands moved. She inquired if these were signs of improvement. They were not; they were involuntary. Still, she read to him and sang a few hymns. Before leaving she held his hand as she said the Lord's Prayer.

For the next three days Obadiah Washington's only visitor was Mariah. She stopped either on the way to work or on the way home. She developed a rapport with his doctors and nurses. Daily, she called his sister with the developments, minute as they were.

On the fourth day his doctor informed her that they'd been monitoring Obie and would soon make a decision about when to disconnect the respirator. "It's not an issue for the moment, but I thought it best to alert you."

Mariah was momentarily speechless. It had never occurred to her that the plug would be pulled. She thanked the doctor for his candor and stumbled to the elevator. In the lobby she called Leonard James. "Have you reached his wife or daughter? Are they coming?"

"Luetta seemed annoyed at the inconvenience, but will be here sometime tomorrow. I can't reach 'Lila, but left messages for her. What's going on? You sound panicked."

"I am. Do you realize that I've made every medical decision for him? The doctors consult with me as if I'm his wife. I thought I was doing what he would have wanted, but expected that once his family was contacted they would take on these responsibilities. Now the doctors are talking about pulling the plug. I don't even know why I was listed as his emergency contact person. Someone from his family needs to be here!" Mariah's voice had escalated into a shrill whine.

"Are you at home?"

"No."

"Call me when you get there, I need to talk to you."

Mariah had intended to return to work but Leonard James's response made her fully aware of how tired and stressed she was. She
called her office, made an excuse, and went home. As she drove, it
occurred to her that even though she had never claimed to be his wife,
Obie's family could conceivably sue her for posing as his wife and
making decisions that weren't her right to make. But why weren't his
family members coming forward?

Once at home she called Leonard James. He came over immediately.

"Listen, Luetta and their son will need a place to stay. Would it be
alright for them to stay in Obie's place?"

Although the idea was a charitable one, Mariah wondered how long
Luetta would stay. She could not afford to not have income from the
apartment. Leonard anticipated her.

"I'll pay the additional month's rent."

"You can afford to do that?"

"As partners, we insure each other. One month's rent won't be a
problem."

"He's not dead, Leonard."

"From what you've said, he will be."

Mariah was irritated by his response. She was worried about the
situation, especially with her increasing involvement.

Porn videos and magazines littered the bedroom. Leonard, who was
peering over Mariah's shoulder, spun her gently back around into the
hallway. "Why don't you check out the kitchen?"

The rest of the apartment was orderly. She would get someone to
clean the bathroom and kitchen and to do a general dusting before
Luetta and her son arrived. Once back in her own apartment, Mariah
asked Leonard what he planned to do with the porn material.

"Trash it, why?"

"Just curious. Obie said the videos and magazines belonged to
you."

Leonard was clearly offended. "I see," he retorted. "I gather you're sleeping with Obie?"

Mariah's expression of dismay made Leonard laugh.

"Now you're getting an introduction into Obie Washington."

"He said that I was sleeping with him?"

"Actually, he was much more graphic." Leonard seemed to enjoy her discomfort.

"Now you begin to see why Obie has no visitors."

"Because he lies?"

"Let's just say, that's the tip of the iceberg."

"But you're his partner…"

"Obie is highly regarded in the trade. He's thorough, his work is excellent, he has connections with churches, ministers, funeral directors and of course, lots of womenfolk. People, including me, use him because he's good, not because he's liked. He's a trickster. And," he added as an afterthought, "he's hard as hell on women." The tension left Leonard's voice. "He's hard on himself, too. With his heart condition he's not supposed to be working, certainly not lifting the weight of some of the bodies we pick up. That alone could take him out of here. Hell, what he eats could take him out of here. I don't think he cares about anything or anyone, including himself."

Leonard paused and with a disapproving scowl mumbled under his breath, "With the exception of Delilah, his first-born."

The hospital called Mariah to let her know they would disconnect the respirator the next day. She called Obie's sister and Leonard.

"I've just come from settling Luetta and her son Jeremiah in the apartment and letting her know when they'll disconnect Obie. I've left a number of messages for Delilah and she hasn't called back, but trust me, if she thinks there's anything to be had, she'll turn up," Leonard said.

"Is Luetta going to come to the hospital?"

"She didn't say."

Besides the medical staff, Mariah was the only one present when the respirator was disconnected. For the last time, she held Obadiah Washington's hand and said the Lord's Prayer.

Mariah did not attend the funeral.

A few days later, Mariah was surprised to see Leonard James barreling up her walkway. His fist was about to pound on the door when she opened it. He rushed in ranting, "You knew all along, didn't you?"

"Knew what?"

"You knew about the insurance policy; you knew he'd changed the beneficiary, didn't you?"

"The only person who ever mentioned insurance was you," Mariah shot back.

"I spent over sixty thousand dollars on his funeral and now the insurance company is telling me that I'm not even on the policy. We bought that policy together, as partners. This is unbelievable!"

"So, who is the beneficiary?" Mariah asked quietly.

"Delilah, that little witch! She got to him."

"Instead of accusing me, you need to be talking to your insurance company; and maybe your attorney while you're at it," Mariah spit out as she headed for the kitchen.

Leonard followed her absentmindedly. "When could she have done it? You said he was in a coma, wasn't he?" He glared at Mariah with bulging eyes and fists held taut at his sides.

Mariah thought for a moment. "Not the time before last when he was hospitalized," she recalled.

Leonard was clearly shaken. Slamming his right fist into his open left palm he continued his rant. "I should have known better, I really should have known… Damn you, Obadiah…"

Leonard was still visibly upset when he left. Midway down the walkway he stopped, turned and walked slowly back to Mariah, who was still standing in the doorway.

"I'm somewhere between a rock and a hard place right now, but I was not raised without gratitude. Thank you for what you did for Obie and his family."

Mariah waited for the question she felt was forthcoming.

"Miss Thompson, how come you stayed the course with Obie?"

Mariah had asked herself that question more times than she could recount. "Because Obie asked me to when he listed me as his emergency contact. He had family and friends, so why did he list me?"

"You're the only person who'd...." With a smile and a gentlemanly bow, he swallowed the words he was about to utter. "In hindsight I'd say he chose well. God be with you, Miss Thompson."

"And with you," she replied, closing the door. She made a mental note to add Leonard James to her prayer list.

SKIP AND DULCIE

E ven though it was a cold day, Dulcie went to the beach to luxuriate in the changing light of the sunrise and the reflections on the water; the rhythm of the waves as they kissed the shore. She needed a place to reflect on Skip's eroding health. The diagnosis of multiple sclerosis had been presented to him three years before but the symptoms had been subtle and slow to manifest. It had progressed from his lack of balance, to the use of a cane, then a walker, and then to a motorized scooter. Over time his body had become one of awkward angles; knees in a bent position, feet rigid and his toes unmoving. His body was twisted into a perpetual S. He still had use of his right hand but his physical mobility was extremely limited. Most of his time was spent in bed or in his wheelchair. But it was the excruciating pain that drove them both to distraction. Although he'd been prescribed pain-killers, the dosage was ever increasing and not always effective. Skip had become more agitated and difficult to live with. MS was taking its toll on her as well. She now found the need to take brief respites to soothe herself.

This beach was where she'd first met Skip. That day she'd arrived at the beach just as the sun was rising. She reveled in the freshness of the salt air and the comforting sound of water lapping the surf. But as the day progressed the sliver of beach became noisy, funky and more crowded with people and portable radios each blasting a different music station. People happily screamed over the din. Dulcie fled. But she couldn't find her car. It wasn't where she'd left it. Or she'd gotten turned around. Or it had been stolen. Or…

Skip had spent the night in his camper further down the beach. As he walked he was mentally designing a yacht for a new client. He saw an attractive woman running from the beach. No one was chasing her. She's cute, he thought to himself. When he noticed her again, she was spinning around in the parking lot. Always one to help a damsel in distress, Skip approached and asked if he could be of assistance.

"I seem to have misplaced my car," she said, glancing up at him. Her attraction to him was immediate. He was so tall and muscled. His clear eyes were mischievous and inviting. She almost forgot the matter at hand.

"What kind of car is it? What color?" he asked as he admired her sweet moon face, petite body and controlled panic.

"It's a yellow Beetle."

He wondered how she could lose a yellow car, but then again she was barely five feet tall. Scanning the parking lot, he spotted it a short distance away. Taking her elbow, he led her to it. He asked if she'd had lunch. She hadn't. He invited her to join him at a nearby restaurant. That was their first date.

Although they had wed eighteen months later the courtship was ongoing even now, twelve years later. He'd taught her how to navigate his cabin cruiser around the ever increasing debris in the water and into and out of the marina. He was pleasantly surprised that she knew how to fish and was not afraid to bait her hook. Dulcie, a nature photographer taught him how to use a camera. He had a natural ability for composition. They both loved the adventure of travel and being outdoors. And they both loved to dance. Their apartment near the Village in New York City made the countless clubs and art galleries easily accessible.

Dulcie remembered that tiny apartment fondly. It was where they'd began their life together, learning to cook each other's favorite foods, pleasantly pressed together getting from the frig to the sink.

Glancing at her watch, Dulcie realized she needed to get back before Skip's caregiver left for the day.

"Were you hanging out at the beach again without me?" he deadpanned when she returned.

"Yes." She knew he longed to be outside, to be in touch with nature. It pained her to see him suffer.

"Do you remember that romantic trip we were going to take, driving up to and across Canada, then down the west coast?" Skip asked.

Dulcie laughed. "Yeah, I do. We took a break from driving, somewhere in Michigan, to walk through the woods, to take a romance moment." She smiled at the memory. "But I kept hearing something so we stopped walking and peered through the trees. Lord have mercy, there were five bears on their hind legs pulling through a trash heap. We scurried back to the car and drove south. We never did get to Canada!"

"And, if memory serves," Skip interjected, "we didn't drive too far before we stopped and found a hotel for our 'moment.'"

"It was more than a moment," Dulcie reminded him.

"I miss our times traveling together Dulcie; swimming in that beautiful blue water off the Isle of Margarita and hanging out with the fishermen, building sandcastles... I'd love to hold you, to dance on the beach one more time..." Skip stopped; he'd promised himself not to be maudlin. "Babe, I don't want to die here. New York can be so hard... I want to be someplace warm, where I can see and hear the ocean, smell the sea air." He turned away from Dulcie briefly – trying to hide his pain.

She allowed him this deception. After all it was much like her out of town assignments – brief escapes from watching the love of her life die an inch at a time. When he turned back towards her he said simply,

"And I don't want to be alone when my time comes." He was not being at all subtle about Dulcie's traveling for assignments.

"We all die alone, Skip. Even if we're in a crowd, our dying is our own." Dulcie knew exactly what Skip was saying, and each time he brought the subject up she thought about Pearl.

She had hired the woman as Skip's caregiver. She was a mature, no-nonsense woman who was not enamored with nor intimidated by Skip and his rants, even those driven by his pain. She made sure he took his meds; she bathed and fed him. She lifted him to and from his wheelchair. She was not interested in idle chit chat. But Pearl had commandeered his TV to watch her religious programs. Skip asked her to watch her shows in the living room.

"Why don't you want to hear the Good News?" she demanded indignantly.

Skip's response was not helpful. "It may be good news to you, but I don't believe in any of that claptrap."

"How can you say such a thing? You're an ignorant man and you'll burn in hell!" she shot back. She was so incensed she left him undressed as she rushed into the living room to call her agency. Dulcie tried to mediate, but neither was willing to hear the other out.

Skip was still angry that evening. "She had no right to take over my television," he lamented.

"Even so Skip, couldn't you have found a less argumentative way of addressing the issue? This is the third caregiver who's quit."

"But she took over my TV! And furthermore, I don't believe in a golden-haired dude sitting on a cloud-propelled throne meting out judgment."

"So, are you saying you don't believe in God?"

Although they'd had this discussion many times during their marriage, this time seemed more relevant.

"No, I'm saying her version is nonsense."

"And your version is what?"

He thought for a moment. "You. I see you as god. You honor nature and all its creatures. You see the good in just about everyone. Even when someone is hurtful you wish them well and remove yourself from their space. You always seek that place of tranquility. Isn't that what it's supposed to be about, moving from humanity to divinity?" He paused again. "And you put up with me," he said, smiling roguishly.

"Well, now that I've been deified..." Dulcie laughed softly. She turn serious. "So who or what are you Skip?"

She left him to think about that while she went to prepare supper.

***

A month later they relocated. The bungalow Dulcie rented on Folly Beach, South Carolina had a screened-in back porch facing the ocean and Skip's bed rolled easily onto it. The salt air enlivened him. Often he slept there, enjoying being greeted by the rising sun, the sounds of the waves, the formation of pelicans flying overhead and the chatter of seagulls.

In the evenings the cooling breezes soothed his spirit as he became more reflective. He questioned Dulcie: "What's the purpose of meditation? How do you meditate? Is it associated with a particular faith tradition?"

Dulcie too was calmed by the sea air, the sun, flora and fauna. Her shoulders relaxed and the frown that had begun forming on her forehead disappeared. There was something familiar and comforting about the place although she'd only been to Folly once before on assignment. Now she relaxed and allowed the ambiance to envelope her.

Skip and Dulcie sat on the porch listening to the sound of the ocean as the sun slid westward. "This is downright heavenly," Skip observed. There was a long silence before he spoke again. "Dulcie, will you return to New York when I'm gone?"

"I don't know. It would be hard to return to the world of concrete and brick after being here." She sighed. Especially without you, she thought, but did not say.

"Ummm." Skip offered and lapsed into another thoughtful silence. "I never did answer your question of 'who or what' I am. So, I quote Exodus 3:14: 'I am that I am.'" He smiled in a playfully roguish manner and waited for his wife to challenge him. She didn't. Dulcie was of the opinion that what a person believes about life, or more importantly, death, is what they'd experience. So, she simply sipped her wine and held her peace. Together they watched the sun meet the horizon. And they gazed serenely as the sky filled with stars. She was glad to be with him in this sacred moment.

THE MAN NEXT DOOR

When the moving van pulled up in front of our door I was puzzled and then curious. Mom had no plans to move – unless she wasn't telling me. But she wasn't even home. Armed with that small bit of confidence, I went outside to see who was moving.

It was a family of four: a girl, about fourteen, my age and a younger boy of about 10 years old. Their parents were too distracted with opening doors and directing the movers to notice me. But Yolanda and Darren were eager to make friends. They were moving from the Bronx to Brooklyn's Park Slope community. The fact that there were mostly brownstones excited them. They had lived in a large apartment building off the Grand Concourse.

Before we became too involved, Mrs. Donaldson called her children to help with the unpacking. She spoke with a sing-song, lilting voice.

In the weeks that followed, Darren made friends with some of the boys his age and never wanted to hang out with me and Yolanda. That certainly pleased her. I took great pride in showing Yolanda the neighborhood, especially the shops on Flatbush Avenue. We loved window shopping and checking out the offerings at the movie theater. Yolanda loved Grand Army Plaza. Sometimes we would sit on the steps of the library for hours watching the flow of people, pets and

cars. And boys. And making plans to go to the zoo or the botanic garden. Much of the time we just sat on the stoop, imagining and designing the dresses we'd make for school or church.

Mrs. Donaldson was nice. She enjoyed teaching us to bake. My
favorite was peach cobbler. Yolanda liked to make sweet potato
pone. (I thought that was cheating since she didn't have to make any
crust!) It was during these times in the kitchen that Mrs. Donaldson
told stories of growing up in Trinidad, and of her dream of becoming
an American citizen; of owning property and returning to her home
country when she retired from nursing. It was a dream she and Mr.
Donaldson shared. She was really proud of their accomplishments.
This was their second property. They owned a small apartment building in the Bronx. It had eight units.

Mr. Donaldson was another matter. He moved around like a shadow. He seemed to appear and disappear at will. And I never understood what he had to say. One afternoon me and Yolanda were walking back home eating our ice cream cones and gossiping. Her father
appeared in front of us. He leaned in towards me and said: "You ought
to take better care of your mother. I've had to take care of her and she
hasn't paid me for the homeopathic remedies I've prepared for her."

Yolanda dropped her cone and ran past her father and into her
house. When he turned his attention back to me his eyes were vacant.
He stepped around me and continued down the street.

My mother didn't know Mr. Donaldson and she wasn't sick. What
was he talking about?

I thought about telling my mother but was afraid she would stop
me from hanging out with Yolanda. My solution was to avoid Mr.
Donaldson – when and if I spotted him before he got too close.
Yolanda never mentioned the incident afterwards.

From my bedroom on the parlor floor, I would sometimes see Mr.
Donaldson in his backyard. He was usually digging around in the dirt
– planting things. He even built a clear plastic-looking greenhouse
in the back corner of their yard. Yolanda said that even though her

father had a passion for growing things, he was a costume designer. On Broadway.

During the latter part of the summer me and Yolanda spent more time in the Brooklyn Botanic Garden or Prospect Park. The heat seemed less intense away from the concrete. And we were less likely to encounter Mr. Donaldson.

September arrived too soon, and we reluctantly went back to school. We were both in the eighth grade, but not in the same class. We'd usually walk to and from school together. Sometimes we had lunch together too.

Just after Thanksgiving, Yolanda was not her cheerful, chatty self. Sometimes she seemed to be miles away. It was a good while before she told me that her parents were not getting along very well; they were arguing all the time. "He's always yelling about something and when Mom isn't around, he tries to beat up on Darren." She was agitated, fidgety.

Mr. Donaldson's erratic behavior and the constant bickering finally got to Mrs. Donaldson. Just before New Year's, a moving van pulled up in front of their house. Mrs. Donaldson, Yolanda and Darren moved seven blocks away, leaving Mr. Donaldson to live alone next door. But Yolanda still attended our same school.

One Friday afternoon after school we saw Yolanda's dad. He seemed sick or something. He was leaning on a fence. Yolanda stopped walking when she saw him. Then she ran to him, almost falling to the ground trying to keep him upright. He was not coherent. She was scared. "Get my mother, hurry," she cried. I ran as fast as I could.

Mrs. Donaldson and the ambulance arrived almost at the same time.

Mrs. Donaldson told my mother her husband was a diabetic and had high blood pressure and some other conditions I wasn't familiar with. The hospital had admitted him. He was in critical condition. "All the years I've known him he's never gone to a doctor. Not even a chiropodist!" Mrs. Donaldson lamented.

Mom was empathetic. Mrs. Donaldson said she'd tried everything she knew to get him to see a doctor. It always ended in an argument. *What's a chiropodist?* I wondered.

The next day I saw Mr. Donaldson coming out of his house and returning a short time later. I thought it odd that he could have recovered enough to be discharged. He must have discharged himself. That same afternoon Darren rang our bell. He was ashen, his voice unsteady. "I don't have my key, and my father is not answering the door."

"Maybe he's not home," I suggested.

"No, he's in there. I can see his feet."

"What?"

"His feet, he's on the floor in the kitchen. I can see his feet from the front window."

My thoughts were scrambled: *Brownstones are not usually floor-throughs; Darren is mistaken; I should look for myself; call the police; call Mrs. Donaldson; call my mother. All of the above, but what to do first...*

I dialed 911. If Mr. Donaldson was on the floor, he needed help. After making the other calls, Darren and I waited outside. He was shaking. The police and EMS arrived quickly.

Mr. Donaldson was dead. *His homeopathic remedies did not work as well as he'd hoped*, I thought to myself.

After the funeral, the Donaldsons moved back into their house. They were all subdued as they resumed their lives without Mr. Donaldson. We, including me and my mother, became very protective of Darren, who'd become quiet and no longer interested in school or sports as he'd been before. He moved around by rote.

Studying for finals was making me cranky but my mother did not accept excuses or grades that didn't include the letter "A." It was late – even my mother, the night hawk, had gone to bed. No longer able to retain what I was reading, I finally turned out the light and opened the window, my nightly routine. I looked out, blinking several times. Mr. Donaldson was in his backyard, digging around in the dirt. My mouth shaped the word, "MOM" but it stuck in my throat. If I moved, he'd disappear. And my mother would never believe what I'd seen. Mr. Donaldson went into the greenhouse. *Maybe I'm dreaming and I don't really see what I'm seeing; but there's a full moon and a light in the greenhouse.* Clouds gradually covered the moon and the light in the greenhouse went out. I stumbled into bed not sure of what I'd seen. I didn't sleep well.

The next day, Saturday, I didn't wake up until Yolanda disturbed me around noon.

"I had the weirdest dream last night," she said, shaking her head as if to remove the images.

"How weird?"

She made a face before continuing. "Dad was in the backyard poking around, then he went into the greenhouse. He was seeding herbs or something – I didn't recognize most of it."

"Maybe it wasn't a dream." I waited for her to say something. She didn't but looked at me expectantly. I told her what I had seen. She glared at me. "You were dreaming."

"No I wasn't!"

"Well, maybe it was Darren," she said, not so convincingly. "Nope," she continued. "He was in bed. I'd have heard him if he tried to sneak out. And besides, I told him what I dreamed and he looked at me like I was crazy."

But me and Yolanda still see Mr. Donaldson in his backyard. And lately Darren has taken an interest in horticulture. He spends a lot of time in the library now, too. Sometimes at night we see the two of them moving around in the yard. Side by side. The taller one seems to give instructions, demonstrating. It's our secret, me and Yolanda's. But I worry. "Yolanda, your dad is passing his passion onto Darren, but it didn't serve him too well."

"That's true," she said wearily. She was quiet for the longest. "Mom is a nurse. Maybe we can start providing some balance to the stuff he's getting from Dad."

"We? Have you figured out how we're going to do that?"

"Not yet, but we will."

"Yeah, we will," my mouth said. That seemed like a project for the long haul. I preferred to think that Yolanda had been right; this was all a dream, and we'd awaken soon. Real soon.

FERN

If the brick of the building opposite them had not been there; if the floor-to-ceiling windows had been cleaned within recent years, perhaps the sun could have entered; the window was certainly large enough. As a matter of fact, the window was the width of one wall of the studio apartment and nearly as high. The many panes however, were small and the glass within each contained the wire mesh of a cage, or prison.

One wall of Beth's tiny room held four rows of books -- all hard-back or leather editions – all scholarly looking. And the subjects confirmed the initial impression: psychotherapy, theology, astrology, numerology. It was, however, difficult to read most of the titles: the dust and lack of light did not permit it.

Directly opposite the dingy window were the mini-refrigerator, the sink and the stove, which was partially hidden by the step ladder that rose from in front of it up into the ceiling. A loft bed dominated the tiny room. Some previous tenant had decided that the only possible solution to the room's lack of space was to build this monstrosity. Perhaps the idea was a good one, but the overall effect, particularly for the present tenants, was claustrophobic. The floor space, what little that remained, was dusty and scattered with notepapers, pencils, and burned candles. The one empty wall served as a backdrop for the mounds of clothes, bed linen and miscellaneous other items of the household.

Actually this wall was not empty. At about 4:15 each afternoon the fading sun cast shadows upon it. Sometimes it looked like a lattice up to the haven of the loft; but most times it was the maze of a spider web holding tight the inhabitants of the room.

Lying on her back in the loft, Beth's arm extended upwards, she could touch the ceiling. And she did quite often – especially when the room began to slowly turn, to take charge of its own movements. The ceiling had become her friend, her anchor, while in the web.

This evening she watched dragons shimmying across the ceiling; watched them shrink into quivering ants; watched them fade and become shimmering children taunting her from their position on the ceiling. She concentrated on the ceiling to avoid looking at Fern.

Normally, a room of these proportions could accommodate only one. Beth and Fern, however, had learned how to live together. In the mornings they shared the precious little light that entered, exchanged small talk, planned the day's schedule and comforted one another. In the evenings and late into the night, after work, after class, and sometimes after concerts in the park, they whispered to one another, sharing secrets, exchanging plans, ideas, hopes and aspirations. And often, they didn't need to speak at all. They did not get in each other's way. They were friends. Fern was always there for her. But tonight, she could not look at Fern.

Fern was directly opposite her, at the window, in the darkened shadows, silhouetted against the cell-like window. She reached again for the ceiling. This time tears flowed from her eyes; her entire body wept, although there was no sound. She knew if she concentrated, if she put her entire being in it, she could and would do something. She had hurt her friend and she knew it. So, she could not, would not face Fern.

She should call for help. Slowly, she turned her head toward the phone. She knew that it was within arm's reach, but it seemed miles away – alien, unreal. Slowly, she removed each finger separately from the ceiling; they felt like grain – liquefied, oozing granules. It took an eternity for the rest of her palm, wrist and arm to follow – to slide down the wall, to gel before moving toward the phone. Even when her arm came to a halt, the granules continued vibrating. Each one, each granule was a beautiful electric color. Each one pulsated more brilliantly than the one next to it: magenta, turquoise, purple, mauve, yellow, red, red, red... She tried to concentrate. Breathing slowly and deeply she counted to ten. First her pinky, index finger, middle finger – each poured across the frame of the bed. The phone moved further away. Yet she needed to help her friend. But wasn't she the cause of her friend's present situation? The least she could do was to face her...

The light of the full moon filtered through the filthy windows just enough to add a silver silhouette to Fern's gray-black color. She looked brittle, hard, fixed in an eternally bent position. She was dead. She was dead and stiff and bore a strange color. Exactly how long she had hung there, in front of the window, at eye level from the loft bed, was a riddle. Who knew the days? They were a series of white pills, multi-colored capsules, pink pills, yellow pills, shadowy blurs of faces and a series of sounds: neighbors shuffling about in their spaces, radios and stereos vibrating at varying speeds, voices, dogs yelping, cats and babies crying. It all blended into a cacophony of piercing sound. How long had it been? How long had Fern hung there, dead?

Her index finger encountered the phone. But how was she to dial? Her fingers were fluid. Whose number was she to call? What was she to say?

Each number she dialed was a reflection: 2 – two other people with her in the mountains popping the mysterious peyote buttons; 4 – four years or so already in school, four more before receiving that precious degree; 3 – three pills each day, or was it three pills three times a day? Each number escaped her after thinking it.

"Hello? Hello? Anyone there?"

"Y-e-s. It's me."

"Me who, who are you calling? Do you know what time it is?"

"No, yes, I mean, she's dead. Fern is dead and I killed her. She's dead! She's hanging in front of me. She's dead and stiff and funny-colored. I couldn't help it. I killed her, I left her and she's dead. But my arm is so pretty. It was lilac and yellow and blue. Now it's all red. The red is so beautiful cascading down my arm, and Fern can't see it. I know she'd like to see it, but she's dead."

"Beth, this is Dr. Henderson. Where are you? Have you taken your medications today?"

"I don't know."

"Beth, try to remember when you last took your medication."

"I don't remember."

"It's okay. Don't worry about Fern. Remember our conversations about having to take responsibility for more than ourselves?"

"Yes."

"Well Fern was your first attempt. You can try again. You just have to remember to water the plant next time. Then it will grow thick and green. You can get another. Now, tell me about the color flowing down your arm. Did you say it was red?"

FOOTBALL

He was not a large man, relatively speaking. He was built like what he was – a running back on a semi-pro football team. He was quite affable; men, women, children and pets all wanted to be around him. He was specialized in his talents. He excelled at three things that I could vouch for: football, partying and sex. I'm not saying that he was deficient in other areas. After all, he was a college grad and had a well-paying professional job, but I can't speak for his expertise in those areas.

For me the entire relationship was a learning experience. Up until my encounter with Cordell I didn't know that the number on a player's jersey indicated his playing position. An "89" indicated a linebacker; a low number like "5" would be the quarterback. Cordell wore a double zero. Beyond that, I figured out that the goal was to get the ball over the goal line at the opposite end of the field. I hadn't figured out what the signals and the flags that the men in black and white shirts meant yet, but I was learning.

Cordell loved to party. But in my mind, he liked getting to and from the party even better. He insisted I drive, even when I had no idea of where I was going. For him this was an opportune time to massage my body; to whisper all kinds of sweet words in my ears. Sometimes it got so intense we'd have to pull off to the side of the road. Often we never made it to the party. The man brought out the wild in timid, inexperienced me. And as quiet as it's kept, I was loving every moment of it.

After a couple of months, I noticed that the guys on the team were tight on and off the field. In fact, several of them lived in the same housing development. It was not unusual for the party to move from one apartment to another. They were always together, touching, patting, congratulating one another for one thing or another. The guys dropped in on each other, often unannounced. I was grateful on more than one occasion that Cordell kept his apartment door locked, at least when I was visiting. His teammates were not at all used to not having immediate access to one another and ribbed him about it at every opportunity.

On this particular occasion I came prepared to stay for the weekend. There would be a football game and an after party. The rest of the weekend we'd make up as we went, which I was sure would not venture too far from the bedroom.

The game was won, the party exhilarating and I was eager for our private "games" to begin.

And they did. Beginning at the front door where Cordell dropped his bag, his jacket and relieved me of mine. We moved into the room, disposing of other items of clothing as we went. It took only a moment to retrieve wine and glasses from the kitchen. A few sips of wine and I was in my underwear – as was he. We stumbled into the bedroom…

In the wee hours of the morning, in a happy dazed state, navigating the darkened hallway to the bathroom, a movement rendered me fully alert. I stood stock-still. Inching closer I realized there was someone on the sofa. The "someone" sat up abruptly, switching on the lamp. It was Neal, one of the guys on the team. I leapt backward at the suddenness of the situation. Neal moved closer, beady red-rimmed eyes piercing my very being.

"You need to clear out. He's mine," he sneered. "I've loved him for years. You just show up and think you can take him from me? It ain't gon happen Honey!"

I could feel his breath on my face. I fell backwards onto the floor, jumped up and ran into the bedroom, locking the door. Cordell sat up in bed on his elbows, "What's going on?"

Before I could respond, Neal was pounding on the door.

"Bring your sorry ass out here you little witch."

"Oh hell," is all Cordell mumbled as he opened the door and stepped back. Neal was thrown off balance having been in the motion of putting his shoulder to the door. I maneuvered past the two men, gathering clothing as I went. I scrambled into some jeans (mine), a sweater (his) and grabbed my purse and whatever pieces of clothing I could on my way out.

The drive home was a blur. My hands strangled the steering wheel. My heart raced, confusion fogging my thoughts. The image of an en-raged Neal kept assaulting my vision. *How had I missed the signs? Had Cordell misrepresented himself? Perhaps not. Maybe, if truth be told, I wasn't all that concerned about it anyway. Maybe I was too busy enjoying it all.* Embarrassment and humiliation engulfed me.

A few days later, going through the clothes I'd hastily grabbed up, I found a pair of men's briefs, red, and a team jacket, navy blue. My new silk blouse and my sexiest underwear had been lost in the melee. As far as I was concerned that weekend was quite the Hail Mary, but I must admit, I still have a fondness for football.

Touch football, anyone?

VISITING ESTILL

Although my Aunt Blanche lived in Chicago we had always been close. Even when she was not physically with me, she spoke to me. I often knew her intent before she spoke it. Aunty would come annually to visit me in South Carolina. This time she was eager to tour. We'd planned day trips to Charleston, Beaufort and maybe even Savannah. But most of all she wanted to visit a former Chicago church member who had moved back to his family home in Estill, SC. I'd never heard of the place and had no idea of its distance from my home, but my love for Aunt Blanche removed any hesitation I might have had in finding it.

I'd always been able to "see" and communicate with entities beyond human, but the car's navigation system was obviously not one of them. The GPS insisted that I'd reached my destination. On my left were railroad tracks. On my right, woods. I began to wonder if the house even existed. If I could find the town's main street, I reasoned, someplace with shops, a gas station, anything – I'd get better directions than the GPS was providing. But driving aimlessly proved to be even more frustrating.

As I drove, Aunt Blanche sat next to me in her 92-year-old splendor; white hair braided and wrapped around the crown of her head, chin forward, a long, slender neck, not at all disturbed at being "lost." She'd been the one to notice a family of pigs, with Momma Pig in the lead, walking single file down the side of the country road. And she'd remarked with a chuckle that there must have been a run on pink paint because "all of the houses since we crossed those railroad tracks are pink. Or trimmed in pink." Observant yes, but she offered no guidance for how to find the home of her former church member, Shadrach.

Finding a clearing I stopped the car and wondered if Aunt Blanche could help me out of my dilemma. Can you let Shadrach know we're lost? Tell him we've pulled into what appears to be an abandoned gas station."

"It's not abandoned!" I heard him shout. "And furthermore if you'd followed my directions–"

"Oh hell no, you will not act as if finding your house is my problem. If you intend to see my Aunt Blanche on this day, you'd better find a better way of talking to me. I am not some wayward child to be reprimanded. And trust me I'll have no problem finding the way back to my home."

Shadrach calmed. "My apologies. If you'll make a U-turn and come up the road about half a mile you'll see a post marking the entry to my driveway on your right."

"Thank you. We'll be in touch if we have a problem." Aunt Blanche had a rather quizzical expression on her face. "Well, now you've met Shadrach."

"Humph! So far I am not impressed."

Aunty found that amusing.

After several more runs up and down the short segment of road, Aunt Blanche pointed to a broken piece of wood sticking up from the ground on the edge of the roadway. It was not what I'd call a 'post' but I slowed. I didn't see a driveway. There was a rutted opening though. I turned the car into the opening. Shrubs and trees engulfed us. After a few feet we were in a well-manicured space. Straight ahead of us was a large, ranch-style house, beautifully landscaped with fruit and flowering trees. There were several well placed shrubs on the grounds. It was surrounded by a high hurricane fence.

As we got out of the car I realized that there were dogs, a lot of dogs inside the fence – about seven or eight that I could count. There were two large dogs, several tiny lap dogs and an assortment of mid-sized mutts. They all were heading toward the gate.

"Aunt Blanche, get back in the car!" There was no need to repeat the command as we both made haste, locking the car doors once inside. We looked at each other. Before we had a chance to make a decision about our next move, a male figure emerged from the side of the house. With the sun behind him, he appeared to be thin and gangly. His clothes hung as if on a hanger. He lobbed along, oblivious to the dogs, who jumped about excitedly as he moved towards us. He waved a shadowy arm. "Come on in." His voice was that of deep wind chimes.

The dogs shot through the open gate jumping on the car. I lowered the car window only a crack, "No thanks. Why don't you join us?" Aunty and I were both afraid of dogs. Having to walk from the car to the house, surrounded by a pack of dogs was not appealing to either of us. I was not having my aunt – or myself for that matter – mauled by a pack of dogs in the middle of nowhere. It would be years before our bodies were found! At least that's the movie that played out in my head.

Our plan had been to reach Estill about 11:00 or 11:30 am and take Shadrach out for brunch. Now I wondered if the town even had a restaurant or diner. Shadrach slid into the back seat. While I was low-rating Shadrach, his town, and his dogs in my mind, he and Aunty were having a lively conversation.

Shadrach talked about how difficult it had been to adjust to living in the country; he wasn't used to having so much space and he was lonely. He asked about members of the church. Aunt talked about how the church had grown and the possibility of having to find a larger building. And although Aunty tried to include me in the conversation, Shadrach ignored me completely. But my attention was held by what was going on in the yard. One large dog was doing something to one of the tiny dogs. It looked as if he was shaking and tossing the small dog around. Maybe he was trying to play, but he was too big. I screamed, "That dog is killing the little one! He's killing him!" Shadrach sauntered calmly from the car and looked down at the limp fur on the ground. He kicked it. "Get up!" he demanded. There was no movement. He picked up the lifeless canine and walked to the rear of the house.

Shadrach returned to the car as if nothing had happened. "Is he dead?" I asked.

"Just about. I'll call a vet."

"Call? When are you going to do that?"

Shadrach rolled his eyes at me. "There's no need," he finally admitted.

I was having a hard time believing what I'd just witnessed but knew it was pointless to inquire further.

It was almost 2 o'clock. When I broached the subject of lunch Shadrach said quite sarcastically, "I always go to Charleston for meals out." I ignored his attempt at wit, if that's what it was.

"We've not eaten since this morning. Is there anything closer?"

He studied me for a few seconds. "Not that would suit your taste."

I didn't like his tone and would have challenged him except that he was probably right. And I had no desire to dine with him anyway.

Aunt Blanche realized the situation was becoming contentious. She put a hand on Shadrach's shoulder. "It's been so good seeing you. We need to head back but I promise to stay in touch."

Shadrach gave Aunty a hug and moved towards his enclave without acknowledging my presence.

I retraced my route back to the main highway, all the while wondering about Shadrach.

"A penny for your thoughts," I heard Aunt Blanche say.

"Is he always like that – shouting at people for no reason? Kicking half-dead dogs?"

Aunty was quietly looking out of the window but I knew she was trying to determine how much to tell me. It was her way – to keep other people's business to herself.

"No, he wasn't always like that. When he joined the church he was quite pleasant. On the quiet side but pleasant. Sometimes he was okay and then other times he seemed impatient or anxious. As time went on he began to change and not for the better."

"So is that when he came to South Carolina?"

"Not quite. One Sunday when he was particularly agitated and argumentative I took him aside to try to calm him. He was in quite a lather. Kept saying something about the doctor being a quack, that he didn't have Irritable Male Syndrome. Shadrach had never heard of such a thing. He was insistent that he was not going to let the doctor 'fiddle with his head or tell him what to eat.' His attendance at church became spotty. I was the only one who kept in touch with him. He moved back to his hometown a few months after that. He's been here ever since."

Aunt Blanche seemed thoughtful, sad. There was something she wasn't saying, but I had no interest in asking what it might be.

We found a quiet restaurant adjacent to the highway and along a marsh where we had a wonderful seafood lunch. Aunty had shrimp and grits, a local specialty and was enlivened. I had a glass of wine with my scallops to rid myself of everything Shadrach. Aunty didn't eat much though. We filled a take home box with most of her meal.

The next day Aunty was relaxing in the garden, intermittently reading the newspaper, when she heard from Shadrach. He was annoyed that I had cut short their visit; that I had not shown him proper respect; that he wanted Aunty to return so that he could show her his home and prepare a meal for her.

"That's very sweet Shadrach, but we've made plans for the rest of the week. I'll give you a call when I get back to Chicago. It really was great visiting with you."

Aunty became pensive. An hour later she exhaled audibly, sat up straight in the lawn chair, and pushed the readers up on her nose.

"Helen," she called, "Would you please call Shadrach's daughter? Her number is in my old address book. She needs to come see about Shadrach."

"Does she even live near here? Doesn't she work?" I was stalling. I didn't want to get any further involved with Shadrach. But Aunty's knit eyebrows told me that she was not going to take 'no' for an answer. I made the call.

"Jamilla, my name is Helen. I'm Sister Blanche's niece. She and Shadrach attended the same church in Chicago..."

She listened as I recounted the experience of our visit. She promised to call on him when she could. She didn't seem eager. Later that evening she called back. We talked deep into the night.

"I haven't heard from Shadrach for several years," Jamilla said. I noticed she called him by his given name, not dad or father. "His behavior had become unpredictable. Mom divorced him and relocated to West Africa. Mom said Shadrach didn't like water so she figured he wouldn't cross an ocean to harass her. She moved on with her life."

Jamilla too had relocated from Chicago to Georgia to be out of Shadrach's ambit. She suggested that I go with her to Estill. I reiterated my disastrous first encounter with her father. After a short silence she said, "How about I visit with you and we develop a strategy for moving forward."

I agreed. The arrangement pleased Aunt Blanche.

It was several weeks before our schedules made her visit possible. By then Aunt Blanche had returned to Chicago. Jamilla arrived driving a bright yellow Camaro. She was short and round with a wide smile, dark laughing eyes and a large Afro that would make Angela Davis weep with envy. Jamilla exuded sensuality.

After getting her situated in the guest room and preparing dinner together, we enjoyed our meal indoors and took our wine outside to welcome the cooling of the day and a memorably colorful sunset.

We tossed around several ideas for addressing "the Shadrach situation" without success.

"Well, from what you've said about your visit with Shadrach, he's worse than ever. What we need is a shaman. A Yoruba priest or priestess."

"Jamilla, I think you've come up with something. Do you know anyone?"

"No, but I know someone who knows someone." She smiled enticingly.

"I do too."

We spent the next hour or so making phone calls.

A week later Jamilla drove me, Mama Arielle, the Yoruba priestess and Olu, a drummer, back to Estill. She entered the home site from a back road. Jamilla took me by the hand as she led the group through a small wooded area. When we reached a clearing, she turned to Arielle and Olu and pointed to a large dogwood tree, indicating the site she'd chosen for the ceremony. Arielle strode forward with Olu following, playing the drum. Arielle placed a white cloth on the ground, along with several symbolic items. She lit sage, poured libation and chanted as she sanctified the grounds. She performed the dance of her Orisha until Oshun came down and mounted her. This, I understood, is how Arielle communicated with the spirits. Jamilla and I held hands for the duration of the ceremony.

I approached Arielle afterwards to thank her for helping Shadrach's spirit find peace. I asked if she knew someone who might help Aunt Blanche to do the same.

She looked at me with knowing eyes. "There's no need. She's here, with Shadrach. They are both at rest now."

There was no way to stop the flow of tears from my eyes. It was hard letting go. Jamilla held me tightly. We've held onto one another ever since.

Shalah.

RASHIDA'S TALE

(For Doris Colbert Kennedy)

It was all too familiar yet disconcerting. It couldn't be the humidity. After all, Rashida was from DC where the humidity could easily rival that of South Carolina. She scanned the churchyard. It had been converted into a festive summer feast. The aromas of Liberian and American southern food wafted gently in the almost breeze; the multicultural congregants milled about holding their plates of food and chatting, moving from one group to another or sitting at the small tables scattered around the grounds. No, it was not the humidity causing her discomfort.

Rashida spotted Stella sitting under a tree focusing intently on the meal before her. Rashida sat down beside her. Stella grunted a greeting. The cousins ate in silence.

The sense of apprehension persisted. Perhaps it was the Spanish moss moving ever so slightly as it hung from the live oak trees. The more Rashida focused on the moss the more she envisioned another time and place – a place where the bodies of her ancestors might have swung from these very trees. The slow twisting movement held her captive.

"You okay Rashida? Are you going to put that food in your mouth or are you holding it aloft for the flies?"

Rashida cut her eyes at her cousin while putting the fork back on her plate. She'd lost her appetite.

Mary Elizabeth waved at them from across the yard. Stella waved back and bent to the task at hand -- eating. Rashida watched as Mary Elizabeth approached, her blond hair tied elegantly with a huge bow at the back of her head. What in the antebellum south is she wearing, Rashida wondered to herself. The Gone with the Wind dress seemed to float about of its own accord. All Mary Elizabeth needed was a broad brimmed straw hat and a shawl. Before either of the women could inquire about the attire, Mary Elizabeth started talking nonstop as she plopped down, fanning herself energetically.

"I've been looking all over for you. I've attended the most wonderful workshop about slavery and the responsibility we white people must take for that part of our history."

Rashida rolled her eyes and bit her lip. Mary Elizabeth rambled on, oblivious to Stella and Rashida's stony silence. Somewhere between the beginning of Mary Elizabeth's new found "insight" and its conclusion, Stella had eased away.

Mary Elizabeth was finally silent – she had spent herself. Rashida took a breath, preparing to excuse herself, but Mary Elizabeth turned abruptly, fixing her intense blue-eyed gaze on her.

"Rashida, I need to beg your forgiveness," she intoned.

"For what?"

"For enslaving you!"

Rashida's eyebrows knit together as her eyes shuttered, becoming thin slits. She exhaled loudly.

"Only if you will forgive me," replied Rashida, pointedly.

"Whatever for?" drawled Mary Elizabeth.

"Don't you remember the slave revolt?" Rashida did not wait for a response. "I killed you!"

Before Mary Elizabeth could recover her composure, Rashida got up and dumped her plate. No, it's not the humidity she thought once again. She went to find Stella.

MEET REGINA

R egina E. Williams is a poet, writer and writing consultant whose poetry and fiction has appeared in such publications as New City Voices: An Anthology, Long Journey Home, an anthology, CONFIRMATIONS: An Anthology of African American Women, Drum, Black American Literature Forum, Central Park: A Journal of the Arts and Social Theory and New Rain.

Regina has performed her work nationally in high schools, colleges, churches, as well as on national radio. She has participated in various panel discussions and dialogues on issues relating to the black community, Womanism, and writing.

As an associate with Writer's Insight, a writing consultant agency, Regina designed and conducted writing workshops for students and teachers in high schools, colleges and various civic and community institutions and organizations. She also served as a Managing Editor for Metro Exchange a monthly newspaper published by Intergroup Marketing & Communications, Inc.

Regina is a founding member of Metamorphosis Writer's Collective and "Ain't I a Woman" Writers Collective, and a member of New Renaissance Writers Guild, and New Bones, a promotion/production group designed to promote black literature and music.

Regina grew up in an immigrant community in Brooklyn, New York. She quickly became fascinated with people: the climates and typography of the countries they came from, the musicality or lack of such in the languages they spoke, the uniqueness of the clothes they wore, the different spicing of their foods; the discovery that everyone did not worship as her family did. Her curiosity led her to travel to many places to broaden her understanding of global customs, art, and culture. Some of her impressions:

Europe: Spain, France, Germany, Switzerland, and *Italy.* Everyone, including children, were multilingual; housing styles tended to be dictated by terrain and climate as much as by history.

Eastern Mediterranean: Egypt, Israel, Palestine, Cyprus, Turkey, Greece, and the *Greek Isles.* The antiquities found in the Cairo Museum brought the world of the pharaohs to life in full vivid splendor. The stark difference between the aridness of Palestine and the lushness of Israel was astounding.

South America: Venezuela and the Isle of Margarita. The isolation and underdevelopment of the island was an unexpected respite from a delightful but crowded Caracas.

West Africa: Ghana, Togo, Benin, Senegal, and the *Gambia.* Art must be functional as well as creative and unique.

India. The plethora of faith traditions was consciousness-expanding.

You are invited to learn more about Regina E. Williams and her work at www.ReginaEWilliams.com.

ACKNOWLEDGEMENTS

A great deal of gratitude to the late Gladys V. Thorne, known affectionately as "Thornie," who introduced me to a remarkable world of black literature, music and dance.

To the many friends and fellow writers who took the time to read, listen and offer suggestions and insights, especially Sister's Righting Salon members, Loretta Campbell and Lora Tucker, and The Main Street Writes writer's group. A special thank you to Shari Stauch, book coach, editor and publisher.

And finally, much appreciation to Winston Kennedy for his artwork and encouragement.

It really does take a village. You are my village...

CPSIA information can be obtained
at www.ICGtesting.com
Printed in the USA
LVHW031658230222
711715LV00003B/246

9 781088 003084